COMPOUND
MURDER

▼

Also by Bill Crider

COMPOUND MURDER

▼

BILL CRIDER

MINOTAUR BOOKS
A THOMAS DUNNE BOOK
NEW YORK

A THOMAS DUNNE BOOK FOR MINOTAUR BOOKS.
An imprint of St. Martin's Publishing Group.

COMPOUND MURDER. Copyright © 2013 by Bill Crider. All rights reserved. Printed in the United States of America. For information, address St. Martin's Press, 175 Fifth Avenue, New York, N.Y. 10010.

www.thomasdunnebooks.com
www.minotaurbooks.com

Library of Congress Cataloging-in-Publication Data

Crider, Bill, 1941–
    Compound Murder : a Dan Rhodes mystery / Bill Crider.—
First Edition.
        p. cm
    (Sheriff Dan Rhodes mysteries ; 18)
    ISBN 978-0-312-64165-8 (hardcover)
    ISBN 978-1-250-02046-8 (e-book)
    1. Rhodes, Dan (Fictitious character)—Fiction.   2. Sheriffs—
Fiction.   3. Texas—Fiction.   I. Title.
    PS3553.R497S45 2013
    813'.54—dc23

                                                        2013018425

Minotaur books may be purchased for educational, business, or promotional use. For information on bulk purchases, please contact Macmillan Corporate and Premium Sales Department at 1-800-221-7945 extension 5442 or write specialmarkets@macmillan.com.

First Edition: August 2013

10   9   8   7   6   5   4   3   2   1

COMPOUND
MURDER

▼

Chapter 1

▼

Sheriff Dan Rhodes sat at his kitchen table and glared at the plastic bottle of Mr. PiBB.

"Go ahead," his wife, Ivy, said. "Try it. You might like it. Breakfast of champions."

"That's Wheaties," Rhodes said.

Ivy ignored that. "Do you think you're going to bring the corporate giant to its knees if you never drink another Dr Pepper? They're not even going to notice."

Rhodes knew she was right. What good would it do anybody if he never drank another Dr Pepper? Would it really punish anybody other than himself? Still, he could never forgive the corporate giant for stopping the Dublin Dr Pepper plant from bottling the drink made with cane sugar the way it should be made. It had been a year now, and he still couldn't forgive and forget. It didn't matter that other bottlers were making Dr Pepper with sugar of some kind or the other. It just wasn't the same.

"Mr. PiBB tastes just like Dr Pepper, anyway," Ivy said. "You won't be able to tell the difference."

Blasphemy. "You might not be able to tell," Rhodes said. "I can."

"You could always try something else. A cola drink, maybe." Worse than blasphemy. "Hah."

"What you need is some solid food," Ivy said. "I'll scramble an egg for you. Fry some bacon. That would do you a lot more good."

"I'm not in the mood," Rhodes said, giving the Mr. PiBB another glare.

Yancey, the poofy little Pomeranian, came running into the kitchen. He skidded to a stop when he saw Sam, the black cat, eating from his bowl near the refrigerator. Yancey had seen Sam there a thousand times, but it always seemed to come as a complete surprise to him that there was a cat in the house. He slid into the leg of Rhodes's chair and yipped in displeasure.

"That's kind of the way I feel," Rhodes told the dog, who sat looking up at him and whining as if looking for a little sympathy.

Sam ignored both of them and kept on eating. Cats didn't care about soft drinks, the presence of dogs, or much of anything else, as far as Rhodes could tell.

Rhodes stood up, took the bottle of Mr. PiBB from the table, and put it back in the refrigerator. He'd been going through that routine for weeks now. He wondered how long it would take to wear out the bottle. Or for him to break down and take a drink of the Mr. PiBB.

Yancey recovered himself and danced around Rhodes's feet, yipping.

"He wants to go out," Ivy said.

"I'll go with him," Rhodes said. "I need to feed Speedo."

He went to the back door, Yancey bouncing along behind. Rhodes picked up the bag of dog food and opened the door. Yancey dashed out and down the steps. He tore across the yard, looking for that squeaky toy that he and Speedo shared. "Shared" wasn't really the right word, Rhodes thought. Each dog seemed to think the toy was exclusively his own.

While Rhodes poured dog food into Speedo's big metal bowl, Yancey's frenzied yips brought Speedo out of his Styrofoam igloo. Speedo charged for the squeaky toy, too, without even shaking himself. Speedo was a border collie, considerably bigger than Yancey, but Yancey didn't appear to notice the difference in their sizes. While he was easily intimidated by the cat, Yancey wasn't intimidated by Speedo at all. Maybe he sensed that Speedo bore him no ill will, whereas Sam almost certainly did, no matter how casual he seemed to be when Yancey was around.

Yancey got to the toy first, snatching it up and sliding right under Speedo's nose. Speedo didn't chase him, because he heard the food being poured into his bowl. He came over and started to eat. Yancey brought the squeaky toy in hopes that Speedo would try to take it, but Speedo was too interested in eating.

Yancey looked so depressed that Rhodes put down the bag of dog food, walked over to Yancey, and snatched the toy from him. Yancey was elated. He danced and yipped as Rhodes held up the toy and pretended to throw it. Yancey wasn't fooled. He'd seen that old trick too many times, so Rhodes had to toss the toy and let the dog romp after it.

Rhodes took the bag of dog food inside and was about to go back to the yard when the telephone rang. Ivy answered it and listened for a bit. Then she said, "He's right here."

Uh-oh.

Ivy held the phone out to Rhodes. "It's Hack."

Hack Jensen was the dispatcher at the jail. He wouldn't call Rhodes at home unless there was some kind of trouble. Rhodes looked at the kitchen clock. Not even seven. It was too early for morning trouble, so this must be something left over from the previous night. Rhodes took the phone.

"What's up?" Rhodes asked.

"Lonnie Wallace phoned," Hack said.

That didn't exactly answer the question, but that was always Hack's approach. He liked to work his way up to the answer in his own way. Sometimes Rhodes thought it was a plot to drive him crazy.

"What did he want?" Rhodes asked.

"Some sheriffin'," Hack said. "Why else would he phone us?"

"I thought maybe there'd been a crime committed. That's usually why people call."

"Yeah, well, there was that, too."

"What was the crime?"

"Hair," Hack said.

"Hair?"

"Must be an echo in here," Hack said.

"You know better than that. Tell me about the theft."

"You don't have to get snippy about it."

Hack always resorted to the snippy defense when he could tell Rhodes was irritated.

"Just tell me," Rhodes said.

"I thought I did."

Rhodes sighed, then wished he hadn't. It would just encourage Hack. "Give me some specifics."

"Lonnie Wallace called."

Rhodes didn't say a word. After a second or two Hack continued. "He said somebody broke into the Beauty Shack and stole his hair."

"*His* hair?"

"Well, he owned it, so that would make it his, right?"

Lonnie was the owner of the Beauty Shack and one of the operators. He'd more or less inherited the place from its former owner, who was no longer in the business. Lonnie had a nice head of hair, but Rhodes didn't think that was what Hack meant.

"I'll go by and talk to him on my way in," Rhodes said.

"Better go on soon as you can. He sounded pretty upset."

"I'm on the way," Rhodes said, but he wasn't.

After he hung up, Rhodes went back outside to fetch Yancey, who had one end of the squeaky toy in his mouth as he tussled with Speedo, who had the other end. Rhodes had no doubt that Speedo could have pulled the toy away at any time, but for the moment he was content to let Yancey appear to be his equal.

"Break it up, guys," Rhodes said, but of course the dogs paid him no attention. They both growled deep in their throats. Even though Yancey's own growl was far from impressive, Speedo's didn't frighten him.

"Time to go in," Rhodes said and picked up Yancey, who tried to hang on to the squeaky toy but couldn't manage it. The dog yipped pitifully as Rhodes carried him across the yard with Speedo walking along behind, looking smug with the toy dangling from his mouth.

Rhodes went in and set Yancey on the floor. Yancey charged off toward the bedroom to hide under the bed and sulk.

"Do you have time for breakfast?" Ivy asked.

Rhodes shook his head. "Not even a swallow of Mr. PiBB. There's trouble at the Beauty Shack."

"Not like the last time, I hope."

"So do I," Rhodes said.

Lonnie Wallace was waiting in the gravel parking lot of the Beauty Shack when Rhodes pulled to a stop. As usual, Lonnie was dressed in drugstore cowboy style: jeans held up by a belt with a big buckle in the shape of the state of Texas, a Western-cut shirt, and ostrich quill boots that cost at least five hundred dollars. Rhodes thought that the beauty business was very, very good to Lonnie.

The last time Rhodes had arrived at the Beauty Shack in the early morning, there'd been a dead woman inside. Rhodes didn't think things were likely to be that serious this time, but you never could tell. He got out of the county car, a white Dodge Charger, his shoes crunching in the gravel that covered the parking lot, and asked Lonnie what was going on.

"Hack said something about hair," Rhodes added.

"That's right," Lonnie said. "We're trying to reach out and get some new customers, so a few weeks ago I started stocking hair extensions and wigs. Made from real human hair. They're very expensive. Seventy-five dollars to start."

Rhodes glanced across the street at the derelict building. "The deputies are still checking that place every night, so your burglars didn't come from there. How did they get in?"

"Let's go inside," Lonnie said. "I'll show you."

They went inside the shop, which hadn't changed much under Lonnie's ownership. It still smelled the same way, which was the way all beauty shops smelled to Rhodes. He didn't know exactly what the smell was composed of, but it was powerful and distinctive. Not unpleasant. More like astringent. Shampoo, nail polish remover, and permanent wave solution all figured into it.

The shop had only one big room, not counting the restroom. The door to the restroom was open, and Lonnie pointed in that direction. Rhodes looked and saw that the window in the restroom was broken. Shards of frosted glass covered the floor. "That's how they got in," Lonnie said. "The hair extensions were over here."

He pointed out a glass case that still held bottles of shampoo, conditioner, hair spray, scissors, nail clippers, and other notions. "The case wasn't locked," Lonnie said, "so they didn't have to break it."

Rhodes thought the whole burglary would have taken five minutes at the outside. Maybe two people involved. Break the window, boost one person through it. That person grabs the extensions, hands them out the window, then leaves the same way. It didn't have to be two people. One person could have done it with something to stand on, say the hood of a car.

"Do you have a burglar alarm?" Rhodes asked.

"Yes," Lonnie said, "but it wasn't hooked to the restroom window."

"Your insurance company might not like that."

"I'm sure they won't. Sandra had it put in. I never updated it."

Sandra Wiley had owned the shop before Lonnie. The insurance company wouldn't care about that. Lonnie should have been more careful.

"Can you catch whoever did this?" Lonnie asked.

People always asked that question, and Rhodes was always honest with them, even when he knew the answer he gave wasn't what they wanted to hear.

"Probably not," he said. "We'll try, you know that, but those hair extensions are likely to be in Houston or Dallas by now. I wouldn't be surprised if they were stolen by someone just passing through town, or someone who came here from out of town especially to steal them."

"I've learned an important lesson," Lonnie said.

"To sleep in your shop with a shotgun?"

Lonnie did a double take. Then he grinned. "I never know when you're kidding."

"You aren't alone," Rhodes said. "I'm going to call Hack and get someone here to work the scene. You might have to cancel your appointments for the morning."

"I'll start making the calls," Lonnie said.

"Use your cell," Rhodes told him. "I doubt that your burglar used the phone, but we have to be careful. You can call in here, but don't touch anything."

"I'll be careful," Lonnie said.

Rhodes went out to the county car, got Hack on the radio, and asked him to send Ruth Grady to the Beauty Shack. "Tell her there's been a burglary. She can get the details from Lonnie when she gets here. I want her to work the scene."

"She's on patrol," Hack said.

"I know, but she's needed here now."

"Take her a while to get there."

"That's all right. Lonnie's closing the shop."

"I'll tell her," Hack said. "Hang on. I got a call coming in."

Rhodes waited. The Beauty Shack was a little past the edge of Clearview's old downtown area, and it was quiet at that time of day. For that matter, it was quiet just about any time of the day. There wasn't much left of downtown, a lot of which was like the building across the street, empty and about to fall down. In fact, some of the buildings had already fallen down. Where there had once been busy stores, there were concrete foundations and floors and nothing more.

A little breeze stirred up a dust devil at the edge of the parking lot, but the breeze didn't do much to cool things down. The day was warm even though it was the middle of October. Rhodes was used to it. The summer had been brutal, the drought had been severe, and there hadn't been much of a fall so far. The weather had been extreme for several years, and Rhodes wondered if things would ever straighten out again.

He didn't wonder long because Hack came back on the radio.

"You better get out to the college," Hack said. "Quick."

"What's the trouble?"

This time Hack didn't obfuscate or beat around the bush.

"In the parking lot in back of the building," he said. "Somebody's dead."

Chapter 2

▼

Rhodes was at the campus in under five minutes. He wasn't sure it was technically a campus, since it consisted of only one building, and maybe it wasn't even technically a community college. The college and its main campus were located in another county. This was a branch campus. It had been in Clearview for several years now, having originally started out in one of the crumbling downtown buildings. When that building became uninhabitable owing to the fact that it was about to collapse, the new building had been constructed on the outskirts of town.

Rhodes pulled into the asphalt parking lot behind the college building and immediately spotted a small group gathered near a couple of big gray-painted metal Dumpsters. Other people were trying to get closer and not succeeding. Seepy Benton was there, doing crowd control. It was probably too late for that, though. There had already been enough trampling and touching to thoroughly contaminate the scene if a crime had been committed, not that many traces would have been left on the asphalt.

Dr. C. P. Benton, known to his friends and acquaintances as Seepy, was a math teacher who'd been in the Citizens' Sheriff's Academy. He now considered himself some kind of unofficial deputy, which could be irritating at times. At other times, however, he'd proved helpful.

Rhodes stopped the county car and got out. Benton came over to him and said, "I've kept everybody away from the crime scene as best I could, Sheriff, but I didn't get here in time to do much good."

"You're sure it's a crime scene?"

"That would be my professional judgment as a graduate of the Citizens' Sheriff's Academy."

Rhodes suppressed a sigh.

"The body's over here," Benton said.

He led Rhodes to the Dumpsters. The body was there, all right, lying on its side between two big containers. A male, probably middle-aged, wearing khaki slacks and a blue shirt.

"Any idea who it is?" Rhodes asked.

"Earl Wellington," Benton said. "English teacher."

Wellington would have looked as if he were sleeping if it hadn't been for the fact that the back of his head was bashed in. The brownish hair was matted with blood that wasn't quite dry. Wellington hadn't been dead long. Rhodes saw that one of the sharp corners of a Dumpster had something on it that looked a lot like hair and blood, probably from Wellington's head.

"Was Wellington married?" Rhodes asked.

"No," Benton said. "Bachelor, like me."

"Family?"

"Not that I know about."

Rhodes nodded. He'd find out about the next of kin later. He didn't know any Wellingtons in Blacklin County.

"Get everybody cleared out," Rhodes told Benton.

"I can move everybody but Dean King," Benton said. "She outranks me."

Rhodes hadn't seen the dean, but he wasn't surprised she was there. "That's okay. Just move the others out of here. Get them into the building. Don't let anybody walk away or leave the parking lot in a car."

Rhodes figured there were at least fifty or sixty students and faculty standing around, maybe more. There was no way he and his small staff of deputies could question all of them, much less everyone who was already inside the building, but he had to make some kind of effort.

"Tell everyone not to leave the campus. Tell them that I want to talk to anybody who might have some information about this. Can you handle that?"

"You know I can," Benton said.

He stepped away and began talking to people, then shooing them inside. As he did, Sue Lynn King came up to Rhodes.

"This is terrible, Sheriff," she said. "Terrible. The college isn't going to look good when the news gets out."

"It's not going to do much for this fella, either," Rhodes said, indicating the dead man.

The blood in Wellington's hair had already attracted a few buzzing flies. An ant crawled across the dead man's cheek and up on his nose.

"Of course not for him," Dean King said. She wasn't looking at the body. "I didn't mean that the way it sounded."

The dean was a statuesque woman a bit past middle age with very black hair stiff with hair spray. Rhodes couldn't see a single touch of gray. He wondered if the dean was a customer at the Beauty Shack.

"Benton told me that his name was Wellington."

"Yes," the dean said. "That's correct. Earl Wellington. He taught English." The dean's mouth twisted into a grimace. "It's always the English teachers."

"You've had other English teachers who were killed?"

"Killed? You mean it wasn't an accident? Or a heart attack?"

"Could be," Rhodes said, "but I don't think so. I think someone killed him. Maybe by accident, but someone killed him just the same."

"Oh, my God. This will really be a black eye for us." The dean put a hand to her stiff hair and gave it a little push. "I didn't mean *that* the way it sounded, either. I'm somewhat discombobulated. I meant that we often seem to have problems with our English teachers."

"What kind of problems?"

"Nothing serious. Academic problems."

That didn't really explain anything, but Rhodes could find out more later if he needed to.

"Was Wellington full-time?" he asked.

"Yes. We have only two full-timers, and he was one of them. I hope he had his grades up to date. I hope I can find someone to replace him this late in the semester."

She seemed a lot more concerned about her own problems than about Wellington, but Rhodes supposed that was only natural. Wellington didn't have problems, not anymore.

"I'll need to see about grief counseling," the dean continued, but she wasn't talking to Rhodes. She was just thinking out loud. "The morning classes will be a mess, but we'll have to try to carry on."

Rhodes interrupted her. "I'll have more questions for you, but right now you need to go on back in the building. I'll come by your office when I finish here. Don't let anyone into Wellington's office, and don't go in yourself. If it's open, close the door and lock it."

The dean looked at him vacantly but said she'd take care of things. Then she turned and left.

Seepy Benton had gotten everyone into the building, and he came over to talk to Rhodes.

"You want me to work the scene?" he asked.

Benton wore a straw cowboy hat, jeans, running shoes, and a blue cotton shirt. His mostly gray beard was neatly trimmed. Even with the beard, he didn't look like Rhodes's idea of a college teacher, but then Rhodes hadn't been to school in a long time.

"I don't want you to work the scene," Rhodes said. "I want you to wait in your office until I come by and talk to you."

"I could handle the scene," Benton said.

"I'm sure you could, but you haven't had the training."

"We did a scene at the academy. I was very good at it."

"That wasn't a real scene, just a setup. I'm going to get Deputy Grady out here to do this one."

Benton seemed pleased by that. "Can she come by and give me the third degree later?"

Benton had been dating the deputy for a while. Rhodes didn't see that they had anything in common, and he wasn't particularly fond of the idea. It was none of his business, however, as he often reminded himself, so he tried to stay out of it.

"We don't do the third degree anymore," Rhodes said. "We ran out of rubber hoses."

"That's too bad," Benton said.

Rhodes heard a siren. "Did someone call an ambulance?"

"Not me," Benton said. "I know better." He looked around. "I'm probably the only one who does, though. There were a lot of people here, and they all have cell phones. Half of them probably called. And took videos."

"Who found the body?"

"I don't know. There was a lot of excitement in the halls just before the bell was about to ring for the eight o'clock class, and I stepped out of my office to see what was going on. Someone said there was a body out here. And there was."

Rhodes could find out from Hack who'd called it in. Even if no name had been given, they'd have the number of the caller. The caller might not have discovered the body, however.

"Do you have any idea what Wellington was doing out here?" Rhodes asked.

Benton smiled. It wasn't quite a smirk, but it tended in that direction. "You don't want me working the scene."

"What does that have to do with it?"

Benton pointed to a cigarette butt that lay not far from Wellington's body. "There's no smoking in the building. If you want to smoke, you have to come outside. The Dumpster's a great big ashtray."

"You don't seem too upset by all this," Rhodes said.

"Danger is my game."

"Sure it is, but there's more to it than that. So tell me."

Benton stared off somewhere to the west. Rhodes looked in that direction. There was a field and then a small housing addition.

Above that, blue sky with some fluffy clouds floating around. Benton wasn't looking at any of that.

"Well?" Rhodes said.

"I thought you wanted me to go to my office."

An ambulance pulled into the parking lot, siren whooping.

"All right," Rhodes said. "I need to send that ambulance away. Don't go anywhere."

The ambulance stopped, and the siren trailed off into a low whine.

"Except to my office," Benton said.

"That's right," Rhodes said.

Benton turned away, and Rhodes started for the ambulance. As he did, a car peeled out of the parking lot, tires smoking and screeching. Someone had been keeping out of sight, waiting for the chance to get away.

"Benton!" Rhodes called. He was already running for the Charger. "Keep the EMTs away from the body. Keep people away from the scene."

"I thought I was supposed to go to my office," Benton said.

"Not now," Rhodes said, his hand on the door latch. He wondered if everybody had been taking lessons from Hack. "I'm deputizing you. Temporarily."

"I'll make you proud," Benton said. He pointed to the badge holder dangling from Rhodes's belt. "Do I get one of those?"

Rhodes ignored him. He opened the door, jumped in the Charger, and took off after the car, which was on the highway headed back toward town. Rhodes was out of the parking lot before he got his seat belt hooked.

The car he was chasing was a gray Chevy Malibu at least ten years old. The trunk had a line of rust across it, and the headliner drooped down. There was nothing wrong with the engine, however. The car was flat-out moving. Rhodes could barely see the top of the driver's head above the headrest.

Rhodes turned on the siren and light bar, then grabbed the radio and called Hack. "Get Ruth Grady out to the college. Tell her it's an emergency. And get the justice of the peace out there."

"What's goin' on?" Hack asked.

"Later," Rhodes said. He hooked the mic, then unhooked it and called Buddy, another of the deputies.

"I'm chasing a gray Malibu," Rhodes said. "It'll be over the overpass in a few seconds. Where are you?"

"Out by the McDonald's."

"That's the way we're headed."

"Hot pursuit?"

Rhodes glanced at his speedometer. It was nearing eighty.

"Yes."

"Roger that," Buddy said. "I'm on the way."

Rhodes hadn't been involved in a high-speed chase in years, and he didn't like them. They were dangerous to him, to the driver he was chasing, and to any citizens who might happen along. Rhodes wouldn't have gone after the Malibu if there hadn't been a dead man involved. Even at that, he wasn't sure it was worth it.

Buddy, on the other hand, loved anything that promised excitement. He'd probably burned rubber for a mile along the highway as soon as Rhodes was off the radio.

The Malibu was down the opposite side of the overpass and nearly to the first stoplight when Rhodes got to the top. The light was red. Rhodes didn't think the driver would stop, but as soon as he thought it, the Malibu's brake lights came on. Rhodes heard the squeal of tires and brakes.

A pickup had gotten into the intersection. The Malibu's driver slid into a turn and almost avoided the truck, but the car clipped the back bumper and spun the truck around. Rhodes had to mash down on his own brakes as the pickup whirled around in the intersection, brakes and tires howling.

The driver of the Malibu kept on turning and made a right onto the street that led through the mostly deserted downtown and into a residential area. Rhodes came almost to a stop. He saw that the pickup hadn't hit anything and that the driver, a young woman, seemed okay. All the other traffic had stopped, and the drivers were already on their cell phones, calling 911 or the ambulance service or their friends. Or taking pictures.

Rhodes stepped on the accelerator and started after the Malibu again.

The Chevy whipped past the law offices of Randy Lawless, past the civic center and the fire station. A couple of firemen sat on the bench outside. They stared after the Malibu and then at Rhodes.

Rhodes heard another siren and looked in his rearview mirror. Buddy was behind him and coming up fast. Rhodes hoped he didn't try to pass. Sometimes Buddy could be overly excited.

They flew past houses and people who gawked at them from the yards. One person was even aiming a cell phone at him. He hoped the video didn't wind up on Jennifer Loam's Web site. At a couple of places dogs sat in the yards, their heads back, their mouths open. Rhodes knew they were howling along with his siren, but he couldn't hear them.

The driver of the Malibu would have to make a choice soon

because if he went straight on, he'd be on a much narrower street, and there was no outlet. However, he could try taking the big curve, an almost ninety-degree turn to the left. He picked the turn. The Malibu leaned over to the right so far that Rhodes thought it would flip. Metal scraped the pavement and sent sparks along the side of the car.

Rhodes braked and slowed to a more sensible speed, hoping that Buddy wouldn't smash into him, but even Buddy knew better than to try that dangerous curve at such a speed. Just a few blocks farther on was a curve to the right, just as dangerous, but the Chevy was around it and gone by the time Rhodes had it in sight.

Now there was nothing in front of the Malibu but a long, straight highway. Years ago, long before Rhodes or anyone else in town had been born, coal had been mined in the southeastern part of the county, and a railroad had been built so that the coal could be transported. The highway was built on the old railroad bed.

The Malibu pulled away. Rhodes wondered what it had under the hood. He pressed down on the gas, and the Charger responded. The speedometer registered eighty-five. Then ninety.

A quick glance in the mirror showed Rhodes that Buddy was still behind him. He checked the speedometer again. Still ninety.

A look ahead gave Rhodes bad news. About a quarter of a mile away, a big green and yellow combine harvester was trundling along, taking up a good bit more than its share of the narrow road.

A farmer was probably moving the combine from one parcel of land to another. It was the kind of thing that had to be done now and then, nothing to worry about in the normal course of events, but this event wasn't anywhere near normal.

The man driving the combine must have heard the sirens. He looked back and saw what was bearing down on him. There was no shoulder on the highway, but as quickly as he could, the farmer moved the combine toward the side of the road that sloped off into a ditch.

The Malibu swerved to pass it, but there wasn't going to be quite enough room. The car's left side went off the highway. The back wheel threw up dead grass, dirt, and rocks, some of which bounced along the highway like little grenades.

One of the rocks came straight at the Charger's windshield, and it took everything Rhodes had in him to keep his eyes on the road and not to duck.

The rock hit the top of the windshield with a sound like a rifle shot. The rock sailed away, and a crack ran down the glass, spiderwebbing off in crazy patterns. Rhodes could still see, but it was tricky.

The Malibu shuddered along, slowing a good bit as the driver fought to get it back on the highway. Rhodes thought for a second he wouldn't manage it, but then he did, and as soon as the wheels grabbed pavement, the car sped up.

The combine was almost entirely in the ditch now, and Rhodes whipped past it. He didn't risk a glance at the driver, who Rhodes figured was pulling out a cell phone.

The highway was clear as far ahead as Rhodes could see, and there were few houses along the way. In places there were fields beside the road. In others trees grew close to the pavement. Farther down the way there were steep drop-offs right beside the road.

At the rate they were traveling, they'd be over the county line in under ten minutes. Rhodes reached for the radio to call ahead to the sheriff's department in the next county, but before he reached it, the casing peeled off the Malibu's right rear tire.

Pieces of rubber spun up in the air. One the size of a bloated water moccasin slammed into Rhodes's already cracked windshield, which sagged inward but didn't break. Rhodes couldn't see a thing.

He held tight to the steering wheel with one hand and pushed the button that let down the driver's window with the other. He stuck his head out, and the wind whipped his hair, what there was of it. Speedo would've loved the feeling, but it didn't have much appeal for Rhodes. A bug slapped his forehead and stung him as if it had been fired from a pellet gun.

In front of him, the Malibu slid at an angle down the road as the driver struggled with the wheel. Rhodes thought for sure that he wouldn't be able to bring the car straight again. Somehow he did, but only for a second. Almost as soon as the car straightened, it slipped into another angled skid, this time in the direction opposite of the first one.

Rhodes was convinced the Malibu was going to roll this time, but it didn't. It slowed down, and Rhodes saw the brake lights as the driver pumped the pedal.

Rhodes slowed, too, and both cars were down to about forty when the Chevy left the road. It bounced through the ditch like a giant oblong basketball. It didn't go far after that because there were trees in the way. It hit the trees sideways, with the passenger side against them. Smoke poured from under the hood. There appeared to be smoke in the passenger compartment, but Rhodes knew that was just powder from the air bag.

Bringing the county car to a stop just off the road about halfway into the ditch, Rhodes got out. Buddy was right behind him, already out of the car and holding his sidearm in a two-handed grip.

"I don't think you'll need that," Rhodes said, looking at the Malibu.

The driver's-side air bag had deflated, but Rhodes couldn't see anyone. The driver might have been injured, unconscious, or just lying low.

"You never know," Buddy said. "How many people in the car?"

"I didn't see anybody but the driver," Rhodes said.

He started walking toward the car with Buddy at his side.

"Why was he running away from you?" Buddy asked.

"I'm not sure. There was some trouble at the college, and maybe he tried to get away from it."

"Seepy Benton at it again?"

"Benton's never caused any trouble." Rhodes paused. "Well, not any *real* trouble. This was something else. There was a dead man in the parking lot."

As they neared the car, Buddy said, "You think the driver here had something to do with the dead man since he fled the scene?"

Fled the scene. Rhodes grinned. Buddy had a fondness for what he believed to be authentic cop jargon.

"Maybe he just wanted to skip class today," Rhodes said. "We'll ask him. Let's stop here."

They were about ten yards from the car. Rhodes heard the hissing of steam escaping from the radiator and smelled burned rubber and hot metal. The trunk lid had popped open, but the doors were still shut.

"Think he's playing possum?" Buddy asked. He still held the pistol in both hands.

"Could be. Let's have a look in the trunk. It's open, so we don't need an invitation."

They circled to the back of the car and peered into the shadowy trunk from a few feet away.

"Good Lord," Buddy said. "He's got somebody's head in there!"

Chapter 3

▼

"That's not a head," Rhodes said. "It's a wig stand. With hair on it. Real human hair, too, I'll bet."

"He scalped his victim?"

Buddy's voice trembled. Rhodes didn't know if the cause was excitement or disgust.

"No," Rhodes said. "His victim was Lonnie Wallace."

"It was Lonnie Wallace's body at the college?"

Rhodes wondered why all his conversations seemed to go this way. Maybe it was somehow his own fault.

"It wasn't Lonnie's body. Lonnie's just fine, but his shop was burglarized last night. Somebody stole some wigs and hair extensions. That's probably one of the wigs. It's on a wig stand. The extensions might be in the trunk, too."

Rhodes knew it was often a mistake to make assumptions, but in this case they seemed warranted.

"Oh," Buddy said.

He sounded disappointed, and Rhodes supposed he was. Capturing someone who scalped his victims would have been a lot more exciting than capturing, or *apprehending,* as Buddy would have put it, someone who'd stolen some human hair extensions and a wig or two.

Rhodes walked to the trunk for a closer look. Sure enough, there were some plastic bags that held what appeared to be hair. He went back to Buddy.

"We'd better see if the driver's okay," Rhodes said. "Keep that pistol handy."

Buddy perked up at the possibility of shooting somebody. "I'm ready."

Rhodes looked through the driver's window. A young man lay against the door, his head just lower than the window. Rhodes couldn't see his face. He wore a baseball cap with the Astros logo on it.

"Is he okay?" Buddy asked.

"I can't tell," Rhodes said.

He gave the door handle a tug, and the door popped open. The driver fell halfway out of the car before Rhodes managed to catch him.

Rhodes laid the young man on the ground, and Buddy moved over to have a look, but he didn't holster his pistol. He didn't get a chance to use it, however. The driver sprang up and hit the deputy in the chest with his shoulder, knocking him aside. Buddy's arms jerked above his head, and he pulled the trigger of the pistol just before he fell. The sound of the shot was like a starter's gun for the driver, who took off at a run. His cap flew off his head as he dashed around the car and into the trees.

Rhodes went after him, and within seconds he was running

over dry leaves with tree branches slapping at him. The driver was younger and faster, but Rhodes was persistent. He tried to think of something to slow the driver down, but nothing came to him. All he could do was hope for good luck. For him, that is. He hoped for some bad luck for the driver.

In the end, it wasn't luck that decided things. It was the driver's youth and overconfidence that did him in. He came to a fallen tree and jumped over it, something Rhodes would never have attempted.

The driver shouldn't have attempted it, either. He hadn't been able to see the low-lying brush pile on the other side. He landed in it, and it tangled his legs and tripped him up. He fell sprawling. The brush crackled around him.

Rhodes took the cautious approach and climbed over the deadfall. Before the driver could get back to his feet, Rhodes was right there, kneeling on his back.

Buddy panted up beside them, holding his pistol. He'd run around the deadfall. "Can I shoot him, Sheriff?"

"Not a good idea," Rhodes said. He was breathing hard himself. Sweating, too.

"Maybe just in the leg," Buddy said. "Or the foot. So he won't run off again."

"He won't run off again," Rhodes said, knowing that Buddy was talking for the driver's benefit. "Will you?"

"No," the driver said.

"Good. I'm going to ease up a little and put some cuffs on you. Put your hands on your head."

The driver did as he was told. Buddy held his pistol in his left hand and handed Rhodes his cuffs. Rhodes pulled the driver's left arm down and slapped on a cuff. He hooked the other on the right. Taking hold of the cuff chain, he stood up, pulling the driver along with him.

When they were standing, Rhodes got his first good look at the young man he'd been chasing. He was around twenty, Rhodes thought, maybe a little older. Hair over his ears and falling in his eyes. A red splotch on his face, most likely where the air bag had hit him. Faded jeans and dirty running shoes.

"What's your name?" Rhodes asked.

"Terrell."

Buddy looked at Rhodes, who knew what the deputy was thinking. They both knew about the Terrells. They were a family of survivalists, living on their own off in the woods and avoiding contact with anybody else as much as they could. All sorts of stories circulated about them. They were running a meth lab. They were farming marijuana. They were guilty of some kind of unspecified crime and would all be arrested if they ever showed their faces in town. Rhodes didn't think that even one of those stories was true.

"Terrell your first name or last?" Rhodes asked.

"Last. First is Isaac."

"People call you Ike?"

"Maybe."

"Good enough. That's what I'll call you. Got any ID?"

"In my back pocket there's a wallet."

Buddy removed a driver's license and handed it to Rhodes, who noted that Ike was nineteen. That would make him an adult in the eyes of the law.

Rhodes handed the ID back. "Are you any relation to Able Terrell?"

"Maybe."

"You take classes at the college?"

"Maybe."

"You need to communicate a little better," Rhodes said. "Might be a good idea to sign up for a speech class."

Ike didn't smile, but Rhodes hadn't expected him to. It wasn't much of a joke.

"You were out at the college this morning," Rhodes said, "and you were in a big hurry to leave. Any reason for that other than the hair you have in your trunk?"

Ike looked down. "I don't know anything about any hair. It looked like there was some trouble at the college, so I thought there wouldn't be any classes. I thought I'd just go home. Then you got to chasing me."

"There was some trouble, all right, and I got the idea you might have had something to do with it."

"Well, I didn't. I just didn't see any reason for staying around if there weren't going to be any classes."

"I'll bet he doesn't take any classes," Buddy said. "Those Terrells are all so worried about the end of the world that they don't put any stock in education. They just hole up in that compound of theirs and wait for the zombies to come after them."

"You live at the compound?" Rhodes asked Ike.

"Maybe." Ike paused. "You gonna read me my rights?"

"I haven't arrested you yet."

"I don't have anything else to say to you, then."

"He lives at the compound, all right," Buddy said. "All the Terrells live at the compound. There's a whole mess of 'em down there."

The compound was what everybody in the county called the place where Able Terrell and his family lived. Able's predecessors had lived on the land for generations. They'd been mostly ordinary country folks as far as Rhodes knew, never bothered anybody, mostly self-sufficient, worked little jobs that didn't pay a lot. Tilled gardens in the spring and killed hogs when the cold weather came around. Even Able had been ordinary for most of his life, until he got the idea that the apocalypse was coming. That had been in 1999, when there'd been a lot of talk about the millennium and how that might mean the end of the world. According to what Rhodes had heard, Able had started hoarding food, buying guns, and training his family for the "end times."

When nothing happened on January 1, 2000, Able had decided that the apocalypse might be a little bit late but that it was still coming. Nobody was sure just what kind of apocalypse Able feared or hoped for. As far as Rhodes knew, Buddy might have been right about the zombies. Whatever it was, Able was going to be ready for it. He had around seventy-five acres of land, and right about in the middle of it he'd built the compound, a living area that was walled off from the rest of the world by a ten-foot board fence.

Not many people visited behind that fence, if any, but the word was that Able taught his family rudimentary martial arts as best he could and had them practice shooting at targets with handguns, rifles, and crossbows. Able had a lot of guns, so the story went. All kinds of guns up to and including assault rifles. Rhodes didn't know how many crossbows there were supposed to be.

The children were homeschooled by Able's wife, Eden, and the family members were seldom seen in town. They'd never been in any trouble with the law, not since Rhodes had been sheriff.

"Able must be your daddy," Rhodes said to Ike. "I know he

had a son who'd be about your age now. Why'd you take the hair from the Beauty Shack?"

"I don't know what you're talking about," Ike said. "You better take these cuffs off or arrest me, one or the other."

Rhodes shrugged. People watched too much television and got too many ideas from crime shows.

"All right, then, I'll arrest you. Ike Terrell, you're under arrest for speeding, reckless driving, public endangerment, leaving the scene of an accident, resisting arrest, and assaulting a law officer. That'll do to start with. We'll get to the hair and any other charges later on." Rhodes read Ike his rights, then said, "Come on and we'll take you to the jail."

"If you lock me up—" Ike stopped talking and turned to go back to the car.

"If we lock you up, what?" Buddy asked.

"Nothing," Ike said. After taking a few steps, he added, "You'll see."

Rhodes and Buddy got Ike settled in the backseat of Buddy's car.

"Take him in and book him," Rhodes told Buddy. "Let him call a lawyer or his family, whichever he wants to."

"His family?" Buddy said. "They don't have phones there in the compound. They don't even have electricity."

"That's just stories you've heard," Rhodes said. "You don't know it for a fact. Everybody has a cell phone now, and that's bound to include Able. He has TV and probably a computer or two. A man's got to have a way of knowing when the apocalypse is about to happen. That's right, isn't it, Ike?"

"I don't have anything to tell you," Ike said.

"I could rough him up, Sheriff," Buddy said. "Get him to talk a little more."

Rhodes hid a grin. "Never mind. Just take him to the jail."

"Good idea," Buddy said.

When Buddy started on the way to town, Rhodes called Hack and told him that Buddy would be in with a prisoner.

"Call for a wrecker to pick up a Chevy Malibu," Rhodes said and gave Hack the location. "Tell him to hurry. I'll wait here for him, and then I'm going back to the college."

"Who'd you arrest?" Hack asked. "Anybody hurt? What's goin' on?"

"Tell you later," Rhodes said and hooked the radio with a good bit of satisfaction.

While he waited for the wrecker, Rhodes picked up Ike's cap and pitched it into the car. Then he had a look in the trunk. Besides the wigs and hair extensions, the trunk held a dirty spare tire with no air in it and a rusty jack. The interior of the car didn't produce anything of interest. There was the Astros cap, along with some jerky wrappers and a couple of empty soft drink cups from the Dairy Queen. Rhodes had thought there might be at least a handgun, if not an assault rifle, considering the rumors about Able's apocalypse arsenal. Rhodes tagged and bagged the hair, and by the time he'd done that, the wrecker had arrived.

The wrecker driver was Cal Autry, who got all the county business. He looked as if he'd gained a few pounds since the last time Rhodes had seen him, and he sported the fashionable unshaven look. Rhodes was sure that in Cal's case, however, fashion had nothing to do with it. Cal just didn't like to shave.

"Take the Chevy to the impound lot," Rhodes said. "You need any help hooking it up?"

Cal pushed back his Detroit Tigers cap. He was the only Tigers fan in Blacklin County, as far as Rhodes knew. Maybe the only one in Texas.

"I can handle it," Cal said. "You can go on about your business.

"I'll do that, then," Rhodes said, and within a couple of minutes he was on his way back to the college.

It wasn't easy to drive the car with his head poked out the window, but at least he could take it slow. He'd have to get the extra car as soon as he could. The county commissioners wouldn't be happy that he'd be filing another insurance claim, but there was nothing he could do about it.

When he got to town, Rhodes discovered that the accident at the foot of the overpass had been cleared, probably by Duke Pearson, one of the other deputies. Rhodes was glad to see it had been taken care of. One less thing for him to worry about. He already had plenty to worry about at the college. He should do something about that.

When he got to the parking lot the ambulance was just leaving. Ruth Grady and Seepy Benton stood near the Dumpsters, talking. Someone was with them, and Rhodes recognized Jennifer Loam, formerly a reporter for the *Clearview Herald* and now the sole owner and proprietor of her own news Web site. She'd been getting a good bit of advertising, thanks to a great kickoff with some photos from a big case handled by the sheriff's department, and Rhodes knew that some of the cell phone photos and video taken of this morning's chase would wind up on the site, along with photos taken of this crime scene.

Ruth had put yellow and black crime-scene tape around the Dumpsters, not that Rhodes believed it would do any good. He parked the county car near the Dumpsters and got out. Heat waves rose from the black asphalt, and Rhodes smelled the faint scent of garbage.

Jennifer Loam had been using a small video camera to record the scene, but she stopped as soon as she saw Rhodes. She came over and started asking him questions before he'd taken more than two steps. She was small, blond, and pretty. She was also very sharp and a good writer. She still held the video recorder in one hand. Rhodes didn't mind helping her with her stories when he could, but he wished she wouldn't use pictures of him on her Web site.

"Who were you chasing?" she asked. "Did you catch him? Did he have anything to do with this murder?"

She held up the video recorder, and Rhodes said, "I was after someone who was speeding. I'm not ready to release his name yet, and I have no idea if he was involved in what happened here."

He stopped, and Jennifer turned off the camera.

"That's not very exciting," she said. "I know there was a wreck. I got video of it from two different people. Did anyone get hurt later on?"

"No," Rhodes said.

Jennifer pointed to his car. "What about that windshield?"

"Hit by a piece of flying tire. I wasn't hurt."

Rhodes turned to Ruth Grady and asked what she'd found out at the scene.

"Not much," she told him. "I've searched the area, and I didn't find anything that looked suspicious. I found a cigarette butt and a coffee cup. That's about it."

"I found a penny," Benton said. He didn't mention that he'd already pointed out the cigarette butt to Rhodes. "A penny's supposed to be lucky."

"It didn't do Wellington any good," Rhodes said, "but it might be evidence. Did you tag it and bag it?"

"I did," Ruth said, "but it wasn't anywhere near the Dumpsters. It looked like it had been out here for a long time. It had turned almost green."

"And that's it?" Rhodes said. "A penny and a cigarette butt?"

"I wish I could say there was more. I took samples of the hair and blood from the Dumpster, but we both know it's going to be from Wellington."

"How about inside the Dumpsters?"

"They were emptied yesterday," Benton said. "The college doesn't have a cafeteria, so it's not so bad in there. I volunteered to climb in and have a look, but Ruth wouldn't let me."

"I climbed in myself," Ruth said. Rhodes gave her a skeptical look, and she added, "Seepy gave me a boost. There's nothing in there."

"Did you search Wellington's clothing?"

"As best I could without disturbing things. I didn't find anything suspicious. Maybe Dr. White will turn up something when he goes through the personal effects. Or in the autopsy. Or maybe the person you were chasing has some information."

"Not likely," Rhodes said. "What exactly do you think happened here?"

"I think I have it worked out," Ruth said.

She showed him the outline of the body that she'd drawn on the asphalt. Jennifer Loam had the video recorder at the ready.

"Here's where the body was," Ruth said. She pointed at the

blood on the Dumpster. "Here's where the victim hit his head. As far as we know, nobody saw what happened. We don't know when he died. Could have been early this morning before anybody came, or late last night after everybody had gone home."

"I stay late sometimes," Benton said. "I didn't see anything, and I'm alert, always watching for battery thieves."

Benton had baited a couple of thieves with his own battery not so very long ago, as Rhodes recalled, but he'd never admitted it.

"Even if you passed by, you might not have seen anybody," Ruth said. She indicated the chalk outline again. "Judging by the position of the body, I'd say the victim was behind the Dumpsters, out of sight. Someone else had to be there with him. There must have been a struggle, and the victim hit his head. Or someone caused him to hit his head. He fell here between the Dumpsters."

"Or he was pushed," Benton said.

Ruth looked at him. "I'm the officer here."

"I'm a deputy, too," Benton said.

"I'm undeputizing you," Rhodes told him.

"You didn't even give me a badge."

"That makes it easier. Let Ruth finish."

"He might have been pushed here," Ruth said. "I think he just fell, though."

"Anything else?" Rhodes asked.

"That's all. How did things work out with the person you were after?"

Rhodes thought about the broken windshield. "Could've been better."

He looked at Jennifer. He might as well let her hear a little about what had happened. She'd find out sooner or later anyway, so he explained that the driver of the car was Ike Terrell.

"Isn't his family the one that lives in the compound?" Jennifer asked. "Waiting for the world to end?"

"That's the family," Rhodes said, "but I'm not sure what they're waiting for."

"They're supposed to have all kinds of weapons there."

"Just a rumor," Rhodes said.

"They never associate with people here in town."

"Ike claims he takes classes here," Rhodes said.

Benton raised his hand. Rhodes looked at him.

"May I speak?" Benton asked. "Strictly as a citizen, and not as a deputy, of course."

"Go ahead," Rhodes said.

"Ike Terrell does go to school here," Benton said. "He's in my calculus class."

"Calculus?"

"Right. You know what calculus is, don't you?"

"Barely," Rhodes said. "We need to talk later. You can go on to your office now."

Benton didn't object. He told Ruth good-bye and left. When Benton was inside the building, Rhodes asked her what she'd found at the Beauty Shack.

"Wait," Jennifer said, holding up her camera. "What's this about the Beauty Shack?"

"Put down the camera, and I'll tell you," Rhodes said. "You can go talk to Lonnie about it later and get some pictures."

Jennifer lowered the camera, and Rhodes filled her in on the burglary. When he'd finished, he asked Ruth again what she'd found there.

"Less than I found here," Ruth said, which was what Rhodes had expected. "Not even an old green penny. We'll never catch the person who did it."

"Oh, I think we will," Rhodes said.

Jennifer turned the camera on him.

Ruth seemed skeptical. "How?"

"A combination of instinct, experience, investigative prowess, and our many coply skills."

"Is that all?"

"Well," Rhodes said, "a little bit of luck wouldn't hurt."

"We don't have that much luck."

Rhodes smiled at the camera. Maybe he liked being on the Internet better than he thought.

"Sure we do," he said. "I already have a suspect in custody."

Chapter 4

▼

Jennifer Loam told Rhodes that she'd put the news about his superb police work in solving the Beauty Shack burglary on her Web site, and Rhodes reminded her that Ike Terrell was merely a suspect.

"I'll be sure to mention that," Jennifer said. "Several times. I'll remember to use the word 'alleged,' too. Frequently. Nobody's going to pay much attention to your superb police work anyway. They'll all be talking about what happened here at the college."

"We don't know what happened here," Ruth reminded her.

"No, but we know that the result was a dead man. People can draw their own conclusions."

"You report," Rhodes said. "They decide."

"Hey," Jennifer said, "that's pretty catchy."

"It just came to me," Rhodes said. "Feel free to use it. Right now, though, I need to get inside and talk to some people."

"Can I come along?"

"Not a good idea. You don't want to interfere with a police investigation."

"No, I don't want to do that," Jennifer said. "I'll just go visit Lonnie and work on the Beauty Shack story. That nobody will be interested in."

"I'd better get back on patrol," Ruth said. "Crime never rests." Rhodes knew she was half joking, but only half. If there were just a burglary or a murder to work on, life would be simple enough, but there was always something else going on. Small things, usually, but plenty of them, and they all took time away from the main investigation. Which was why he didn't often get a day off.

He went into the building and was chilled by the air-conditioning. It wasn't a bad feeling after standing in the hot parking lot. The concealed fluorescent lights overhead reflected off the polished floors. The doors to the classrooms were closed, but Rhodes could hear the low hum of voices. He looked up to see if there were any security cameras in the hallway. There were, but there hadn't been any outside. The college had been planning to install some for a while because of the battery thefts, but Rhodes had put a stop to those, and the cameras hadn't been installed, as far as Rhodes knew. Saving money was always a consideration in the academic world, or so Seepy Benton had told Rhodes on several occasions when his salary was mentioned.

Rhodes's first stop was the dean's office. The administrative assistant told him that the dean was on the telephone but that she wanted to see Rhodes. He said he'd be back later and went on up to the second floor to see Seepy Benton.

Benton's office always looked as if a tornado had blown through it. Papers and books were piled on the desk, on the chairs, on the floor. The shelves might once have looked orderly, but that had been long ago. A guitar case leaned against the desk, with a guitar beside it. Benton was at the desk, tapping away on his computer keyboard. A new addition was a white dry-erase board. It was covered with equations that looked like something from a cartoon drawing. They were meaningless to Rhodes.

"Uploading a new song video to YouTube?" Rhodes asked Benton from the doorway.

Benton thought of himself as the greatest singing and songwriting math teacher to come along since Tom Lehrer, a major difference being that Lehrer played piano and Benton allegedly played guitar.

"No," Benton said.

He'd taken off his straw hat, and Rhodes noticed that he'd had a haircut recently. That and the neatly trimmed beard indicated that dating Ruth was having a good effect on him.

"I can show you a video of my latest composition if you'd like to see it," Benton said. "It's a surreal country-western song called 'Drowning in a Stream of Consciousness.' "

Seeing it wasn't the bad part. Hearing it was, so Rhodes said, "Not now. We have more important things to do."

"I've been doing some of them already," Benton said.

"Like what?"

"Wellington and I are Facebook friends. I've been looking at his Facebook page."

"I got the impression that you didn't care much for him."

"Being friends on Facebook doesn't have anything to do with being real friends. It's completely different. But sort of the same."

"Thanks for clearing that up. Did you find anything?"

"No. Most teachers have learned to be discreet on Facebook, or not to have pages at all. Or to have one under a fake name."

"You think Wellington did that?" Rhodes asked. "Used a fake name?"

"I can't say. If he did, we won't be likely to find it. His Facebook page is useless anyway. He never posted anything."

"What about a Twitter account?"

Benton looked at Rhodes with feigned surprise. "Wow. You're learning about this computer stuff, aren't you."

"Slowly," Rhodes said. "Very slowly."

"In this case, it doesn't matter if you're slow. I can't find a Twitter account for him."

"Unless he used an assumed name," Rhodes said.

"It's always a possibility, but it's doubtful. I can't really see Earl as a fan of social media."

"Why didn't you like him?"

Benton changed the subject. "Have you searched his office?"

"Not yet. The dean was on the phone when I went by, and I didn't get the key."

"I'll call and see if she's off the phone," Benton said. "I'm sure she'd like to talk to you."

Benton didn't wait for Rhodes to respond. He picked up the phone and punched in some numbers. He talked to the administrative assistant for a few seconds and then hung up.

"She can see you now," Benton said. "I think you should talk to her about the students. She's worried about keeping them here. A lot of them have jobs. They can't just stay on campus all day."

"I'll go see her," Rhodes said, wondering why Benton was so eager to get rid of him. "You wait for me here."

"I wouldn't think of leaving," Benton said.

●   ●   ●

Dean King was agitated and animated. She waved her hands and spoke a little too loudly for the small office, which was much neater than Benton's. She was obviously one of the clean-desk crowd.

"I've been on the phone all morning," she said, "trying to find a replacement for Mr. Wellington. English teachers are usually a dime a dozen, but just try to find one in the middle of the semester. It's not easy, let me tell you."

"I'm sure it's not," Rhodes said.

"That's not all," the dean said. "We have to let the students leave. We can't have classes as usual, not with what's happened. It's not respectful, and they're not paying attention to the instructors. Besides, there's no way you could question all of them."

"I know," Rhodes said. He'd thought about it on the way back to town, and he knew the situation was impossible. "How about this. You make an announcement and say that I need to talk to anybody who might have some helpful information. That includes the faculty members. Everyone else can go."

It wasn't a good solution. Rhodes knew it was likely that the person having the most information would leave with the rest.

The dean leaned back in her chair, her relief obvious. "Thank you. That will help me get things back on track. I'll announce it right now. I'll dismiss classes for the rest of today and tomorrow. I can have anybody with information meet you here. I can give you some privacy."

"That'll be fine," Rhodes said. "I'd like the key to Wellington's office, too, if I have your permission to search it."

"Of course." The dean opened a desk drawer and got out a key. She handed it to Rhodes and said, "This is a passkey. I'll need it back."

"I'll bring it by," Rhodes said. "When I do, I have some questions for you."

"Me? What have I done?"

"Not a thing, but I need to find out about Wellington."

"I'm not sure what I can tell you."

"Me either," Rhodes said, "but we'll find out. I do have your permission to search Wellington's office, right?"

"Certainly."

"Good. I'm going to talk to Benton now. Be sure to make that announcement."

"I will," the dean said.

She was quick about it, too. Rhodes heard it over the speaker system as he went up the stairs to Benton's office, and he wondered who would come by to talk to him, or if anyone would.

By the time Rhodes arrived at Benton's office, the dean had finished the announcement, and almost immediately there was the rumbling noise of chairs being shoved back, followed by doors opening and students rushing into the hallways and chattering away on their cell phones. Most of the classrooms were on the first floor, so Rhodes was able to get Benton's door closed before any of the students saw him.

Benton had cleaned off a chair by his desk, where he sat clicking a computer mouse.

"Take a look at this," Benton said.

Rhodes sat down and looked at the computer screen.

"All right," he said. The screen was a little blurry. "I'm looking. Now tell me what I'm supposed to see."

"It's a Web site called ProfessoRater. Students can rank their instructors on a scale of one to five and make comments about them. This is a page of my rankings."

"So?" Rhodes said.

"In the comments you'll notice several occurrences of words like 'awesome' and 'great' and 'best.' "

"I don't see 'modest,' " Rhodes said.

"That's strange," Benton said. "Modesty is one of my most outstanding qualities."

"Right. And you're showing me this because?"

"Because I want you to see Wellington's rankings." Benton made a couple of clicks with the mouse and wound up on a new page. "What words do you see there?"

"I get the feeling you have them memorized."

"As a matter of fact, I do," Benton said. " 'Worst.' 'Terrible.' 'Avoid at all costs.' If I were the dean, I wouldn't worry about lining up any grief counselors."

"People can grieve even for someone they didn't like, especially when he's killed outside their school."

"That's true," Benton said. "I wasn't thinking. He wasn't well liked, though."

"Okay, I can see that the students didn't think he was a very good teacher, but can you rely on what students think?"

"You saw what they said about me." Benton clicked back to his own rankings. "Absolutely correct. Case closed."

"If you say so. Is there supposed to be a motive for killing him hidden in his rankings somewhere?"

"Let's take another look," Benton said. He clicked the mouse and moved the cursor to a comment. "How about this one."

Rhodes had to unbutton his shirt pocket and get out his reading glasses. He leaned forward and read the sentence that Benton held the cursor on. It said, "He is not only the worst teacher but he's picky. Picky, picky, picky."

"I'm guessing that being picky isn't good," Rhodes said, taking off his reading glasses and returning them to the shirt pocket.

"Your guess is correct," Benton said. "Wellington was a little too strict. He was hard to like because of it."

"These postings are anonymous, I take it."

"That's right. People might not be honest if they had to give their names."

"Did the dean know about Wellington's bad habits?"

"Everybody knew. Wellington didn't have many friends on the faculty. You might want to ask the dean about it."

"You can count on it. You said that Wellington didn't have many friends. He must have had one or two."

"The chair of the English Department is Harold Harris. He was as good a friend as Wellington had, but that wouldn't mean they did more than speak in the halls. I think they had their problems."

Rhodes stood up. "Let's go have a look at Wellington's office."

"There's one more thing I want to show you. Well, I'd better not. You're just a civilian when it comes to the college, and I can't deputize you. I'm not a civilian, though, so I can look at a student's class schedule. I checked out Ike Terrell's."

"And?"

"And he was in one of Wellington's classes." Benton smiled. "Am I deputized again?"

"I'm not so sure it's legal," Rhodes said.

"Oh, come on. Do you watch TV?"

"I hardly ever have time."

Rhodes could remember the days when he had time to slip home and watch an old movie now and then. An old, bad movie, his favorite kind. It had been too long since he'd done that.

"TV is very educational. If you watched, you'd know that Steven Seagal gets made a special deputy all the time. That sheriff in Arizona had him working in the danger zone, and I'm a lot better qualified than Steven Seagal."

"He's an accomplished martial artist."

"So am I," Benton said. "I've told you before that I studied with Professor Lansdale and learned his system."

Benton had indeed told Rhodes that before, more than once. Anybody could study martial arts. That didn't mean he'd learned anything.

"Want me to bust a few moves?" Benton asked as if sensing Rhodes's skepticism.

"Not right now," Rhodes said.

"I've been through your Citizens' Sheriff's Academy. Can Steven Seagal say that?"

"He might have been through some other county's academy."

"I don't think so. How about it? Can I be a deputy again?"

"Temporarily," Rhodes said.

"But no badge?"

"No badge," Rhodes said.

Wellington's office was much neater than Benton's, if not as immaculate as the dean's. Rhodes had brought Benton so he could have a go at the computer. It belonged to the college, not to Wellington, but Wellington might have used it for personal things.

While Benton was on the computer, Rhodes looked around

the office. He didn't see anything that looked unusual. The bookshelves were crammed with things like *The Norton Anthology of American Literature,* several editions of different grammar handbooks, and novels by mostly American writers. Hemingway, Faulkner, and Fitzgerald were prominent. The only surprising thing was a copy of a brand-new hardback with the snappy title of *Piney Woods Terror Attack.* Rhodes pulled it off the shelf.

"The latest Sage Barton thriller," Benton said. "Even English teachers love them."

A few years earlier, two women named Jan and Claudia had been in a writing workshop in Obert, a little town not far from Clearview. There'd been a murder, and in the course of solving it, Rhodes had met the women. They'd eventually written a novel about a heroic Texas sheriff, a retired Navy SEAL who went about his job while armed with twin Colt Peacemaker revolvers. Barton fought terrorists, captured serial killers, and outran explosions that left craters the size of small lakes. Everyone in Blacklin County liked to claim that Rhodes was the model for Sage Barton, though Rhodes and Barton weren't alike in the least. The claim had made the books hot sellers in the county; in fact, they sold well all over the country.

"I didn't think English teachers read stuff like this," Rhodes said, putting the book back on the shelf.

"You think they sit around reading Shakespeare all day?" Benton asked.

"I don't guess I ever thought about it."

"Everybody needs a break," Benton said. "Have you read *East Texas Terror Attack?*"

Rhodes wasn't a fan of the books, but Jan and Claudia always sent him a signed copy of the latest one. Ivy had read it. Rhodes hadn't. When he told Benton that, Benton said, "You should. It's about a terrorist plot to destroy the Big Thicket."

Rhodes couldn't imagine why the terrorists would want to do that. He also didn't know how the Big Thicket had moved to the county where Sage Barton was the sheriff. He wasn't going to ask, however.

"There are lots of explosions," Benton said. "Every good book has lots of explosions."

Rhodes wasn't sure about that, but he wasn't a literary scholar. Neither was Benton, for that matter. Rhodes changed the subject. "Did you find anything on the computer?"

"No," Benton said. "Just the usual stuff. I thought there might be something encrypted or secured by a password, but everything's right there in plain sight. You're not going to find anything helpful there."

"I need a copy of his class rosters."

"You'll have to get them from the dean. I'm not sure that I'm allowed to pass along that kind of thing, even if I am a deputy."

Rhodes looked through the desk drawers and found a folder marked ATTENDANCE.

"I won't need the rosters," Rhodes said, removing the folder. He opened it to be sure it held what the cover said, and it did. "I have what I need right here. Let's make a copy on your printer."

"You'll never be able to interview all those students."

"I'll narrow things down."

"How?"

"I'll think of something," Rhodes said, though he had no idea of what it might be. He put the rosters back in the drawer. "Or not. I don't think this was a student argument, anyway. Let's check the messages on the phone."

"I can do that," Benton said, but he didn't find anything. All the messages, if there had been any, were gone.

"Now what?" Benton asked.

"If I were Sage Barton, I'd blow something up and that would solve everything."

"You keep telling everybody you're not Sage Barton, though."

"Sometimes I wish I was," Rhodes said.

Chapter 5

▼

Only one person was in the dean's office waiting for Rhodes, and he wasn't there voluntarily. The dean introduced him as Harold Harris, the chair of the English Department. He looked like an athlete who'd let himself go a little, and he was dressed like Rhodes expected a college teacher to be dressed. He wore a navy blazer, a striped tie with a light blue shirt, khaki slacks, and penny loafers. His hair was brown with a little bit of gray at the temples. He had even more gray in his Vandyke. Or maybe it was a goatee. Rhodes had never been clear on the differences.

"I asked Dr. Harris to come by to talk to you about Dr. Wellington," the dean said. "He was Dr. Wellington's department chair. I'll leave you two alone now."

"I'll need to keep the key to Wellington's office," Rhodes said, "and I need to know one other thing from you. Which car in the lot belonged to Wellington?"

The dean frowned. "I suppose the office is not to be opened."

"That's right. Now about that car."

"I don't know about the car. We don't require parking permits. Maybe Dr. Harris can tell you."

She left, and Harris moved immediately to the chair behind the dean's desk to assume the seat of power. It didn't work out too well, because Rhodes stood beside him and loomed over him.

"I have a lot of questions," Rhodes said, "but we'll start with the car first."

"Wellington drove a little Ford Focus," Harris said. His voice was deep, deeper even than Seepy Benton's. He seemed nervous. Rhodes didn't blame him. "Red. There aren't too many of those in the lot, I'm sure."

"I'll find it," Rhodes said. He could get the license plate number later if he needed it, which he doubted. There couldn't be more than a couple of those cars in the whole county. "What about family? Did Wellington have any kin that you know about?"

"That information would be in the HR office," Harris said. "He was originally hired for the home campus, and he just came here at the beginning of the spring semester this year. This is only his second semester on this campus."

"Why did he come here?"

Harris rubbed his hands together. "We needed another full-time instructor, and we advertised the position. Wellington was teaching part-time at the main campus, and he was one of the applicants. He had a good reputation there and seemed solid. The hiring committee voted to recommend him."

"Had any of them read his rankings on ProfessoRater?"

"He had very few from his previous job," Harris said, looking at the floor. "We have other ways of determining an instructor's effectiveness."

Rhodes wondered about Harris's rankings. He didn't mention Benton's. It might be a good idea to talk to someone at the home campus about Wellington and see if there was some reason he'd been eager to leave town.

Rhodes sat on the edge of the desk and continued to loom.

"The dean said Wellington had been in a little trouble already. Tell me about that."

"It was nothing, really," Harris said, not quite meeting Rhodes's eyes. "Earl was harmless, but he was also somewhat irascible. We have a few students who complain about anything they think is an unkind word, and several of them didn't like the way Wellington handled certain things. He was very picky."

"So I've heard," Rhodes said. "Can you give me an example?"

"For one thing, he was very outspoken when students came late to his class. He believed they should be on time, every time. He didn't hesitate to make some comment to any student who was late more than once. He was even more outspoken if a cell phone rang during a class meeting. He was quick to let the offending students know about their transgressions, and he did it in front of the class. The students were embarrassed."

Rhodes recalled some of his own teachers and the things they'd said on occasion. There were any number of them who'd been outspoken when students did something they considered wrong, either in class or out of it. They didn't care in the least if someone was embarrassed.

"Students complain to you if they're embarrassed?" he asked.

"All the time," Harris said, in a tone that indicated he was resigned to an endless stream of student complaints. "And it's not just the students. It's the parents, too."

Rhodes tried to remember if his parents had ever complained about any of his difficulties at school. He couldn't think of a single time that they'd ever even entered the building. Maybe they'd attended a PTA meeting or something, though he didn't remember that, either.

"The parents complain?"

"If a student has any little grievance at all, the parents are in my office or the dean's office almost instantly. 'We pay taxes here,' they say. 'You can't tell our child he has to be in class on time.' Or, my favorite, 'We pay taxes here. You have to see to it that my child doesn't fail.'"

"Not that you're bitter," Rhodes said.

"I don't mean to sound that way, but I suppose I am. I'm old enough to remember when my job was to teach classes, make schedules and budgets, and order books. Now I sometimes feel that I spend most of my time settling disputes."

"What do you do about it when parents and students complain?"

"Usually I try to have the student talk to the instructor first. If that doesn't work, then I talk to the instructor myself. When that doesn't satisfy everyone, we have a meeting with the student. Sometimes the dean is in the meeting. Sometimes the dean and the instructor are there."

"How did you handle Wellington? Any meetings?"

"I talked to him and told him to restrain himself during class. I told him to speak to students privately so they wouldn't be embarrassed in front of their peers. Things usually went smoothly for a while after our little talks, but then he'd forget."

Talking hadn't relaxed Harris any. He dry-washed his hands as he talked, and he seemed happier when the topic wasn't directly related to Wellington.

"Was Wellington irascible in other ways?" Rhodes asked. "I've heard he wasn't well liked."

Harris squirmed a little in the chair. "What do you mean?"

"I mean that neither the students or the faculty liked him very much. You must have had some complaints about his bad behavior."

Harris was plainly uncomfortable with the conversation. "He did make some inappropriate comments to students. I handled all of those personally. I didn't see any need to involve the dean. When I had discussions with him about the problem, he said he was only teasing the students."

"Give me an example," Rhodes said again, then realized it was the kind of thing his English teachers used to write on his essays when he was in school. Harris should have known to give examples. He was probably avoiding them deliberately.

"I can't go into personnel matters," Harris said, confirming Rhodes's suspicions.

"You can when there's a death involved. I'm going to need names."

"I'll give you an example, and then you decide whether you need the names. The most recent incident was with a young woman with red hair and freckles. She was very upset that Wellington referred to her as 'his speckled friend.'"

"That's it?" Rhodes said.

In his school days, teachers had said things that were considerably worse. Nobody had thought anything about it. Rhodes felt old and out of it.

"That's it. She cried in my office."

If that was what the student remark had to do with, Rhodes wasn't at all sure it was the kind of thing that could lead to a scuffle that ended with someone dying. Maybe he didn't need names after all.

"How did you find out about Wellington's death?"

Harris brushed a hand across his forehead. "I arrived only a few minutes ago, and Dean King told me about it. Terrible, terrible. I can't understand it."

"What about enemies other than his offended students?" Rhodes asked, though he already knew the answer. Nobody ever had any enemies, at least not according to the people Rhodes questioned. "Faculty members, maybe."

"Just Dean King," Harris said.

"Tell me about that," Rhodes said.

Dean King wasn't any happier talking to Rhodes than Harris had been. Rhodes didn't loom over her, however. He was tired of looming. She sat at her desk, and he sat in one of the chairs put there for visitors to the office.

"Wellington's been quite a problem for you, hasn't he?" Rhodes asked.

The dean nodded. "Yes, he has. I've found a replacement for him, though, and his grades are all in the computer and up to date, so the problem is solved."

"That's not the kind of problem I meant," Rhodes said. "I meant that he's been a problem ever since he came to the campus. Lots of complaints from the students."

Dean King fidgeted. "Listening to students' problems is part of my job. It's not a part I enjoy, but I think I handle it well."

"Parents, too?" Rhodes asked.

"Sometimes parents are involved, yes. Again, that's part of the job."

She seemed more philosophical about it than Harris did.

Rhodes wondered if she really was or if she was just better at hiding her feelings. Or maybe Harris was able to take care of most of the complaints before they ever got to the dean's office.

"You've talked to Dr. Harris about Wellington more than once. You even said that you wished he hadn't been hired."

The look on King's face indicated that she might be wishing she hadn't hired Harris, either.

"Sometimes we make a mistake," she said. Rhodes figured she was talking about Wellington. "In spite of the interviews and the recommendations. It can happen."

"What about ProfessoRater? Ever look at that?"

"You can't believe those things. The only students who use them are the ones who want to praise an instructor or damn him. We have our own system for evaluation."

"Did the problems turn up in those?"

"Yes, sometimes, but Dr. Wellington's evaluations were mostly good ones. He's been here only one full semester, though, and we prefer to look at several semesters before arriving at any conclusions."

That seemed fair to Rhodes, but they weren't going to have that opportunity with Wellington.

"Were you in on any discussions with Wellington and Harris?"

"Dr. Harris prefers to handle his departmental matters himself if possible. If there's something he can't resolve, then he comes to me."

"I don't suppose you ever had any disagreements with Wellington yourself?"

Dean King looked surprised that he would ask such a question. "What do you mean by that?"

"I mean did you have any arguments that might have gotten a bit loud. Arguments that others might have overheard."

Dean King sighed. "You've been talking to my administrative assistant."

Rhodes had heard about the argument from Harris, who'd gotten it from the administrative assistant. So he said, "No, it's general knowledge around here. What were you arguing about?"

"I wasn't arguing. Dr. Wellington was."

"What about?"

"Plagiarism. He'd accused one of his students of plagiarizing a paper. The student insisted he hadn't done any such thing. I took the student's side in the matter."

That was interesting. Rhodes had always believed that administrators took the side of the instructor. He asked what King's reasoning had been.

"We have ways of checking online to see if a student's plagiarized a paper. In this case, Dr. Wellington couldn't find any proof. I suggested that the student had simply worked especially hard on the paper. Dr. Wellington didn't agree, but in light of the fact that we had no proof, I had no choice but to take the student's side. Dr. Wellington just couldn't let it go, however. I insisted, and that resulted in the argument."

"Didn't Dr. Harris handle this kind of problem?" Rhodes asked.

"He tried, but the student wasn't satisfied with Dr. Harris's answer. He insisted on a meeting with me."

"I'll need the name of that student," Rhodes said.

"I can't tell you that."

"I can find it out easily enough."

"Then you'll have to find it out. I can't give out information like that because of the laws about confidentiality."

"That's okay," Rhodes said. He knew that students talked

among themselves. He could ask a few and get the name. If not, Benton probably knew. Or maybe Rhodes could just make a guess. "It was Ike Terrell, wasn't it."

Judging from the look on the dean's face, Rhodes knew that he wouldn't have to ask anyone else after all.

"I'm not saying you're right," the dean told him.

"That's all right. Dr. Harris said something about having meetings with parents about certain problems. Did you have a meeting with Ike Terrell's parents about the plagiarism accusations?"

"I didn't mention any names," the dean said. "I really can't discuss things of that nature."

"You can answer yes or no. That's not a discussion."

"Then without mentioning any names, the answer is no. I . . . the student involved asked me not to get in touch with his parents, and I didn't. I didn't see that it was necessary since Dr. Wellington had no proof of his accusations."

Rhodes thought it over. He decided he didn't have any more questions for the time being, so he thanked the dean for her help.

"Did you find any grief counselors?" he asked before he left.

"I'm still working on that. It might not be necessary."

Rhodes didn't ask why. Benton had already given him the answer to that one.

"If any of the students happen to mention anything helpful, you'll let me know, I'm sure."

"I'll call if I hear anything," Dean King said. "Some things might have to remain confidential."

Rhodes thought the college was too concerned about confidentiality and not concerned enough about who had killed Wellington. He thanked the dean again and left her office.

On his way out of the building, Rhodes stopped by the HR office and checked on Wellington's family connections and address. The HR director was Susan Owens. She'd worked in the public schools before coming to the college. Rhodes had known her for years, and she was happy to cooperate with him. She looked up Wellington's file on her computer.

"Dr. Wellington lived at the Forest Apartments on Pine Street," she said. She gave Rhodes the apartment number. "He's not from Texas. He's from Arkansas, and his contact information is a brother there. I'll give you the address."

She wrote the address on a notepad, tore off the sheet, and handed it to Rhodes. He folded it and put it in the pocket with his reading glasses.

"The college will be notifying him," she said. "If that's all right with you."

Rhodes didn't mind at all. "Did you know Wellington?" he asked.

"Not well," Susan said. She wore old-fashioned half-glasses with plastic frames. She pushed them up on her nose. "Just to speak to in the hall."

"What did you think of him?"

"*De mortuis nil nisi bonum.* I learned that in an English class, believe it or not. Part of it was the title of a story we read. Do you know what it means?"

"I think we must have read that same story when I was in school," Rhodes said. "I don't remember anything about the story, but I remember the title means that we should say nothing but good about the dead."

"Very good. I'm impressed with your memory. I believe in that saying, by the way, so I'm going to tell you that Dr. Wellington had very nice posture."

"A good quality in anybody," Rhodes said, standing a little straighter.

"Yes," Susan said. "I think so, too."

Chapter 6

▼

The radio on Rhodes's car started to squawk as he opened the door. He got in and grabbed the mic. Hack came on and said there was another emergency.

"You got to get over to Hannah Bigelow's house," Hack said. "Quick."

"What's happened?"

"Wild hog in the house."

"Hogs are Alton Boyd's job."

Boyd was the county's animal control officer. He'd dealt with hogs before. Also cows, goats, and lots of dogs and cats. Not to mention an alligator.

"Alton's out somewhere around Milsby with Duke. There's a bunch of cows loose on the road, and Alton's tryin' to round 'em up while Duke keeps people from havin' wrecks. Ruth's down around Thurston, and Buddy's workin' a fender bender out east of town. The hog's up to you."

Rhodes thought of a television character whose lament was that it was always something. Roseanne Roseannadanna or some odd name like that. The name didn't matter, though. She was right. In Blacklin County, it was always something. Murder investigations sometimes had to come to a stop because of mundane troubles like hogs in the house. Not that there was anything mundane about a hog in the house.

"I'm on my way," Rhodes said.

Wild hogs covered Blacklin County and Texas like fleas covered a stray dog. They were starting to cover a lot of the whole country, for that matter. Rhodes had seen reports of them from as far north as New York. They tore up pastures, killed calves, ruined crops, and multiplied faster than rabbits. They were beginning to move into urban areas, and Rhodes figured the damage inside a house would be considerable.

The state of Texas had tried all kinds of things to get rid of the hogs, but so far nothing had been truly effective. Rhodes had experienced plenty of problems with them himself, but this was the first time he'd heard of one being inside the Clearview city limits, much less inside someone's house. He supposed it had been just a matter of time until it happened.

Hannah Bigelow didn't live far from Rhodes, only about a half mile, but that put her house a half mile closer to the edge of town. Rhodes hoped he wasn't going to have trouble with hogs in his house or yard. Speedo wouldn't like that kind of visitor at all. Ivy wouldn't be too thrilled about it, either. Rhodes would have to see about having the fences strengthened, not that fences stood much of a chance against a determined hog, and if there was anything the wild hogs were, it was determined. And unrelenting.

Rhodes parked in front of the Bigelow house and got out of

the car. The house was an old one, built sometime during the 1920s, Rhodes thought. One Bigelow or another had owned it all that time, and they'd managed to keep it in fairly decent shape. Hannah was the last of the Bigelows, though, and she was a Bigelow only by marriage. Her husband, Lawrence, last of the true Bigelows, had been dead for a couple of years.

Hannah was waiting for Rhodes on the concrete porch outside her front door. She was short, a little over five feet tall, but stout. She wore her gray hair pulled back into a tight, neat bun at the back of her head.

"It's about time you got here," she said. "If my Lawrence were here, you'd have a little more snap to your service. My Lawrence wouldn't have tolerated a slow response time like this when there's an emergency."

"I'm sorry I took so long," Rhodes said. "I was working on another case. Where's the hog?"

"Inside, like I told that Hack Jensen when I called. I'm scared to go in there with it. Do you know how dangerous those wild hogs are?"

"Yes, ma'am, I sure do."

"Then where's your rifle? You did bring a rifle, didn't you? You can't kill a hog with your bare hands."

Rhodes heard a crash inside the house.

"That sounded like my china cabinet," Hannah said. "You'd better get in there and put a stop to things."

She was right, but Rhodes had to ask a question first. "How did a wild hog get inside your house?"

"You know about Donnie?"

Rhodes said that he knew. Donnie was the Bigelow family dog, or had been. He'd passed away not long after Lawrence.

"Donnie was a good dog, and we trained him to come inside through a doggie door in the back. I never thought a hog could get in through it, though."

"So the hog's not very big," Rhodes said.

"I didn't say it was big. I said it was tearing up my house. Now are you going in there or not? If my Lawrence were here, you wouldn't be standing out here talking. You'd be right in there after that hog."

"I'm going in," Rhodes said.

"What about your rifle?"

"I wouldn't want to kill a hog inside your house if I could help it. You'd have blood and hair all over the floor and the walls."

Hannah looked thoughtful. "That would be bad. It's bad enough he's tearing up my house. I can see why you don't have a gun. You better not come running out and leave him in there, though. My Lawrence wouldn't stand for it if you didn't get that hog."

"I'll get him," Rhodes said, hoping he sounded a lot more confident than he actually was. He opened the door and went inside the house. He left the door open, in case he needed to make a quick exit, no matter what Lawrence might have thought about it. His hope, however, was that the hog would be the one making the exit.

The light in the front room was dim even with the door open because the shades, old-fashioned shades like you didn't see much anymore, were pulled down. In the light that slanted across the room from the doorway, Rhodes could make out a bookcase, a piano, and a writing desk. A small table lay overturned by the piano, and a broken lamp lay on the floor. The breaking lamp, not the china cabinet, had probably been the crash they'd heard.

There was no sign of the hog, but Rhodes heard something

snuffling around in another room. A crash came from the back of the house. Not much of a crash, but it was followed by renewed, and louder, snuffling. Rhodes went through a hallway with a chest of drawers and a coat tree and into a kitchen. Light came in through a window over the sink, and Rhodes spotted the rear end of a black hog.

The front end of the hog was inside a plastic trash can in which the hog was rooting around for food. The hog snuffled and snorted and kicked back its trotters as it tried to get a better grip on the slick vinyl floor and push itself deeper into the trash can. It had no idea that Rhodes was anywhere around. All it cared about was whatever it had found in the trash.

"My Lawrence would get that critter right now," Hannah said at Rhodes's back, and Rhodes didn't jump more than a foot. He turned to look at her.

"What are you doing in here?"

"I thought you might need some help. Sure didn't hear you doing anything about that hog. Next thing you know it'll have the refrigerator open."

The hog was still busy in the trash can and either didn't hear them or didn't care that they were there.

"I don't need any help," Rhodes said. "You go on back outside. Your Lawrence wouldn't want you to get hurt."

"You got that right. He always took care of me. Now that he's gone, I have to rely on the officers of the law, and from what I've seen so far, there's not much to 'em."

"We do the best we can," Rhodes said. "You go on back to the porch, and I'll see what I can do about this hog."

"You sure you don't need my help?"

"I'm sure."

"Well, if you say so."

Hannah left by way of the hall, and Rhodes turned back to the hog. The bristles on the hog's back end didn't seem nearly as coarse as they should have, and the animal lacked the overpowering smell of the wild variety. Rhodes thought that what he had here was an impostor, someone's pet potbellied piglet that had escaped its home and decided to see what the rest of the big wide world had to offer.

That was good news, since it meant that Rhodes wouldn't have to kill it, not that he had anything to kill it with, and he wouldn't have to worry about being ripped to shreds by its tusks. In fact, he very much doubted that the hog had any tusks at all.

The bad news was that he still had to do something about it. The pig might be tame, it might even be housebroken, but that didn't mean it would be easy to handle. Rhodes wished he hadn't asked Hannah to leave. He wished Alton Boyd were there to help him. He wished he had the telephone number of the hog's owner. For that matter, he wished he knew who the owner was, but the wishes weren't doing him any good. He was going to have to do something, and do it before the pig decided to come out of the trash.

He wondered if Hannah had really gone back outside.

"Hannah?" he said.

"I knew you needed some help," she said from the hall, and she came back into the kitchen.

"Do you have any duct tape?" Rhodes asked.

"Of course I do. My Lawrence always said you could fix anything with duct tape. Duct tape and WD-40. He always had to have those two things in the house. What he couldn't fix with one of them—"

Rhodes held up a hand. "Could you bring the duct tape in here? Fast?"

"It's in there." Hannah pointed to a cabinet drawer. "Right in there. My Lawrence said to keep it handy because you never know when you'll need it, so that's what I do."

The pig lunged forward, pushing the trash can a foot or more. There must have been something really tasty down in the bottom. Rhodes didn't think the pig would hear him, so he stepped around him and opened the cabinet drawer. Sure enough, a roll of silver duct tape lay right in front. Rhodes took the tape and went back to Hannah. While she watched, he stripped a long length of tape off the roll and tore it free. It wasn't a quiet process, but the pig wasn't bothered.

As Rhodes handed the length of tape to Hannah, the pig began to back out of the trash can. Rhodes tossed the roll of tape in the general direction of the stainless steel kitchen sink. It landed with a clang, and Rhodes grabbed hold of the pig's back legs.

The pig reacted instantly, squirming and squealing. Rhodes kept his grip, forced the legs together, and upended the pig into the plastic can while bringing the can into a standing position. The pig snorted and kicked with its front feet, but without much effect since they were restrained inside the can. It tried to kick with its back feet. Rhodes held tight. The pig writhed. Rhodes pushed down and kept it in the can.

Hannah stood by calmly with the tape, watching.

"Wrap the legs!" Rhodes said. The struggling pig was dragging him away from her. "Wrap the legs!"

"Oh," Hannah said.

She stepped over, and Rhodes tried to hold himself away from the legs so she could pass the tape around them. After she'd made a couple of rounds, Rhodes squeezed the legs closer together. Hannah made three more rounds. It wasn't easy, as the pig never gave up. Its exertions carried Rhodes to the right and to the left, and he slid around the kitchen, with Hannah calmly following along and continuing to wrap the legs.

Rhodes knew they weren't going to get the front legs wrapped. There was just no way. Maybe if they'd had the defensive line of the Houston Texans with them they could've managed it, but he and Hannah weren't up to the job.

Hannah had finished the wrapping, but Rhodes couldn't let go. He said, "Call the sheriff's department. When you get Hack Jensen, hand me the phone."

"You have your hands full already," Hannah said.

"Don't worry about that. Just make the call."

An old black handset hung on the wall beside the refrigerator. Rhodes wouldn't have been surprised to see a dial on it, but when Hannah took the receiver off the hook, he saw the pushbuttons.

"What's the number?" Hannah asked.

Rhodes gave it to her, speaking up to be heard over the squealing of the pig, and she punched it in. When Hack answered, she said, "Mr. Jensen, this is Hannah Bigelow again."

She listened for a moment and then said, "Yes, the sheriff is here. He's holding on to the wild hog right now, but he wants to talk to you."

"Never mind," Rhodes said as the pig surged to the side, pulling Rhodes right along. "Just ask him if anybody's called in about a missing potbellied pig."

"What's a potbellied pig?"

"It's what I have my hands full of. Just ask him, please."

Hannah asked Hack, listened, and turned to Rhodes. "He says yes, someone's just called in about a missing pig."

"Ask who it was," Rhodes said.

He was a little short of breath now, and sweating as much as he had when he'd chased Ike Terrell. He didn't know how much longer he could hold on to the pig.

Hannah asked Hack about the owner. "He says it's Paul Wooton."

Wooton lived not far from the Bigelow house, about a block closer to town.

"Have him call Wooton and tell him to come get his pig," Rhodes said. "Tell him to bring a rope and to make it snappy."

"My Lawrence used to say that. 'Make it snappy, Hannah,' he'd say." Hannah's eyes got a faraway look. "I haven't heard that expression in years."

Sweat ran out of Rhodes's hair and down his forehead. "Just tell Hack." The pig jerked him to the left. "Please."

Hannah spoke into the phone again and hung up. "He says he'll do it. He doesn't know how long it might take Mr. Wooton to get here."

Wooton couldn't come too soon for Rhodes. He wasn't going to be able to hold on to the pig for much longer. Wild or not, it wasn't happy inside the trash can now. Rhodes had to try something different.

"Go open the back door," he told Hannah. "I'm going into the yard."

Hannah didn't question him. "This way," she said.

She opened the kitchen door and went out onto a screened-in porch. Rhodes followed her, holding the pig's legs tight against his chest and pushing the trash can along in front of him on the vinyl flooring as if it were a wheelbarrow. Once on the porch, he saw the back door with the doggie door in the bottom.

"You should nail that thing shut," Rhodes said, "or replace the whole door."

Hannah gave him a sad smile. "My Lawrence would do that if he were here. He was handy with things like that. He's the one who put the doggie door there in the first place. But he's not here."

She opened the door, and Rhodes pushed and dragged the pig out onto a small porch. He wasn't sure he could bump the plastic trash can down the steps without breaking it, and if he did that, the pig would escape for sure.

Only three steps, he told himself. *You can do it.*

He did, but when he got to the bottom, he had to sit down on the steps while the pig struggled madly inside the trash basket as Rhodes clung to its legs.

Hannah stood on the porch above him. "What's a potbellied pig?" she asked again.

"It's a kind of miniature pig that people have as pets," Rhodes said. "Lots of people have them. Not here in Clearview, but other places."

"I never heard of such a thing. I thought it was a wild hog, like we have roaming all over the county. Why would anybody want a pet pig?"

"You'll have to ask Mr. Wooton," Rhodes said. "Why don't you go out front and see if he's here yet."

Hannah walked down the steps, past Rhodes and the canned pig, and down the driveway to the front of the house. Rhodes sat on the step and thought about pork chops, baby back ribs, ham, and bacon.

He wasn't sure how long it was until Wooton arrived, maybe

five more minutes. Wooton was a small man with a wrinkled face and faded jeans that were too long for his legs. They drooped over the tops of his shoes and dragged on the ground. He held a loop of white nylon rope in his right hand. At the end of the rope was a metal clasp.

"That my pig you got in that trash can?" he asked.

"I hope so," Rhodes said. "We can worry about the identification later. Let's see if we can get it out of this thing."

"Pig's name is Susie," Wooton said. "'Cause of how people call pigs. Soooooeeeeee. Like that. So I named her Susie. Name's on her collar, if that's her."

"The pig has a collar?" Rhodes asked.

"Sure. So I'll know it's my pig if it happens to wander off."

Rhodes wondered how many pigs Wooton thought wandered off in Clearview.

"You're going to need a better fence," Rhodes said. "We can't have pigs strolling around the neighborhood."

"Thought I'd locked my gate. Hadn't. I'd pull that trash can off 'er, but you got 'er mighty stirred up. She might not know me."

Rhodes didn't think it mattered if Susie knew Wooton or not. As soon as the can was off, she was going to make a break for it.

"Her front legs aren't taped," Rhodes told Wooton.

"Figgered they weren't. You hang on to the back ones, and I'll snap this clasp on her collar. Then we'll be all set."

Rhodes had his doubts about that, but he didn't see that he had much choice in the matter. He renewed his grip on Susie's back legs, and Wooton pulled on the trash can. The pig was wedged inside tightly enough so that Wooton had to strain a little. When the can popped off, bits of paper scattered. There wasn't much else left inside the can. Whatever had been in there was now inside

Susie, who emitted a high-pitched squeal and tried to run as soon as her head cleared the trash can. Her front trotters didn't get much traction on the driveway, however, so Rhodes was able to hang on while Wooton snapped the clasp to a silver ring on the metal-studded collar.

When the clasp was secure, Wooton wrapped the rope around his arm. He reached into his pocket and came out with a knife. He pitched it to Rhodes and said, "Cut the tape."

Rhodes caught the knife in one hand, keeping one arm wrapped around Susie's legs. "Are you sure?"

"Sure I'm sure. Go on. It'll be okay."

Rhodes let go of the legs. He opened the blade and sliced through the tape. Susie's legs snapped apart, and she kicked backward, narrowly missing Rhodes, who'd quickly leaned to one side. Susie's hooves hit the ground, and she plunged forward, jerking Wooton nearly off his feet.

Wooton held on to the rope and talked to Susie in what Rhodes assumed were supposed to be soothing tones as she dragged him along.

"It's all right, Susie," Wooton said. "It's all right. The mean sheriff won't hurt you any more."

Rhodes folded the knife blade into the handle. He didn't mind that Wooton wanted to calm Susie, but he did resent the "mean sheriff" crack somewhat. He stood up and watched the pig drag Wooton around the yard.

"What about my damages?" Hannah asked. "Who's going to pay me for that?"

"That's between you and Mr. Wooton," Rhodes said.

"I'll pay," Wooton said. "You just send me a bill."

He had Susie almost under control now and was guiding her down the driveway toward the front of the house. Or maybe she was dragging him. It was hard to tell. Rhodes followed along behind. Hannah was beside him.

"You heard him, Sheriff," she said. "He's going to pay. You're my witness."

"All right," Rhodes said. "I'll hold him to it."

"You see that you do. My Lawrence would hold him to it if he were here, but he's not. So I need all the help I can get."

Rhodes thought Hannah did very well for herself and didn't have any trouble getting help.

"I really thought that was a wild hog in my house," she continued. "I never dreamed it could be a pet pig. Will wonders never cease."

"I doubt it," Rhodes said.

"You doubt what?"

"That wonders will ever cease. If you do get a wild hog in your house, you be sure to give us a call."

"I'll do that." Hannah stopped and plucked at Rhodes's sleeve. "Look. There's another wonder."

Wooton opened the door of his old black pickup and helped Susie climb inside by pushing her from behind. When she was on the bench seat she settled down and lay quiet. Wooton closed the door.

"Thanks for helping me out, Sheriff," he said. "I'll remember it next election day."

"I'd appreciate that," Rhodes said.

He handed Wooton his pocketknife. As Wooton put it away and got in his pickup, Hannah said, "I'll remember, too, Sheriff. My Lawrence and I always voted for you. Every single time."

"Thanks," Rhodes said. "I need all the help I can get."

"I can see that," Hannah said. "I surely can."

Chapter 7

▼

Rhodes was closer to Wellington's apartment building than he was to the campus, so he checked in with Hack.

"You catch that wild hog?" Hack asked.

"It wasn't a wild hog. It was Paul Wooton's pet pig. You know that."

"It'd sound better on that Web site of Jennifer Loam's if it was a wild hog. If it was Sage Barton doing the rescue job, that's what it'd be."

"It was a pet pig, and I'm not Sage Barton. I'm going to Wellington's apartment. Did Buddy get Ike Terrell booked?"

"Yeah. The kid's a model prisoner."

"Good. Did he make any calls?"

"Just one, to his daddy."

"You know what he said?"

"Nope. I'm just the dispatcher, not a spy. You want a spy, you go to the county and get me a raise."

"I'll see about that at the next meeting."

"What meeting is that?"

"Never mind. I'm going to Wellington's apartment. I'll come back by the jail when I've finished searching it."

"We'll all be looking forward to seeing you," Hack said.

The Forest Apartments on Pine Street weren't located in a forest or anywhere near one, and in fact Pine Street wasn't lined with pines. Rhodes had never seen a pine tree anywhere near it, and he thought that the street must have been named for someone named Pine, though he didn't know that anyone named Pine had ever lived in town, either.

The apartments were some of the first ever built in Clearview, which meant that they were over fifty years old, just one long building, two stories tall, made of faded red brick. The social elite didn't live in Forest Apartments or even come near them after dark.

The manager was Marty Sewell, and Rhodes had dealt with him only about a couple of weeks ago when someone had stolen the copper out of several of the apartment air conditioners in the wee hours of the morning. Sewell's tenants weren't known as model citizens of the town, and the place was a bit run-down. Maybe it was the best place Wellington could find on short notice.

Sewell's thin brown hair was combed over his scalp in a vain attempt to cover its barren, speckled landscape. It reminded Rhodes of the thin spot on the back of his own head.

Sewell's sunken eyes stared at Rhodes from above purplish bags. His big ears and pointy nose gave him the look of a sad weasel.

"What'cha want today, Sheriff? You caught those good-for-nothin's that messed up my air conditioners? I'm still waitin' for the insurance to pay off on those things."

"Haven't caught up to them yet," Rhodes said, "but we're still looking."

Sewell didn't appear thrilled with Rhodes's answer, or with Rhodes himself, for that matter. He stood inside his apartment with the door about halfway open, and it was clear that he didn't intend to open it any farther. A sour smell of greasy cooking and dirty laundry wafted through the opening.

"I need to get into Earl Wellington's apartment," Rhodes said.

"Wellington?" The possibility of scandal seemed to spark Sewell's interest. "What's he done?"

"Nothing, as far as I know," Rhodes said. "Except die."

"He died?" Sewell didn't seem surprised, or maybe he just didn't care. "What happened? Heart attack? He was a smoker, you know. They're prone to heart attacks."

"I don't know the cause of death yet," Rhodes said, which if it wasn't exactly the truth was as much of it as Sewell needed to know. "I'd like to get a key to his apartment. Maybe I'll find a clue."

"Just a minute," Sewell said.

He closed the door, but he was back in a few seconds with a key, which he handed to Rhodes.

"Here it is. Apartment 212. You bring it back when you're through up there."

Rhodes said he would and left Sewell standing there, staring at his back.

.   .   .

The first bad news that Rhodes got was that Wellington had a cat. Rhodes knew it even before he entered the apartment because he started to sneeze. The cat greeted him just inside the door. It was small, probably not more than eight pounds, if that. It was black and white, a tuxedo cat. Rhodes thought about his responsibilities as sheriff. The cat wasn't included in them. It was Alton Boyd's job, but Boyd was probably still out herding cows, or off on some other mission.

It wasn't just the cat that had made Rhodes sneeze. The apartment smelled of stale cigarette smoke. Wellington hadn't bothered to go outside to smoke when he was at home.

The cat looked up at Rhodes and meowed.

"I'm sorry about your human friend," Rhodes said, "but I can't take you with me. I already have a cat at home, not to mention a couple of dogs. You and the dogs wouldn't get along."

"Meow," said the cat.

"I know the smell is irritating," Rhodes said. "It bothers me, too, but you should be used to it by now."

"Meow," said the cat.

Rhodes knew what would happen if he took the cat to the city's animal shelter and nobody adopted it. He didn't like to think about that. Surely somebody would adopt it, though. It was a good-looking cat, glossy coat, sparkly eyes, tail sticking straight up. Wellington had taken good care of it, except for making it live with secondhand smoke, and it was friendly, not in the least intimidated by Rhodes.

Rhodes went through the small living area and into the kitchen with the cat right behind him. The cat's food bowl was empty, but it had plenty of water. The kitchen door opened onto a little balcony. Rhodes stepped out on the balcony and took a look. A hibachi sat against the wall. That was all. There wasn't even a chair. Rhodes closed the door. The cat sat a few feet away watching him.

"No clues out there," Rhodes said.

"Meow," the cat said.

Rhodes sneezed.

Rhodes and the cat went back to the living area. It held an old couch, a scarred coffee table, and a chair that must have come from a thrift store. A makeshift bookcase of concrete blocks and unvarnished pine boards held a lot of books in the Sage Barton vein, along with several by someone called Joe Lansdale. Rhodes wondered if he was any relation to the professor with whom Benton claimed to have studied martial arts. Not that it mattered. At any rate, Wellington's reading tastes weren't exactly highbrow, as far as Rhodes could tell. He must have needed a break from the writers in the books Rhodes had seen on the shelves in his office at the college, as Benton had suggested.

A small flat-screen TV and DVD player sat on a table near the bookshelf. A few DVD cases lay beside it. Special-effects-heavy thrillers. Nothing that would have interested Rhodes, whose tastes ran more to old and bizarre movies like *The Alligator People* or *I Married a Monster from Outer Space*.

Rhodes went into the bedroom with the cat right at his heels. The cat's litter box was in the bathroom just off the bedroom. There was barely enough room for it. Rhodes checked out the medicine cabinet. Aspirin, mouthwash, toothpaste, razor and blades, shaving cream. A tube of antiseptic cream. Aftershave.

"No help here," Rhodes said.

"Meow," the cat said.

The bedroom was no help, either. No gun under the pillow or

mattress, no drugs hidden in the sock drawer. The only thing that might be helpful was the laptop computer on the bedside stand. Rhodes bagged it. He'd take it with him and have Ruth look at it. Or Benton, as a last resort.

He took the computer to the county car and came back for one last check. The cat sat and watched him.

"I'll have Buddy come and take a look," Rhodes told the cat. "He can question the other people living here. They might be able to tell us something useful."

"Meow," the cat said.

Rhodes almost sneezed, but he managed not to. Maybe he was getting used to the cat.

"I've already told you I can't take you," he said. "Maybe Buddy needs a feline companion."

He'd managed to palm off a dog on Seepy Benton. If it had worked once, it might work again. Seepy, however, was single, and Buddy wasn't. That might make a difference.

"Meow," the cat said.

"I told you the reasons I couldn't take you," Rhodes told it. "Those dogs at my house are savage beasts. They'd tear you limb from limb."

The cat looked skeptical. Rhodes didn't blame it. The thought of Yancey confronting it made Rhodes smile. The only thing Yancey could tear limb from limb was a rag doll. The cat would terrorize him.

"You're right," Rhodes said. "You'd scare the dogs."

The cat moved its head. Maybe it was a nod. Rhodes wasn't sure. He wasn't fluent in cat sign language.

"My wife would kill me if I brought in another cat," Rhodes said.

It wasn't really his fault that he'd taken in two dogs and a cat already. They hadn't had anywhere else to go. Or so he'd told himself. He wasn't going to take them to the animal shelter, so he hadn't had much choice.

"I have to go to the college and look at a car," Rhodes said. "You can't go with me. You'd have to ride in the county car. You probably don't like to ride in cars."

"Meow," the cat said, looking up at him.

"Okay, maybe you do. We'll see."

Rhodes reached for the cat. He told himself that if it shied away from him, he'd leave it in the apartment and send Alton Boyd for it later that day.

The cat stood up. Rhodes slipped his hand under its stomach and picked it up. The cat began to purr.

"Maybe the dogs will be okay with you around," Rhodes said, "but Sam won't. He's a territorial animal. You won't even be able to get close to him."

The cat purred.

Rhodes took it out to the county car and set it inside. It pawed the seat a time or two, then curled up on it and lay down, as comfortable as if it had been living in the car for years.

"I'll be right back," Rhodes said.

The cat closed its eyes. Could it already be asleep? Rhodes didn't know. He went to Sewell's apartment and knocked on the door.

"Find anything?" Sewell asked when he opened the door.

"Nothing much. I'll have to keep the key for a while."

"I need to get the place cleaned out. Get it rented. Can't have it vacant."

"You'll survive. We'll finish with it as soon as we can. Right now I need to ask you some questions."

Sewell looked doubtful. "You wanna come in?"

Rhodes got a whiff of the sour smell. "I'm fine right here. What kind of visitors did Wellington have?"

"You think I keep a watch on visitors?"

"We've been through this a time or two," Rhodes said. "I know you do."

"Only when they make noise. I don't stand at the window and peep out."

Rhodes knew that was true, but he also knew that Sewell kept up with the comings and goings better than he was admitting.

"You're not in any trouble," Rhodes said. "Yet. Now tell me about Wellington's visitors."

Sewell shrugged. He patted his thinning hair. He rubbed his earlobe.

"Well?" Rhodes said.

"All I can remember is that he had a woman up there a week or so ago. I don't know who she was. Wasn't any of my business."

"What did she look like?"

"Do I look to you like the kinda guy who's an expert on women? She was a woman. That's all I know. It was a weekend, and they were quiet. The neighbors didn't complain. As long as the neighbors don't complain, I don't nose into things."

"Right," Rhodes said. There was no reason a man couldn't have company in his own apartment. "What kind of car did she drive?"

"What makes you think—"

Rhodes cut him off. "I just do. Now tell me."

"Looked like a Chevy to me. Wasn't a car, though. Was a pickup. Black Silverado."

That was no help. The county was full of black Silverados.

"Anybody else?" Rhodes asked.

"I don't remember anybody. Like I said, I don't keep a watch."

"Maybe you should," Rhodes said.

Riding in the car didn't bother the cat at all. It didn't even wake up when Rhodes started driving. The only thing to do, Rhodes thought between sneezes, was to drop off the cat at his house. Maybe it would run away. If it didn't, maybe Ivy, Yancey, and Sam wouldn't even notice it.

Maybe Rhodes would win eight million dollars in the Texas Lottery.

He parked in his driveway and slid a hand under the cat, which woke up and said, "Meow."

Rhodes picked the cat up and carried it into the backyard. Speedo gave them a suspicious glance but otherwise ignored them. Rhodes went on into the kitchen, where Sam was asleep in his usual spot by the refrigerator. At the sight of Sam, the cat started to squirm in Rhodes's hand, so he set it on the floor.

Rhodes heard Yancey's toenails clicking on the floor, and the cat turned toward the door into the kitchen. Yancey bounded through it and stopped short, skidding again as he had that morning. He looked a bit like a character in an old Warner Bros. cartoon. As soon as he was able to stop the skid, he turned and ran from the room.

"He's not your biggest fan," Rhodes told the cat.

The cat didn't seem to care. It walked over to Sam's food bowl and started to eat. Sam opened an eye to have a look, then closed it. The cat finished eating and drank some water. After it had finished, it sat down and groomed itself for a while, keeping an eye on Sam, who didn't budge.

Grooming complete, the cat walked over to Sam and curled up against his back. Sam opened his eyes, thought things over, and went back to sleep. Rhodes couldn't believe it. Weren't cats supposed to be intensely territorial? Weren't they supposed to resent any intruders into their space? What was going on here? It was as if these two had been litter mates, but the possibility of that was so small that it couldn't be seen with the naked eye. Rhodes decided that they were acting contrary to their nature just to spite him. On the other hand, maybe they were just weird, like every other cat in the world.

"This arrangement might work out after all," Rhodes said. "What do you think?"

Neither cat bothered to answer him.

Chapter 8

▼

On his way back to the college campus, Rhodes realized that he'd missed lunch. It happened all the time, and he couldn't understand why he never seemed to lose any weight. Not that he needed to lose weight. He still weighed the same as he had for the last fifteen years or so. However, he was losing the battle with gravity, and he couldn't see his belt buckle.

Thinking about food made Rhodes hungry, so he stopped by the Dairy Queen and went to the drive-through window. Ivy tried to keep him on a diet of healthy foods. He remembered the meatless meat loaf without affection, and he told himself she'd never know if he had a cheeseburger now and then. And some french fries. Maybe a Blizzard with Reese's Peanut Butter Cups.

After he had his order, Rhodes sat in the parking lot and ate his meal while he thought about the day so far. An apparent murder, a wild hog that wasn't, and a cat adoption, and the day wasn't over yet.

He hadn't really learned much about Wellington, and he was suspicious of some of the things he'd heard. Some of what he'd been told didn't seem quite right, but if he listened long enough to enough people, he'd eventually get to the truth, or that was the way it usually worked. He hoped it would work again.

It didn't take long for him to finish his meal, and he felt much better afterward, considerably better than he had after the meatless meat loaf, which lacked the proper amount of fat and calories to sustain a man of action. He drove to the college and spotted Wellington's red Ford Focus immediately. It was one of the few cars left in the parking lot, and it was the only Focus there.

Rhodes didn't think it would be a good idea to search it on the lot. He got Hack on the radio and asked him to call for the wrecker to pick it up and to have Ruth look it over in the impound lot.

"You're sure spendin' the county's money freely," Hack said. "How am I ever gonna get a raise?"

"You worry too much about money," Rhodes said. "Think of all the fringe benefits you have."

"Ha," Hack said.

"Get Buddy to go out to the Forest Apartments on Pine and question the residents about Wellington if he's done with that fender bender."

"He's been finished with that for a while. Moved on to a suspicious man out near Obert."

Rhodes knew better than to ask about the suspicious man. If he did, he'd never get off the radio. He told Hack he'd come to the jail as soon as he could and signed off.

Cal Autry showed up about ten minutes later, and Rhodes told him to take the car to the impound lot.

"Place is getting crowded," Autry said.

"Let's hope we don't have any more customers for you for a while," Rhodes said.

"You need to do something about that windshield on your own car."

"You got that right," Rhodes said.

He thought about what he needed to do next. So many things came to mind that he was almost overwhelmed, but he thought he'd start by having a talk with Ike Terrell. After he did something about the windshield.

"When you drop that car off," Rhodes said to Autry, "come by the jail and pick this one up."

"Another customer already," Autry said. "Business is sure good."

"Take it to the Burgess Body Shop. They'll know what to do."

"Be pretty hard not to," Autry said.

Rhodes drove to the jail and parked out front. He'd use the spare cruiser for a day or so while the windshield was being replaced. He didn't think he'd even mention the windshield to Hack. No use to give him an opening for criticism.

When Rhodes opened the door and entered the jail, he saw Hack at his desk. Lawton, the jailer, stood outside the door to the cellblock. As soon as they saw Rhodes, both men started to whistle the same tune. It was familiar, but Rhodes didn't quite recognize it. He stood and listened for a few seconds, and then it came to him. It was *"El Degüello,"* which Rhodes had heard many times while watching a movie called *Rio Bravo*.

He walked to his desk, put Wellington's laptop on it, and sat down.

The whistling continued.

He started working on the form to log the laptop into evidence.

The whistling continued.

Rhodes knew that if he gave in to Hack and Lawton, it would be a while before he found out the reason for the whistling. Was it worth the aggravation? He decided that it was either give in and be aggravated or continue to listen and be even more aggravated, so he turned in his chair.

"All right," he said, "what's up with '*El Degüello*'?"

The whistling stopped.

"You ever see *Rio Bravo*?" Hack asked.

"Not more than a dozen times."

"Then you oughta know," Lawton said. "It means—"

Hack glared him into a quick silence. Hack was always the leader in these things, and he didn't like for Lawton to give the game away so soon.

"I know what it means," Rhodes said. "No quarter."

"Yeah, that's it, all right. In the movie. But do you know what it means to us?"

"Who's us?"

"Us right here in this jailhouse."

Rhodes thought it over. He said, "It means that I'm John Wayne, Lawton's Dean Martin, and you're Walter Brennan."

Lawton started to laugh, looked at Hack's red face, and nearly choked trying to stifle his laughter.

"The question is," Rhodes said, ignoring both of them, "who's Ricky Nelson and who's Angie Dickinson?"

"That ain't what it means," Hack said, his face still dangerously red. Rhodes hoped he wasn't going to have some kind of episode.

"I had a feeling it didn't really mean that," Rhodes said. "So what *does* it mean?"

Lawton wisely kept quiet. Hack said, "You remember how in that movie John Wayne arrested this kid whose daddy was comin' to get him out of jail?"

"I remember," Rhodes said.

"Well, you got Able Terrell's kid here. What if his daddy comes after him?"

"They say he's got rocket launchers down there in the compound," Lawton said. "He could blow the walls of this jail right down."

"I don't think he has rocket launchers," Rhodes said, though he wasn't really sure. There was no telling what somebody might need in case of the zombie apocalypse. "We don't have to worry about that."

"Maybe he has 'em and maybe he don't, but he's got all kinds of guns," Hack said. "He could come in here and wipe us out."

"Runs a meth lab back in those trees," Lawton said. "That's what they say."

Rhodes had often wondered about how the Terrells survived. Fishing and gardening wouldn't be enough to get by on, not unless they were very good at it. He was almost certain, however, that they weren't selling meth. If they were, there'd be a steady stream of customers into the compound. Nobody knew of anybody who visited the compound, and nobody had ever reported heavy traffic in the area.

"Oughta go in there and arrest the whole bunch of 'em," Hack said.

"I'll tell you what, Stumpy, you get some dynamite lined up, and we'll be all set. He won't stand a chance."

"You can make fun if you want to, but it could happen like I say. What this county needs is a SWAT team. That'd do the job."

Rhodes wondered if Hack had been talking to Mikey Burns, one of the county commissioners. Burns would love the idea of a county SWAT team.

"We don't have one, though," Rhodes said. "What about that suspicious stranger Buddy was checking on?"

Once Hack was given the opportunity to hassle Rhodes, his mood improved immediately, as Rhodes had known it would.

"Mighty suspicious, all right," Hack said. "Just down the road from Miz Killen's house. She lives not too far from the old college out there."

"Lots of trees on that road," Lawton said. "Stranger could hide in 'em and not be seen for a while."

"That's right," Hack said. "A woman livin' alone can't be too careful. Gotta keep an eye out for suspicious strangers."

" 'Specially one that just stands around all day lookin' right at her house," Lawton said.

"Buddy was ready, though," Hack said. "He had that cannon of his loaded up and primed. Got a hair trigger on that pistol, he tells me."

"Be against the law to kill the stranger," Lawton said. "Seein' as how he was federal."

"Wait a second," Rhodes said. "Are you telling me there was a federal agent in Obert? Spying on somebody's house?"

Hack looked at Lawton, who shrugged and grinned.

"Well, now," Hack said, "that's not exactly what we said."

"What we said was—" Lawton began, but Hack cut him off.

"What we said was, the suspicious stranger was federal and it would be a crime to shoot him."

"A federal crime," Lawton said. "Serious business."

As usual when Hack and Lawton were doing their routine on him, Rhodes felt slightly disoriented, as if he'd wandered into an old comedy routine by Abbott and Costello, whom Hack and Lawton happened to resemble in their physical appearance as well as their conversations. Hack was a slightly shorter version of Abbott, mustache and all, and Lawton a somewhat less rounded Costello.

"Who's on first?" Rhodes asked.

Hack looked at Lawton. "Do you know what he's talkin' about?"

"Not me," Lawton said. "I thought we were talkin' about the suspicious stranger."

"Just tell me," Rhodes said. "Is Buddy in federal custody for shooting a federal agent? Is Mrs. Killen a spy?"

Hack tried to look surprised that Rhodes could be so dense. "We never said any of that."

"Then what did you say?"

"Well—" Lawton started, but Hack cut him off again.

"What we said was that Mr. Gore—you know Mr. Gore? Lives right down the road from Miz Killen?"

Rhodes knew Gore. He'd owned a lumberyard at one time and had retired to Obert several years ago, but Rhodes knew Gore because of something else.

"He called us about some vandalism a while back."

"That's the man," Lawton said. "The very one."

"Somebody ran over his mailbox," Rhodes said.

"Crime against property," Hack said, "and a federal offense, too, since a mailbox is used to hold mail."

"We caught the perp," Lawton said. Rhodes wondered if he'd been hanging around with Buddy. "Wasn't really vandalism, though."

It hadn't been vandalism, and they hadn't caught anybody. The school bus driver on that route had called in and confessed. He'd hit a pothole in the gravel road, swerved, and taken out the mailbox. Nobody had been hurt or even shaken up, and the driver hadn't called when it happened because he had to finish his run on time and didn't want to get the students home late. He'd paid Gore for the mailbox the next day.

"I think I know where this story's going now," Rhodes said. "Mr. Gore got a new mailbox."

"Nice sturdy one," Hack said. "Standin' tall. Lookin' right at Miz Killen's house."

"No wonder she was nervous," Lawton said. "What with that stranger not movin' all mornin' long."

"Buddy didn't shoot it, did he?" Rhodes asked.

"Nope," Hack said. "He went by Miz Killen's house and had a little talk with her. Told her it might be a good idea if she paid a visit to Dr. Fiddler."

Fiddler was the optometrist who had an office attached to the local Walmart.

"What did she say to that?" Rhodes asked.

"She told Buddy she could see as good as anybody and that he was a smart-alecky young whippersnapper."

"She called him a whippersnapper?"

Rhodes hadn't heard the term in years. The last time had been when Gabby Hayes had used it in some movie Rhodes had seen about ten minutes of on TV.

Hack nodded. "That's what Buddy said she called him, and you know Buddy don't lie."

"So Dr. Fiddler shouldn't be expecting her to show up at his office."

"I don't think so," Hack said. He grinned. "I don't think Miz Killen's gonna be callin' about any mailboxes for a while, though."

Just another day in Blacklin County, Rhodes thought. Maybe he could get a straight answer to another question now that Hack and Lawton had had their fun, so he gave it a try.

"Who called in the dead man at the college?"

Hack looked frustrated. "Ever'body in town. Well, that's what it seemed like. Phone just started to ring till ever' line was full. One of 'em was your pal Seepy Benton, but there was plenty of others."

Rhodes hadn't been hopeful that knowing who'd called in the death would be of any help, so he wasn't too disappointed in what Hack told him. He turned back to his work just as the phone rang.

Hack answered, listened. "You sure about that? You could drive into town, tell him right here."

The speaker on the other end got loud and angry then. Rhodes could hear the tone but not the words.

"You could even tell him on the phone," Hack said.

The voice on the phone was loud and angry again in response.

"No need to get snippy," Hack said. "I'll tell the sheriff and see if he can make it."

The same angry tone came from the phone.

"You have a nice day, now," Hack said and hung up.

In all his years in office, Rhodes had never heard Hack say that before.

"That was your friend Able Terrell," Hack said. "Well, it wasn't him, exactly. It was some guy said he was callin' for Able. Able wants you to come out to the compound for a little visit. Wants to talk about his son."

That wasn't protocol. "We don't go to him," Rhodes said. "He comes to us."

Hack looked frustrated. "I told the fella that. Did you hear me tell him that?"

"I heard you. It's too bad Able won't come. He should visit his son."

"What he should do and what he's gonna do is two different things. The fella said he didn't leave his place for anybody but that you'd want to come down there and see him."

"What's this fella's name?" Rhodes asked.

"Duffy, I think he said. Sounded like that, anyway."

Rhodes didn't know anybody named Duffy who was associated with Terrell, but that didn't mean much. Nobody knew who was at the compound.

"Did he say why I'd want to make that visit?"

"He said he has something to tell you about the dead man," Hack said.

That did put a different spin on things.

"He could've told me on the phone."

"I know you were listenin'," Hack said. "I know you heard me tell the fella that. Able won't talk on the phone. Says he doesn't trust phones."

"Did he mention where they heard about Wellington?"

"Same place me and Lawton did," Hack said. "You sure didn't tell us. It's on Jennifer Loam's Web site."

"She already has a story about that?"

Rhodes supposed he shouldn't have been surprised. News had always traveled fast in Clearview, and with the addition of the Internet to the town's life, it traveled even faster.

"Has one about that and the car chase, too," Hack said. "Sounds like somethin' Sage Barton would've been in."

Rhodes didn't want to talk about Sage Barton. "Did Duffy mention what kind of information Able had?"

Hack shook his head. "Just said he had it. You gonna go?"

"I guess so." Rhodes stood up. "I might as well hear what he has to say. First I need to put this laptop in the evidence room and then talk to our prisoner."

"He ain't doin' much talkin'," Hack said. "Buddy couldn't get a word out of 'im."

"Maybe I can be more persuasive," Rhodes said.

He put the laptop away. When he came back, he told Hack to have Ruth check it over, and then he headed for the door to the cellblock. As he went through the door, Lawton and Hack started to whistle *"El Degüello."*

Chapter 9

▼

The cellblock, like beauty shops, had its own unique smell, and it was just as hard to describe. It was composed of powerful cleansers mixed in with what seemed to be the smell of a few generations of prisoners who'd been housed there over the years, along with some industrial-strength air freshener that Lawton used too much of to suit Rhodes. Maybe it covered some other, even less pleasant smells, though.

Ike Terrell lay on his bunk, staring at the bottom of the unoccupied bunk above him. He wore the county's orange jumpsuit, which it occurred to Rhodes might have passed as fashionable street wear in the seventies. A long time gone, and probably for the best.

Ike didn't deign to acknowledge Rhodes's appearance at the cell door, so Rhodes tapped on the bars.

"Yeah?" Ike said.

"We need to talk," Rhodes said.

"I don't have to talk to you."

The kid had plenty of attitude. Rhodes had to give him credit for that.

"Not if you don't want to. If you'd like to have a lawyer, we can get one here. I wouldn't be surprised if the judge had already assigned one to you."

Ike swung his legs off the bunk and sat up, leaning forward so as not to bump his head. He pushed his hair out of his eyes and said, "Lawyer or no lawyer, I don't want to talk. What is there to talk about?"

"There's that stolen hair in your car, for starters," Rhodes said. "After we get that subject out of the way, we could talk about Earl Wellington. Your English teacher. You remember him, don't you?"

"I remember him."

"You know he's dead, right?"

Ike looked surprised. "I knew something bad was going on. I didn't know Dr. Wellington was dead."

"You must have known. Otherwise you wouldn't have left the college so fast."

"I don't know what you mean. I left because it didn't look like classes would be meeting, so I figured I could just go home."

"With a car full of stolen hair."

"I don't know how that hair got in my trunk. Somebody must've put it there."

He sounded so convincing that Rhodes almost believed him. Not quite, however.

"I didn't mention it was in the trunk," he said.

"It wasn't in the car with me, so it must have been in the trunk."

Good recovery, Rhodes thought. "Where were you going to sell the hair?" he asked.

"What hair?"

All Rhodes really wanted out of life was a straight answer to a simple question. He was pretty sure he was never going to get it. Certainly not from Ike Terrell.

"I'm going to pay a visit to your father," Rhodes said. "He has some information to give me. You have any idea what it is?"

"My father doesn't give information to anybody," Ike said. He clearly didn't want to talk about Able. He leaned back, swung his legs up, and lay down in the bunk, resting his head on the jail-house pillow, which was about as thick as a dime. "He doesn't have visitors, either. I'd stay away if I were you."

Rhodes tried to get him to say more, but Ike closed his eyes and pretended to be asleep. Rhodes left him there and went back to the outer office.

Hack was busy on the computer, and Rhodes stopped to tell him to have Buddy interview the residents at the Forest Apartments. Hack nodded, and Lawton said he had to clean the cells, so Rhodes was spared any more whistling.

Cal Autry had picked up the cruiser with the broken windshield, but that was all right. The spare car was ready to go, and Rhodes headed southeast again. It was a much less stressful trip this time, and if he hadn't been involved in the car chase earlier, he'd never have known that it had happened. He passed the same houses and yards, but now he could look at them without worrying about having a dog run in front of the car. A woman in front of one house was watering flowers with a hose. She waved as Rhodes passed by. No one had waved that morning. They'd all been too shocked at what they were seeing.

While he drove, Rhodes thought things over. He couldn't quite figure out what was going on with Ike Terrell. There was something between him and his father, that much was certain. Beyond that, Rhodes didn't have any idea. Maybe Able Terrell would enlighten him.

Then there was the dead man, Earl Wellington. Judging by what he'd seen, Rhodes thought the man's death was likely an accident, though caused by some kind of struggle. An argument of some kind? That's what it appeared to be, but if that was right, the argument had gotten far too physical.

Rhodes didn't know what to think of a man who liked cats and Sage Barton books being killed in a struggle. It didn't seem in character, somehow.

Rhodes would need to get the official time of death, but he didn't think Wellington had been dead for long before his body was found. If that was correct, something had happened only shortly before people had begun arriving at the college.

Wellington and someone else had been there, but they must have come in early, well before classes started. Rhodes wondered if that was a habit Wellington had. He'd have to ask Seepy Benton and see what he knew.

As for why Wellington might have been involved in an argument, Rhodes had already thought of several possibilities. The one that concerned him most was Ike Terrell. Obviously he'd had a problem with Wellington because of the paper that Wellington believed was plagiarized. Would that have been enough to set Ike off if he'd encountered Wellington in the parking lot?

What about Wellington's supposed pickiness and difficulties with students? Lately Rhodes had seen story after story about teachers who'd gotten into sexual tangles with their students, but that didn't seem to be Wellington's problem. Most of the incidents he'd read about had to do with high school teachers, and a surprising number of them were about relationships in which the aggressor appeared to be a female teacher who had ongoing encounters with a male student. That wasn't the problem here, or didn't seem to be. Rhodes thought he needed to find out more about Wellington's relationships with his students and whether they'd extended beyond what Wellington had told Harris was merely "teasing."

It was clear that the dean and the department chair weren't going to reveal much, certainly nothing more than they absolutely had to, but that didn't surprise Rhodes. In any institution, there was a lot of covering up when things went wrong. A college wasn't any different.

Rhodes would get it all uncovered, one way or another. He hoped. Seepy Benton would help, and Rhodes knew he could find out a lot from the students. They wouldn't be interested in covering things up. They might even get a kick out of the possible scandal.

Rhodes passed the spot where the piece of Ike's tire had hit his windshield. It lay over beside the road, nearly in the ditch. Rhodes wondered how long it would lie there before somebody picked it up. Nobody had adopted this section of the highway.

A little farther along he came to the spot where Ike's car had gone off the road. He could see a clear trail where it had plowed through the grass to the trees. The trail would be gone soon enough if they ever got any rain.

Able Terrell's compound was a few miles farther on. It was well off the main road, and to get there Rhodes had to turn off the pavement and drive down a sandy, rutted track that wound along for about half a mile. Trees grew so close to the ruts that

Rhodes could have reached out and touched them if he'd rolled down his window, but if he'd done that he'd have been covered in the fine sand that the car's tires were churning up.

At the end of the track, Rhodes came to a large clearing where a ten-foot fence of thick boards walled the Terrells off from the rest of the world. It would provide good protection from the zombies when they attacked, too, Rhodes figured, unless zombies could climb.

The fence was covered with hand-painted signs that didn't do much to encourage visitors. One of them read BEWARE OF THE DOG. Right next to it was one that read DON'T WORRY ABOUT THE DOG. IT'S THE PEOPLE HERE WHO HAVE GUNS. Another read GO AWAY. OR STAY AND GET SHOT. YOUR CHOICE. THIS PROPERTY PROTECTED BY SMITH & WESSON was another one. All of them expressed similar sentiments.

Even though he was there by invitation, Rhodes didn't feel welcome. He sat in the car with the engine running and sand settling on the roof and hood. He wondered whether he should ram the gate or just turn around and leave. Before he'd come to a decision, the gate began to swing open. When it had opened all the way, a man came into sight and waved Rhodes through.

Rhodes decided he'd rather walk. No use to have his car trapped in there if someone decided to close the gate. He got out of the car. A little of the sand still hung in the air, and he brushed a hand across his face.

It was getting on toward late afternoon, and the sun slanted through the trees, making long shadows all around. Rhodes wasn't sure it was a good idea to go inside the gate at all, even walking. He waved for the man in the entrance to come out to meet him.

The man didn't move. For a while the two of them stood there looking at each other. Rhodes had never met Able Terrell, but he knew the man in front of him wasn't Terrell. Terrell was supposedly fairly small, and this man was, too, in a way. He wasn't tall, but he was wide, and his arms looked as if he'd pumped a lot of iron with them. He looked tough enough to hunt wild hogs with a willow switch. Terrell wasn't like that, by all accounts.

Rhodes realized that he didn't know how many people lived in the compound. He doubted that anyone knew other than the ones in residence, not even the census takers. Especially the census takers, considering Terrell's alleged antigovernment beliefs. Rhodes didn't think Terrell would've filled out any census forms, not in a long time, if he ever had. He probably didn't pay taxes, either. Rhodes knew for sure that Terrell, his wife, and several children lived in the compound, and supposedly there were others of like inclination.

The man finally got tired of looking at Rhodes and walked in his direction. When he got to within ten yards, he stopped.

"You the sheriff?" he asked.

He was even broader than he'd seemed at a distance. A Western-style straw hat that might once have been white was perched on his head, so Rhodes didn't know if he was bald. The hair that showed was brown, mixed with a little gray. He wore a camouflage shirt and pants and pointy-toed black cowboy boots. He could've used some dental work.

"Sheriff Dan Rhodes," Rhodes said. "Able Terrell said he wanted to talk to me. I expect you'd be Duffy."

"That's me," the man said. He didn't mention whether that was his first name or his last. He sniffed, grimaced, sniffed again.

"Hay fever?" Rhodes asked.

"Yeah. Can't shake it."

"Sorry to hear it," Rhodes said, though he wasn't, not really.

"You want to talk to Able, you'll have to come on in," Duffy said and sniffed. "He don't come outside the fence. He stays inside, and that's just the way it is."

Rhodes thought it over. He didn't see any real reason not to go ahead. Terrell hadn't made any threats, and things looked peaceful enough.

"Lead the way," Rhodes said, and Duffy turned around and walked back through the gate.

Rhodes followed him, and when they were inside the fence, Rhodes noticed that each section was double braced with heavy boards. No zombies were going to push that fence over. They might *pull* it over, but Rhodes didn't bring up that point. He didn't think it would be appreciated. Duffy turned and started to close the gate. The hinges didn't make a sound.

"Able don't like people to wander in," Duffy said.

Rhodes gave him a look, but Duffy just went on and finished closing the gate. Rhodes didn't really mind that the gate was shut. What he minded was the gun that was leaning against the fence until Duffy picked it up. Rhodes wasn't a firearms expert, but he knew an AR-15 when he saw one. This one had a fixed stock, a twenty-inch barrel, and a rifle-length gas system. It wasn't a Smith & Wesson, however, as the sign outside might have led someone to believe. It was made by Colt.

For just a second, Rhodes thought he could hear someone whistling "*El Degüello.*" The rifle's magazine didn't look as if it held more than five rounds, so it was legal. That didn't mean Duffy didn't have another magazine or two or a dozen around somewhere.

"Hunting rifle," Duffy said, picking it up. His hands were large and calloused.

"Right," Rhodes said.

The rifle looked like a toy in Duffy's big hands. He pointed with the barrel. "Able's house is the one in the middle."

Rhodes looked in the direction Duffy had indicated. There were three houses, one of them larger than the others. All three were painted with camouflage colors, even the roofs. They looked to be in good repair, but Rhodes supposed that the people in the compound had plenty of time to work on them. A satellite dish was perched on the edge of each roof, so the compound wasn't entirely cut off from the rest of the world. Probably got both TV and the Internet by way of the dishes. Rhodes saw the front end of a military-style jeep near the back of the biggest house, along with an old gray Pontiac. The Pontiac was dusty but looked serviceable. It wouldn't have been out of place on the streets of Clearview. A couple of men were standing outside one of the houses watching Rhodes and Duffy. Rhodes heard dogs barking somewhere in back of the houses. The dogs didn't sound friendly at all.

"Who are those fellas?" Rhodes asked, inclining his head in the direction of the men who were watching him.

"Nobody you need to worry about." Duffy snuffled and wiped the back of his hand across his nose. "They live here and don't bother anybody."

"Right," Rhodes said. "What about the dogs?"

"Got four of 'em. Leopard hounds. Big suckers. They're real friendly."

"I can tell they're friendly," Rhodes said, wondering if the phrase *release the hounds* was spoken often in the compound.

Duffy shot him a look.

"From the sound," Rhodes said. "They sound friendly and happy."

Duffy just looked at him. Rhodes smiled and said nothing. He looked around the compound some more. Besides the houses and vehicles, there were several archery targets and some bales of hay. Rhodes didn't see any animals that the hay would feed, and he supposed it served as backing for rifle and crossbow targets. He caught the scent of wood smoke and noticed a faint curl of gray from a stovepipe on one of the houses.

"Smells good," he said.

"Getting to be about suppertime," Duffy said. "We use a woodstove for some of our cooking. Let's go."

The AR-15 dangled from his hand as he walked past Rhodes and led the way to the biggest house, which sat on concrete blocks. A set of concrete steps stood in front of the door. Duffy didn't bother with the bottom step. He didn't need it. He might have been short, but he was stout and agile. He stepped right up on the top step and rapped on the door with his free hand.

The door swung open and Able Terrell stood there. He was about Duffy's height, but not nearly as broad. His brown, wrinkled face reminded Rhodes a little bit of a monkey he'd once seen in a photo in some magazine or other. He wore camos like Duffy, but no hat. His black hair was clipped short and had a gray streak through it. Skunk and monkey, Rhodes thought. Not a good combination. Terrell didn't offer to shake hands, and neither did Rhodes.

"Come on in," Terrell said, stepping aside.

Duffy went in, and Rhodes followed him. The room they entered was large, with a high ceiling. The floor was bare wood, polished but not gleaming. It held a couch, three sturdy wooden chairs, some end tables, and a TV set. In spite of the satellite dish, nobody was watching TV. There was a wide fireplace that would come in handy in the winter.

Rhodes smelled something cooking. Beans of some kind. It was a homey smell, but the atmosphere seemed anything but homey to Rhodes.

Duffy walked over to sit in one of the chairs. He placed the AR-15 across his knees.

"You have a seat, too, Sheriff," Terrell said.

Rhodes sat in one of the chairs. He expected Terrell to sit in the empty one, but Terrell preferred to stand. It wasn't really an advantage for him. He wasn't built for looming the way Rhodes was. Neither was Duffy, but he could make up for his lack of height with his attitude. Rhodes thought he could loom with the best of them if he had a mind to. For that matter, he was practically looming while he sat in the chair, without even trying. The sniffling detracted a little from the image, however.

"You said you had some information for me," Rhodes said to Terrell. "It must be good since you wouldn't tell me on the phone."

"I don't tell anybody anything on the phone," Terrell said. "You should know why."

"Sorry," Rhodes said. "I don't."

"Tell him, Duffy."

"The gover'ment," Duffy said. "A man can't have a private conversation in this country anymore. They listen in on everything."

"They?" Rhodes said.

"You know what I mean," Duffy said. "The gover'ment. It's in all the papers. They say they're listening for terrorists, but that's just an excuse. You county people are in on it, too, just like the ones in Washington."

"We don't tap phones," Rhodes said.

"So you say. You probably record everything that comes into your jail, right?"

The county had thought about setting up that system up a few years ago, but it hadn't been done yet.

"Not us," Rhodes said, "but we might be before long."

"See?" Duffy said. "Even us paranoids are right some of the time. The gover'ment is always spying on the public, even the ones that just want to be left alone."

"Like us," Terrell said. "We just want to be left alone."

"If you want to be left alone," Rhodes said, "what am I doing here?"

"You have my boy locked up in your jail. I want you to let him out."

"You know I can't do that," Rhodes said. "He has too many charges against him. He must have told you what happened."

"It was your fault he ran. He was scared. Anybody'd run in that situation."

"Ike ran because he burgled the Beauty Shack."

"If he did it, and I'm not saying he did, maybe he had a good reason."

"You want to tell me what it is?" Rhodes asked.

"That's up to Ike," Terrell said. "If he did it."

"Everything will come out at his trial."

"Shouldn't be any trial. You need to let him go."

Rhodes stood up. "I told you. I can't do that. If he makes bail, that's a different story. You go in and post his bond, then he can come home. He'll still have to stand trial, though."

"You think he killed that teacher, don't you. Well, he didn't. I can promise you that."

Rhodes hoped they were finally getting to the information that Terrell had told Hack about. So far he hadn't learned anything at all.

"If you know anything that will clear this up," Rhodes said, "tell me now. Otherwise I'm leaving."

Duffy angled his AR-15 in Rhodes's direction. "I wouldn't get too sure about that," he said.

Chapter 10

▼

It occurred to Rhodes that he'd made a rookie mistake. Going to talk to Terrell wasn't it. Going alone was. It had been that way most of Rhodes's career. He'd seen far too many of the things people were capable of at their worst, but he somehow remained trusting and hopeful about nearly everybody he encountered. He'd even thought only minutes before that there was no reason not to go into the compound.

He'd been expecting a pleasant conversation, or at worst something along the lines of the wild hog in Hannah Bigelow's house. Knowing what he knew about Terrell, he should've thought it through better. He should've expected something like Duffy. There was always an enforcer, and in Terrell's compound, it was Duffy. Not that Rhodes was going to let Duffy or his rifle bother him.

"Like I said, I'm leaving," Rhodes told Duffy. He looked at Terrell. "Unless you have something to tell me."

Terrell nodded at Duffy, who moved the rifle barrel until it was pointing at the wall. Rhodes sat back down.

"I didn't want Ike to go to the college," Terrell said. "He got all his other schooling right here in this house."

"Good schooling, too," Duffy said. "I was the math teacher."

Duffy didn't look like any math teacher Rhodes had ever known. It would be fun to introduce Duffy to Seepy Benton. They could sit around drinking green tea and discussing the finer points of the Fibonacci number or the binomial theorem.

"I don't like government schools," Terrell said, and Duffy nodded. "What Ike was getting off the Internet and from Duffy and others was good enough. I don't like the liberal ideas that they teach in colleges, but Ike said he wouldn't pay any attention to that kind of thing. He said he needed more education than we could provide for him. There might be more to it than that. He might've wanted to be one of the elites, maybe, instead of living here in the woods."

Rhodes wasn't sure that you could call community college students the elites, but if Able wanted to believe they were, Rhodes wasn't going to discourage him.

"Anyway," Terrell said, "I let him go. I believe in personal freedom, and if the boy wanted to go, well, it was up to him. He was doing pretty well, to tell the truth, until he got into it with that English teacher of his."

Maybe now Terrell was going to tell Rhodes something. Finally.

"What kind of trouble?" Rhodes asked, even though he was sure he already knew the answer.

"It was that paper he wrote," Terrell said. "The teacher said it was stolen off the Internet. He couldn't find any proof of that, but he said he knew Ike didn't write it. He reported Ike to the higher-ups and got him in trouble with the college, all because he couldn't believe some kid from the sticks could write a decent essay. That's how those liberal left-wingers think."

"Did Ike write it?" Rhodes asked.

"Are you asking me if my boy would tell a lie?"

"I guess that's what I'm asking you. Would he?"

"We taught him better than that," Duffy said. His hands twisted on the rifle. "You could ask Eden. She'd tell you." Terrell looked at him. "I mean you could ask her if she was here, which she's not. She was his English teacher."

Rhodes figured that the women had been sent elsewhere while this meeting was taking place. Terrell wouldn't want them around if things got out of hand and there was a body, namely his, to dispose of.

"Eden's my wife," Terrell said. "She knows all about writing, where to put the commas, what a semicolon is, all that stuff. Ike does, too."

Rhodes seemed to recall from his own schooling that there was more to writing a good essay than knowing about commas and semicolons, but he didn't think this was the time to mention it.

"Ike was pretty upset about being accused of cheating, I guess," he said.

"Now there you go, Sheriff," Duffy said. His voice was harsh, and his eyes, though nearly hidden under the brim of his hat, were hostile. Duffy was on the edge of losing his temper. "You lawmen are always trying to trick somebody into saying something wrong."

"Just asking a question," Rhodes said.

"Ike wasn't as chapped by that teacher as I was," Duffy said. "I don't like it when some ivory-tower elitist accuses somebody of something he didn't do."

Wellington wasn't there to defend himself, and Rhodes didn't know who was right about it. Maybe Ike was an excellent writer, but if he was, Wellington should have known it from other writing samples. The paper must have been really well done.

"How upset were you?" Rhodes asked.

"Sheriff, you aren't half as smart as you think you are," Duffy said. His voice now was not just harsh but angry. "You should know better than to ask something like that. Didn't I tell you that Able don't ever leave this place? He's not going to go into town to meet with somebody and risk the government arresting him on some piddling little charge just because we don't believe the way they want us to."

There were lots of ways to resist the government, but Rhodes didn't see Terrell as much of a threat. He wasn't bothering anybody. He was just living in the woods and minding his own business, unless there was more going on around the place than Rhodes could see.

"I didn't mean to imply you'd killed anybody," Rhodes said. Of course, all three of them knew that wasn't the truth. The apology seemed to be accepted, though, and it smoothed things over for the moment.

"Like Duffy told you," Terrell said, "I don't ever leave this place. Ike shouldn't have, either, but you can't keep a kid away from town until he's learned what it's like. Anyway, you need to be looking at the college for whoever killed Wellington. They didn't like him there."

"Who's 'they'?"

"Nobody liked him," Terrell said. "Students didn't. Other teachers didn't. He didn't fit in. That's why they killed him."

Rhodes leaned forward. This was the first interesting thing Terrell had said.

"Who's 'they'?" Rhodes asked again. He was getting tired of asking people to be specific.

"If you don't know already, you aren't much of a sheriff. You ought to find out more about that kind of thing, see who's spreading lies. Then you might get somewhere."

Terrell had a point, but he hadn't told Rhodes anything new. Terrell didn't have any information. All he wanted was to get Rhodes there and try to talk him into releasing Ike.

"I'll check into it," Rhodes said.

"That'd be a good idea. Meantime, you can let Ike out of the jail."

"Not until somebody posts his bail. You know that."

It occurred to Rhodes that Terrell might not be able to afford bail for his son. Rhodes didn't know the amount, but Terrell couldn't have had much disposable income, considering that he didn't do any work. Rhodes wondered again if the rumors about the meth lab were true, even it there was no evidence of it. Nothing was being cooked up at the moment, or Rhodes would have caught the odor. There was no hiding it. All he could smell was the beans.

"That's why people don't like the justice system," Terrell said. "A poor man hasn't got a chance. Neither does an innocent man, once he's accused."

"If Ike is innocent," Rhodes said, "we'll find out."

"You must not hear the news much, Sheriff," Duffy said. "How many men have been let off death row in this state in the last few years? Five? Ten? Every one of 'em innocent based on the DNA evidence when it finally got used, but every one of 'em convicted by a jury, every one of 'em behind the walls for half their lives."

That was a little exaggerated, but there was enough truth in it to make Rhodes uncomfortable.

"None of those men were from around here," Rhodes said, knowing as he said it how weak it sounded.

"There's always a first time," Able said, "but it better not be my boy."

"It won't be," Rhodes said, and this time he was certain.

"I'm taking your word for that," Able said. "There's another thing, Sheriff."

"What's that?"

"You could talk to the judge, tell him to let Ike out on a personal bond. Ike's never been in trouble before. He's not down on your books for anything. If he stays locked up, he's going to fail all his classes at the college, and you'll be the one to blame."

Rhodes didn't feel guilty about Ike being locked up or about the college classes. Nevertheless, Terrell had a point. Ike was just a kid, really, and his record was clean. Letting him out on a personal bond wasn't a big risk at all since as far as Rhodes knew none of the Terrells had left the county in the last forty years or so, much less the state. Odds were that Ike would come in for his court dates even if he were released.

"I'll think about it," Rhodes said. "Maybe it'll work out."

"I'd appreciate that," Terrell said. He stood up, and Rhodes knew it was time for him to go.

"Duffy'll show you to the gate," Able said as Rhodes got to his feet.

Rhodes didn't much care for Duffy's company, but somebody had to open and close the gate. It might as well be Duffy.

Duffy stood, the AR-15 still in his right hand. "Let's go, Sheriff," he said.

"You first," Rhodes said.

Duffy looked at Able, who nodded. Duffy went to the door, opened it, and went outside.

"You do the right thing by my boy, Sheriff," Able said.

"I always try to do the right thing."

"That's what I've heard. We'll see how it works out this time."

Rhodes didn't know what to say to that, so he followed Duffy out the door. Duffy was at the bottom of the steps, and he fell in beside Rhodes as they started toward the gate. Rhodes could still smell dust in the air even though it must have settled back to the road by now. Maybe it was just his imagination.

After they'd walked a few yards, Duffy dropped back, and Rhodes felt the barrel of the AR-15 poke him in the back.

"You know, Sheriff," Duffy said, "I don't like you much."

Rhodes kept on walking. "You aren't the only one."

"Yeah, that figures, you being a sheriff and all, but the rest of 'em aren't here. I am, and I'm the one with the gun. You do what Able said, or you're gonna be sorry."

Rhodes didn't know what Duffy was trying to prove, but Rhodes didn't like threats, and he wasn't going to let Duffy get away with one.

Rhodes had made a rookie mistake by coming without backup, though things had turned out all right. Now Duffy had made a mistake by getting too close to Rhodes with the rifle. Rhodes wasn't going to let that one turn out all right. Not for Duffy, anyway.

Rhodes stopped abruptly. When the rifle poked him in the back, he turned around and grabbed the rifle barrel in his right hand, pushing it up and causing the butt to swing down. He took the butt in his free hand and twisted to the left as hard and quickly as he could. Duffy's finger made a satisfactory *snap,* and Rhodes took the rifle from him.

Duffy bent over, his hands clutched at his belt. He sucked in a deep breath and let it out slowly.

"I know what you're thinking," Rhodes said. "You're thinking you like me even less now than you did a few seconds ago, and I don't blame you a bit. What you have to consider, though, is that you brought this on yourself."

Duffy stared at him as if he'd like nothing better than to break Rhodes in half like Rhodes had broken his finger. He was strong enough to do it easily, but now Rhodes was the one with the rifle.

"You might even be thinking about police brutality," Rhodes said. "If you are, you ought to be thinking about what a judge would say to a man who was poking the sheriff in the back with an AR-15. I have a feeling he'd have some harsh words for you. Do you want to find out?"

Duffy thought it over. He wasn't entirely stupid, so it didn't take him long. "You mean you're not going to arrest me?"

"I might. I haven't decided. Maybe you've learned an important lesson and won't do anything stupid again."

"What if I have?"

"Then we'll just forget this ever happened. I can understand why you're upset. Your friend's son is in jail, and you think I haven't done enough for him. I said I'd consider talking to the judge. That should be good enough for you. Threats don't work very well."

"Yeah, I guess not."

"You might want to get a splint on that finger. I know you folks don't go in for doctors, but that's all one would do for you anyway. You have anything else to say?"

Duffy shook his head. "Can't think of anything."

"I'll be leaving, then," Rhodes said. "If you ever come to town, you can drop by my office and see about getting your rifle back."

"You're taking it with you?"

"That's right," Rhodes said. "It's not that I don't trust you." He paused. "Well, I guess that's not true. It *is* because I don't trust you. You're the one who was poking a gun in my back."

Duffy just nodded. Rhodes turned his back to him and went to the gate. When he got there, he turned and said, "You going to open this for me, or shall I do it myself?"

Duffy didn't bother to answer. He turned and went toward the house.

"That's okay," Rhodes called after him. "I can let myself out."

So that's what he did. Then he locked the rifle in the trunk of the county car and got out of there.

Chapter 11

▼

As Rhodes drove back toward town, he got Hack on the radio and asked for an update on the investigations. Hack told him that both Ruth and Buddy had left reports for him.

"Won't do you any good, though," Hack said.

"Why not?"

Rhodes didn't expect a straight answer, but he got one. More or less.

"'Cause there's nothing in 'em."

"There has to be something in them if they're reports."

"The somethin' is nothin'," Hack said.

"You mean there's no evidence or information that will help us."

"That's what I said."

Rhodes said that was too bad. He'd hoped that either Ruth would find something in the cars or Buddy would get some information from Wellington's neighbors. Anything that would help point the investigation in some direction or other would have helped.

"Any problems while I was out of touch?" he asked.

"More loose livestock. Duke and Alton took care of it. Seems like a lot of cattle are on the prowl today. Maybe we'll get a change in the weather."

"I thought it was turtles on the prowl that meant a change in the weather," Rhodes said.

"Cows, turtles, doesn't matter," Hack said. "They get on the prowl, there's gonna be a change. You'll see."

"I hope so," Rhodes said. He was tired of the heat and the dryness. "That all?"

"That's all. You want another killin'?"

"No thanks. One is more than enough. I'm going home. If you need me, you know where I'll be."

"Unless you're somewhere else. You don't hardly ever eat supper at home."

"I'll have my cell phone with me," Rhodes said.

"You hate that cell phone."

"I'm trying to join the twentieth century."

"You're one century behind," Hack said.

"Story of my life," Rhodes said, and he signed off.

Before Rhodes could do any more work on the investigation, he had to go home and face Ivy. It might have been a good idea to let her know that another resident had joined the household, but that would have spoiled the surprise. Rhodes hoped the new cat wasn't too big a surprise. He supposed he'd find out.

He knew things had changed in the house as soon as he got to the door. Yancey almost always came to meet him, but this time he didn't hear any little toenails on the floor or any excited yipping. He didn't hear anything at all except a car that passed on the street. He was reminded of the old cliché about things being too quiet.

He opened the door and didn't see or hear Yancey or anyone else. He knew Ivy was at home. He knew Yancey was in the house. It was too quiet, all right. Rhodes thought maybe he should have gone to the jail and locked the AR-15 up instead of leaving it in the car. Something at the jail might have needed his attention, and he could have stayed there for a while. He could have read the reports that Ruth and Buddy had turned in. Even if they'd told Hack they hadn't found anything useful, Rhodes might spot something that would help.

He hadn't gone to the jail, however. He'd come home, and now he had to face the consequences of his actions.

Rhodes walked into the kitchen. Sam was asleep near the refrigerator. Yancey was nowhere in sight. Ivy sat at the table. Something was asleep in her lap. Rhodes didn't have to ask what it was, but he did anyway.

"Is that a cat in your lap?" he asked. He sneezed.

Ivy reached down and rubbed the cat's back. "What do you think it is?"

Rhodes looked around the kitchen as if puzzled. "I wonder how it got in here."

"I'll just bet you do," Ivy said.

"Hannah Bigelow thought she had a wild hog in her house today," Rhodes said. "It came in through the pet door."

"We don't have a pet door," Ivy said.

"I thought maybe you'd had one installed."

"You might as well give up," Ivy said. "I know you're guilty, just like you're guilty of several other things." She rubbed the cat's back. "I forgive you, but I'm not sure Yancey will."

"Speaking of Yancey," Rhodes said, "where is he?"

"Under the bed. What's this cat's name?"

Rhodes sneezed and admitted that he didn't know. He explained how he'd come by the cat, not forgetting to add that if he'd left it in Wellington's apartment it would have starved and if he'd taken it to the shelter it might not have been adopted.

"We couldn't have that, could we," Ivy said.

"No," Rhodes said. "We couldn't have that."

"You're sneezing. I thought you were getting better around Sam, but this new cat is going to be a problem. I suppose you'll get used to him, too."

Rhodes sneezed. "I'm sure I will."

"I'm going to call him Jerry," Ivy said.

"It's a boy?"

"Yes. You didn't even check?"

"I didn't think about it."

"He's been fixed," Ivy said. "He and Sam get along just fine."

Rhodes had seen that for himself. "He and Yancey, on the other hand . . ."

"Yancey will come around." Ivy paused. "Well, maybe not, but he'll get used to things. Where are you taking me to dinner to make up for bringing in another stray?"

"Wherever you want to go," Rhodes said.

"That's the right answer," Ivy said.

Ivy's choice was Max's Place for barbecue. Maybe she was getting as tired of meatless meals as Rhodes was. He tactfully didn't mention the cheeseburger he'd had for lunch. As they drove, Rhodes told her about his day, making it sound a lot less stressful than it had been. She was more curious about Wellington than any of the other events, naturally enough, and she asked about the cause of death.

"We don't know for sure," Rhodes said. "I don't have an autopsy report yet. We might stop by Ballinger's after we eat and see if it's ready."

Clyde Ballinger ran a local funeral home, and since there was no county morgue, and since Ballinger was a civic-minded kind of guy, he let the county perform autopsies there free of charge.

"We won't have to look at anything, will we?" Ivy asked. "Not right after we eat."

"Just the autopsy report. And Clyde Ballinger. He's not so bad, though. You can probably stand it."

"I never know when you're joking."

"Join the club," Rhodes said.

When they got to the restaurant, Rhodes could smell the tangy smoke. He could almost taste the barbecue. Max greeted them at the door. As he led them to a table, Rhodes asked how the barbershop chorus was doing. Max sang baritone in the chorus, and he'd been a bit involved in one of Rhodes's previous investigations.

"We're doing all right," Max said. "I think I'll invite the group to sing here some night. What do you think? Good idea?"

"You let Seepy Benton sing here," Rhodes said, "so why not the chorus?"

Benton sang bass in the chorus, and he didn't have a standard lead singer's voice, but he did have his own YouTube channel. He played guitar and wrote his own songs, and somehow he'd persuaded Max to give him a regular gig at the restaurant. To say that Rhodes wasn't a big fan of his alleged singing was a considerable understatement, but Ivy seemed to like it, and so did Ruth Grady. Maybe some of the other customers did, too. Rhodes knew there was no accounting for taste, but still . . .

"Might not be room on the stage for the chorus," Max said, "but it wouldn't hurt if we spill off onto the floor. I think I'll do it."

"What nights?" Rhodes asked.

They were at their table, and Max held Ivy's chair for her. An old-fashioned gentleman all the way. Rhodes seated himself.

"Are you asking because you want to come or because you don't want to come?" Max asked.

Ivy kicked Rhodes's ankle under the table.

"I want to be sure to hear you sing," Rhodes said.

Max handed him a menu. "I'll let you know what I decide. Enjoy your meal. I still have the best smokers and the best sauce in Texas. Those are the two big secrets of the barbecue business."

Max left the table, and as Rhodes watched him leave, Seepy Benton came into the restaurant. Max met Benton with a menu. Benton took the menu and headed for Rhodes's table.

"Mind if I join you?" he asked.

Ivy kicked Rhodes again. He'd never worn boots because they hurt his feet, but he might have to consider buying a pair just to protect his ankles.

"Have a seat," he said.

"Thanks." Benton pulled out a chair and sat down. "Good evening, Ivy. How are you tonight?"

"I'm fine," Ivy said. "And how are you?"

"Great. Life is good. It would be better if I were singing tonight, but this isn't my evening for that."

Rhodes waited for Ivy to kick him again. When she didn't, he said, "How are things at the college?"

"We need to talk," Benton said.

Rhodes thought that was a good idea. He had a lot of questions for Benton about the way things worked at the college and about Wellington's relationship with the rest of the faculty and administrators. He wanted to know more about the rumors, too.

"I've been doing a little investigation of my own," Benton continued.

"That's not a good idea," Rhodes said, but he didn't explain why because the server arrived to take their order. Rhodes said he'd have a sliced beef plate with pinto beans and coleslaw with the barbecue sauce on the side. Ivy decided she'd just visit the salad bar, and Benton joined her. If that was what they wanted, Rhodes didn't object, but he was sticking with real food.

When the waiter left to fill Rhodes's order, Rhodes said, "I know that amateurs do just fine in the movies, but you could get in trouble nosing around at the college."

Benton raised his eyebrows. "Amateur? I'm a deputy."

"No you're not."

"Yes I am. You forgot to undeputize me. I'm going to get my salad."

Benton had made two trips to the salad bar by the time Rhodes's meal arrived. Ivy was still working on the small bowl of salad she'd created on her first visit. Rhodes added some sauce to his sliced beef. Max was right: The secret was in the sauce. The meat was lean and tender, but the sauce was just the addition it needed. Not too much sauce, though. It wouldn't do to overpower the smoky flavor of the meat. For good measure Rhodes put a little of the sauce in his pinto beans.

Between bites of his salad, Benton told Rhodes what he'd found out at the college. "I talked to a lot of people who don't have to keep things confidential," he said. "One of them was the bookstore manager, Mary Mason. She says she knows you."

Ivy gave Rhodes a look, but at least she didn't kick him.

"I wouldn't say I know her," Rhodes told Benton. "I know who she is."

"Everybody knows who she is," Ivy said with a little edge in her tone.

Who Mary Mason was was one of Clearview's most eligible women. Mary had appeared in town a year or so earlier for unspecified, but widely speculated upon, reasons. She was from a college town called Pecan City, which Rhodes had never visited, though he'd met Boss Napier, the chief of police, once.

There were rumors that Mary had left town after a clandestine affair with someone at the college in Pecan City, possibly the president, but no one had ever confirmed it. She was blond and buxom, and she'd become quite popular with the young men about town, of whom there weren't many. Wellington would have been one of them, though as far as anyone knew he wasn't much interested in women. Or maybe it was that they weren't interested in him.

"Does Ruth know you talked to Mary Mason?" Rhodes asked.

"I haven't told her yet," Benton said, "but she won't mind. She knows I'm as pure as the driven snow."

Rhodes hadn't seen a lot of snow in his lifetime, most of which had been spent in Texas. He'd always wondered why driven snow was supposed to be so pure. Now probably wasn't the time to get into that, however, though he knew Benton would have an opinion. Benton had an opinion on just about everything.

"Did she know Wellington?" Rhodes asked.

"I didn't think to ask her about that," Benton said.

Amateur. "Did you get distracted?"

"No," Benton said. "Anyway, there wasn't any need to ask that. She worked in the bookstore, and Wellington was a teacher. She knew him, all right."

"I didn't mean being acquainted," Rhodes said. "I meant did she know him well."

"I didn't find that out. I got what I wanted, though. I found out about Ike Terrell's bookstore bill."

Maybe not such an amateur after all. Rhodes wouldn't have thought of that, but then he didn't quite see what it had to do with anything.

"What did you find out?" Rhodes asked.

"Ike's made only a partial payment for his textbooks. He's not going to get his grades at the end of the semester if he owes the college money, and it looks like he does. He might owe even more. I'd have to check with the dean of students to find out. In a couple of days anybody who hasn't paid his tuition is going to be forced to drop out of classes. Ike might not have paid up."

Rhodes had figured out what Benton had been after, and it was a point in Benton's favor that he'd thought of the bookstore bill.

"So you think Ike might have stolen that hair to help pay his bills," he said.

"I've heard a little bit about his family," Benton said. "Judging from what I've been told, Ike's about as likely to be taking out any student loans or applying for a government grant as I am to fly to the moon under my own power." He paused. "That's not out of the question, you know. It could happen."

Rhodes started to say something, but Ivy kicked him again. He looked at her. She was having trouble keeping a straight face.

"So I suppose Ike could pay his bills, too," Benton said, "but I think he might have needed to get some money, fast, to pay them with. Hair extensions are easy to get cash for, according to the news reports. People are stealing them all over the country. Wigs, too."

He was right, and Rhodes had to give him credit for coming up with a motive for the theft. It didn't make Ike any less guilty, but it did help explain why he'd committed the burglary. He must have been desperate. Able didn't appear to be withholding financial support from his son, but there might not have been enough money to pay for tuition and books. Ike would have had a tough time getting a job in town, not because nobody would hire him but because Able would've objected. Not that there were a lot of jobs to be had anyway.

Everyone had finished eating now, but Rhodes wasn't ready to leave. He wanted to hear what else Benton had found out, and he wanted to hear it now. The waiter had come by and left their bills, separate checks without even being asked. He deserved a good tip.

"What else did Mary Mason know?" Rhodes asked.

"Nothing much," Benton said. "She'd heard that Wellington and Dean King had a big fight about something and that the dean and Dr. Harris were planning to get rid of Wellington at the end of the year."

Part of that was news to Rhodes. He knew about the plagiarism argument but not that the dean and the department head were planning to get rid of Wellington. Neither King nor Harris had mentioned it. Trying not to draw suspicion to themselves,

Rhodes was sure. Mary Mason might have been doing the same, but Rhodes couldn't be sure since Benton hadn't asked about any possible relationship with Wellington. Rhodes would have to find out about that.

"Anything else?" Rhodes asked.

"She'd heard the same things we've all heard," Benton said. "That's all."

Rhodes had been wondering about those rumors. Everything had to start somewhere, and while rumors usually seemed to spring up without any particular origin, they didn't just happen. They had an origin, even if it was almost always impossible to find.

"Where do you hear all that stuff?" Rhodes asked.

"In the faculty lounge," Benton said. "A lot of the people with early classes like to have coffee in the lounge and talk to their friends. It's a nice way to start the day. Not today, of course, but most days. Sometimes there's a little gossip. Teachers love gossip, and that's where Wellington got raked over the coals."

"He wasn't there?"

"He comes in, or came in, early, but he never came by the lounge. Maybe he didn't feel comfortable with the rest of us. You know how it is. The ones who've been around for a few years don't always welcome the newcomers. It took me a while to be part of the group, but I won them over with my natural charm."

Rhodes waited for Ivy to kick him, but she just grinned at him.

"Besides," Benton said, "Wellington liked to go outside and have a smoke before class. You know that already."

"Who's in the lounge in the mornings?" Rhodes asked. "Other than you."

"The regular crowd is me, Tom Vance, Harry Harris, Charlotte

Wilson, George Lewis, Beverly Baron, and Will Tracy. Do you know any of them?"

Rhodes knew Vance, a biology teacher and paleontologist who'd helped him out a little once upon a time when there was a mammoth involved in an investigation. He didn't know the others, but he was sure he'd be talking to some of them. If they were in the lounge, though, they hadn't been outside with Wellington.

"Oh," Benton said, "Mary Mason comes in sometimes, too. She's not faculty, of course, but she fits right in."

"I'm sure she does," Ivy said.

This time it was Rhodes's turn to grin.

Chapter 12

▼

After they left Max's Place, Rhodes drove to Ballinger's Funeral Home, which had at one time been a mansion occupied by one of Clearview's wealthiest families. Ballinger lived in back in the servant's quarters. If there was any symbolism in all of this, Rhodes preferred not to think about it. Rhodes saw a light in Ballinger's window, so he parked the car and asked Ivy if she wanted to go in.

"That's his house, right?" Ivy said.

"That's it," Rhodes said. "You didn't think he lived in the funeral home, did you?"

"I just want to be sure there won't be any surprises."

"Clyde might be wearing his drop-seat pajamas."

"That's not the kind of surprise I meant, and you know it. Besides, nobody wears that kind of pajamas anymore."

"Let's go find out," Rhodes said, and Ivy got out of the car.

They went to the door, and Rhodes knocked. Ballinger called for them to come in.

He wasn't wearing drop-seat pajamas. He had on a pair of shorts and a Hawaiian shirt that was predominantly blue, with some palm trees and leis and waves as decoration.

Rhodes looked at Ivy. "Surprised?"

"At least it's not drop-seat pajamas," Ivy said.

Ballinger, who had been sitting at his desk, stood up and said, "Sometimes I get the feeling that I came in on the middle of something."

"It's nothing," Rhodes said. "I hope we're not bothering you."

"Nope, I've been expecting you. Not Ivy, though. This is a rare pleasure. Have a seat."

Rhodes and Ivy sat on a short sofa, and Ballinger sat back down in his desk chair. For years his desk had often been covered with copies of the kind of old paperbacks that he loved to read, but now there were none. There was just an e-book reader and several stacks of paper.

"Nice shirt," Rhodes said. "Have you been hanging around with Mikey Burns?"

Commissioner Burns had a penchant for colorful shirts.

"Nope," Ballinger said. "Just relaxing after a long day. You probably had one, too, considering that I have an autopsy report on the late Mr. Wellington for you."

"All his days are long," Ivy said. "I'm lucky to see him at all."

"Always on duty or on call," Ballinger said. "Not unlike a funeral director."

"Did we interrupt your reading?" Rhodes asked.

"I was just seeing what I could pick up for free tonight. How is it that writers can just give their books away?"

Rhodes had to admit that he didn't know.

"They do it all the time," Ballinger said. He picked up his

e-reader. "I've nearly filled this thing up with free books, and I just keep getting more. I'll never get around to reading all of them."

"Are they the kind you like?" Rhodes asked, remembering having seen the desk littered with books with lurid covers and titles like *Park Avenue Tramp, Halfway to Hell,* and *Campus Doll.*

"Sure," Ballinger said. "Lots of old books are free, but I can get new ones for free, too. I don't know how they do it, but if they're going to give them away, I'm going to take them."

"I should get one of those readers," Ivy said.

Rhodes was sorry he'd brought it up, so he changed the subject by asking Ballinger about the autopsy report.

Ballinger tapped a small stack of paper. "Here it is. Dr. White said to tell you that it's about what you'd expect. No surprises."

Rhodes got up and took the report. He flipped through the pages. Wellington had died because of the blow to the back of his head, all right, possibly as the result of being knocked into the Dumpster during a struggle. The time of death was approximately seven fifteen. No students would have been arriving at the time. The early-bird faculty would already have been in the lounge.

The report didn't mention any bruises that might have resulted from blows to Wellington's head and face, but there was a bit of bruising on his arms that suggested he might have been gripped tightly.

"Any help?" Ballinger asked when Rhodes was done.

"You never know," Rhodes said. "What about personal effects?"

"Got 'em right here," Ballinger said.

He reached down beside his chair and picked up a clear plastic bag. It was sealed and had a paper attached. That would be Dr. White's statement that the bag held all of Wellington's effects.

Ballinger held the bag up, and Rhodes saw that it contained a cell phone, a wallet, some coins, a wristwatch, a package of filter-tip Camels, and a small pocketknife.

"Not many people still wear a watch," Ballinger said. "They all have the time on their phones now."

Rhodes took the bag and thanked Ballinger for his help.

"Drop by anytime at all," Ballinger said.

Rhodes's next stop was the jail.

"I'm getting the grand tour tonight," Ivy said when they stopped outside. "I haven't been here in a long time."

"They should have a Take Your Spouse to Work Day," Rhodes said as he opened the trunk of the county car. It was all right to drive the car to dinner, he figured, as long as he made sure to do some official business along the way.

Ivy got out of the car and joined him. "What's in the trunk?"

Rhodes reached in and took out the AR-15.

"Where did that come from?" Ivy asked.

"I picked it up along the way today," Rhodes said. When he'd told her about what he'd been doing, he'd omitted his little tussle with Duffy. "I'm going to lock it up where it'll be safe."

"I should hope so," Ivy said, but she didn't question him any further about it.

They went inside the jail, and Hack seemed glad to see her, though not quite so glad to see Rhodes.

"Where'd you get the rifle?" he asked.

"Just happened to find it," Rhodes said, hoping Hack would let it drop and knowing all along that he wouldn't.

"Find it where?" Hack asked.

"Down at Able Terrell's place," Rhodes told him. "I'm going to lock it up now."

He got the keys to the evidence room, ignored Hack's looks, and locked the gun away. When he came back with the keys, Ivy was sitting at his desk, and Hack was still curious. He said, "Terrell just let you walk off with one of his guns?"

"He might not even know about it," Rhodes said, and that was true. Duffy might not have told him.

"Able Terrell never let anybody walk off with a gun in his life."

"It wasn't Able. It was Duffy."

"Guy who called here today? He sounded big as a house."

"Not quite," Rhodes said.

"I don't want to hear about it," Ivy said.

"Don't worry," Rhodes said. "You won't."

They'd been married for a while now, but Ivy still had trouble dealing with some of the things that Rhodes got into. It was like the cheeseburger he'd had for lunch. He tried not to tell her more than she needed to know.

"Did Ike Terrell get his bond set today?" he asked Hack.

"Not yet. Judge's gonna see him first thing tomorrow."

"Don't let him get away before I talk to him," Rhodes said.

"Better be here early, then."

"I'll be here," Rhodes said.

He and Ivy told Hack good night and left the jail. Rhodes was through for the night unless he got a call. It wouldn't be unusual if he did. The county wasn't always quiet at night. The metal thieves were still going after copper all the time, and they liked to vandalize air conditioners at deserted buildings in the wee hours. Churches were a favorite target. Rhodes had pretty much shut down the local outlets for illegally obtained metal, but the thieves could always go elsewhere—and would, as long as they got paid.

Lately there'd also been a rash of tailgate thefts. It took a skilled thief about fifteen seconds to remove a pickup tailgate, toss it into his own truck, and drive away. Rhodes didn't know where the tailgates were being sold, but so far he hadn't caught anyone in Clearview selling them. He'd keep looking, though.

Driving home, Rhodes thought about the day He had more to worry about than tailgates and copper, including a dead body, but no real suspects unless he counted Ike Terrell, and he was by now convinced that while Ike might have burgled the Beauty Shack, he hadn't killed anyone, even by accident.

Seepy Benton had given him some people to talk to about the rumors surrounding Wellington, but Rhodes didn't know where that would lead him. He didn't have great hopes that he'd find out anything useful. On the other hand, Benton had mentioned once before that the faculty members loved gossip. Maybe talking to them would lead to something.

"You have a lot on your mind?" Ivy asked when they reached the house.

"No more than usual," Rhodes said.

"Maybe I can take your mind off those things and put something else on it."

"That sounds promising."

"You better believe it, pal," Ivy said in her best Cagney voice. Or maybe it was her Bogart voice.

Rhodes couldn't tell the difference, but that didn't matter. He believed it.

•   •   •

The next morning the phone rang just as Rhodes finished feeding Speedo. He was in the kitchen, watching the two cats sleeping by the refrigerator, perfectly at ease with each other. The animal who wasn't at ease was Yancey, who wouldn't come in the kitchen. He hadn't even crossed it to go outside for a little romp with Speedo earlier. Rhodes figured that the dog's feelings were hurt but that he'd get over it.

Ivy answered the phone, then handed it to Rhodes.

"It's the mayor," she said.

Great, Rhodes thought. Just what he needed. The mayor, Clifford Clement, wasn't one of Rhodes's biggest fans ever since a previous case in which he'd been a suspect. It never paid to suspect the mayor, especially when the city contracted with the county to provide law enforcement. Rhodes didn't know why Clement was calling, but he was sure it wouldn't be to tell Rhodes what a wonderful sheriff he was and what a fine job the department was doing.

Rhodes was right. At first, however, Clement wasn't upset. It took him a while to work up to that state.

"I understand you have someone in jail for the killing at the college," he said after Rhodes took the phone.

"There are several people in jail," Rhodes said, "but I don't think any of them killed Earl Wellington."

"I was told that you had one of the Terrells. Everybody knows they're all crazy down at that compound."

"They aren't crazy, just a little odd, and the one in the jail's not a killer. I don't think any of them are killers. They want to be left alone, that's all."

"This is terrible publicity for the city and the college," Clement said. "What if the college decides to pull out of Clearview? We can't have that."

Like the dean, the mayor seemed more interested in how Wellington's death would affect his own bailiwick than in seeing justice done. It was an attitude that Rhodes understood but didn't appreciate.

"You'd better get this wrapped up quickly, Sheriff," Clement said. "If you don't, the city council will have to reconsider Clearview's relationship with your department."

Rhodes had to smile because it wasn't much of a threat. The city was about as likely to create its own police force as Seepy Benton was to fly to the moon, though of course that was always a possibility.

"The department is devoting all its resources to solving the case," Rhodes said. That was the kind of phrasing that the mayor understood.

"It had better, and while you're at it, you might want to do something about that Web site the *Herald*'s ex-reporter has. She's sensationalizing everything, and it's not good for the town or anybody in it."

Rhodes wasn't sure what Clement thought the sheriff's department could do about a Web site. He looked across the kitchen at Ivy, who smiled at him. The cats slept on. Yancey had disappeared. Rhodes couldn't count on getting help from any of them.

"What should I do?" he asked. "Arrest her?"

"Are you trying to be funny?" Clement asked.

"No," Rhodes said. "Just asking for some idea of what I should do."

"Never mind. I'll talk to her myself."

Rhodes would have paid to be at that confrontation. Jennifer Loam could stand up to anybody, and would. Clement wasn't going to win that one.

"Great idea," Rhodes said. "I'm sure she'll be reasonable."

"She'd better be," Clement said, "and you'd better get things wrapped up out at the college."

"Count on it," Rhodes said.

"I will," Clement told him, and he hung up.

"Great way to start the day," Rhodes said as he hung up his own phone.

"How about some Mr. PiBB to keep that feeling going," Ivy said.

"You're not any funnier than I am," Rhodes said.

When he left the kitchen, Yancey looked up at him with big, sad, accusing eyes.

"You need to get used to having another cat in the house," Rhodes said. "It's not like you haven't learned to deal with Sam. You'll figure out Jerry, too."

Yancey hung his head, and he didn't even bother to yip.

Chapter 13

▼

Before he went to the jail, Rhodes stopped by the courthouse. He had an office there as well as his desk at the jail, but he didn't spend much time at the courthouse. He wasn't there to visit his office. He was there to talk to the judge, the prosecutor, and Ike's court-appointed lawyer. Rhodes recommended to them that Ike Terrell be released on his own recognizance. Ike had no record of any previous run-ins with the law, and Rhodes left the meeting convinced that Ike would get a break.

When he got to the jail, Hack and Lawton were ready for him. He could tell by the way they looked that something was going on. He put off letting them get started on him by securing Wellington's personal effects in the evidence room.

When he got back to his desk, he avoided looking at Hack and Lawton. Instead he checked to see if Ruth had examined Wellington's laptop. She had, and Rhodes looked over her report. She'd found nothing of interest other than the fact that Wellington must have liked games. He hadn't even searched any porn sites.

Rhodes put down the report. Having put it off as long as he could, he asked Hack and Lawton what they had for him.

"Had some more copper thefts last night," Hack said. "Just like the others this week. They got the air conditioner at the Baptist church. Pulled all the coils out. Duke's on it already. He'll check by the recycling center, too, after he's finished at the church."

The recycling center's actual name was the Blacklin County Environmental Reclamation Center. Rhodes was pretty sure that any criminal activity had stopped there after his last run-in with the people in charge. It wouldn't hurt for Duke to pay them a visit, however.

Hack's straightforward answer had been encouraging. Rhodes thought he might get through the day without having to listen to any of Hack and Lawton's complicated tales of wrongdoing in the county. Then he made the mistake of asking if anything else was going on.

"Got a water problem," Hack said. "Over at Mr. Murphy's house. Dwight Murphy. You know him?"

Rhodes never knew where Hack was going when one of these conversations got started, but this time he was more puzzled than usual.

"I know Mr. Murphy. He used to deliver the mail on one of the rural routes."

Murphy had retired from his job with the postal service several years ago, maybe ten years. Rhodes wasn't sure.

"Did he call the Water Department?" Rhodes asked.

"Nope. He says this is a job for the sheriff."

Like Hannah Bigelow's wild hog, Rhodes thought. *Everything was a job for the sheriff, no matter what else he was dealing with at the time.*

"It's his water heater," Lawton said, picking up the story.

"Okay," Rhodes said. "I can see that a water heater's not a job for the Water Department. It's a job for a plumber. I'm not a plumber."

Truer words had never been spoken. The last time Rhodes had tried a "simple" plumbing job was when he'd bought a new faucet for the kitchen. After a couple of hours, with Ivy offering helpful advice and commentary throughout the process, Rhodes had given up and called a plumber. He'd felt lucky that the plumber hadn't charged him extra for the job after the mess Rhodes had made of it.

"Mr. Murphy doesn't think a plumber can handle this job," Hack said. "It's not like the water heater's leaking or anything."

Rhodes had never heard of any other kind of problem with a water heater, though he supposed if it was a gas heater, it could've exploded.

"Did the thing blow up?"

"Nope," Hack said. "It's all in one piece, far as I know."

"I give up," Rhodes said, and he meant that in more ways than one. "What's the problem with the water heater?"

"It's talking to him," Hack said.

"Talking to him?"

"That's what he said."

"Is it speaking a language he can understand?"

"I guess it is. He said it was using cuss words. You wouldn't think a water heater'd know words like that."

"Didn't have a good upbringin'," Lawton said. "That's what I think. It's a shame what this country is comin' to when even the water heaters can't be civil."

"What does Mr. Murphy want us to do?" Rhodes asked, though he had a feeling that he knew the answer.

"Wants you to come over and talk to the water heater," Lawton said. "Maybe arrest it for abusive language."

"Scare it straight," Hack said. "Tell it if it doesn't shape up, you'll lock it up and throw away the key."

Rhodes sighed. "I have other things to do."

"I know that," Hack said. "That's what I told him. You don't need to worry about it. I sent Buddy over."

"Uh-oh," Rhodes said. Buddy had a puritanical streak. "You know how Buddy feels about cussing."

"You don't have to worry about that, either," Hack said. "I told Buddy not to shoot it, even if it got smart with him or said a few bad words. He won't let it get to him. You can rest easy."

Rhodes hoped so. Wild hogs were one thing. He could deal with those. Talking water heaters were something else entirely.

"If Buddy blows up the house, it's on you," Rhodes said. "He has to be back here to escort Ike to the courtroom, too."

"Buddy'll be fine. He'll take care of Mr. Murphy and be here on time. Trust me."

Rhodes didn't see that he had any choice.

"I need to have a little conversation with Ike Terrell before he goes before the judge," Rhodes said. "Is he okay this morning?"

"As okay as anybody who's spent his first night in the jail," Lawton told him. "He's not happy."

"Maybe he'll be happier after I talk to him."

"You're always a ray of sunshine," Hack said. "Ever'body's always happy to see you comin'."

"Not everybody," Rhodes said.

Rhodes hoped he hadn't made a mistake in trying to get Ike released on a personal bond, but he did have an ulterior motive. He thought that if he talked to Ike again, maybe he could use the bond as leverage to get some more information.

Ike sat up on the edge of the bunk when Rhodes tapped on one of the bars of the cell door. Ike's hair was a mess, and he didn't look quite as chipper as he had the previous day. The night in jail seemed to have taken away a little of his cockiness, which Rhodes thought was most likely a good thing.

"Ready to go before the judge?" he asked.

Ike ran his fingers through his hair, but that didn't do much for it.

"I guess I am. What happens then?"

"That depends," Rhodes said.

Ike perked up a little. "Depends on what?"

"It might be that I can get you a personal bond. No money involved. All you have to do is swear before the judge that you'll appear in court on the date and time he appoints."

"I don't know if I can promise that."

"Sure you can. If it's your father you're worried about, there's no problem. I've talked to him. He's the one who suggested it."

Ike looked skeptical. "You talked to him?"

"I went to the compound. Met with him and a friend of his called Duffy, who says he was your math teacher when you were being homeschooled."

"Duffy? I guess he tried. I learned most of my math off the Internet, but I needed somebody to help me with the stuff, and Duffy had trouble with most of the problems. That's why I wanted to go to the college, to get some real help. Dr. Benton's really good about that. He knows what he's doing."

Rhodes didn't know if he'd bother to pass along the compliment. Seepy's opinion of himself was already high enough.

"I didn't meet your mother," Rhodes said. "Duffy told me that she was your English teacher."

"They believe in keeping women out of sight," Ike said. He was loosening up a little, and Rhodes hoped he could keep him talking. "Their opinions don't amount to much."

"Your mother knows how to use a semicolon, though."

"She's a good writer. Better than my father and Duffy, that's for sure."

"I guess she taught you about plagiarism, then."

Ike frowned. "You're not going to start about that, are you?"

"It's important," Rhodes said. "If you're going to get that personal bond, you need to convince me that you didn't have anything to do with Earl Wellington's death. From all I've heard, you're the only one with a motive."

"I knew I shouldn't have started talking to you. I don't even have a lawyer. I was an idiot."

"We're just having a friendly conversation," Rhodes said. "You don't have to talk if you don't want to. I'm just trying to help you out."

"Maybe. My dad says I shouldn't trust any representative of the government, and that's what you are."

"The county pays me, all right, but you have to remember that your father trusted me. He even invited me to his house to talk."

"He didn't come to town, though. He never comes to town. That's because he doesn't trust you or anybody else."

"If that's the way you feel . . ."

"I didn't cheat on that paper. I wrote it all myself. I'm a good writer, and Dr. Wellington just didn't want to admit it. He thinks that because I come from an unusual family and was home-schooled that I can't write. He's wrong about it, though."

Rhodes remembered enough from his own English classes to know that Ike was using the wrong verb tense. Maybe that was because the reality of Wellington's death hadn't sunk in on him yet because he hadn't been involved in it.

Or maybe Rhodes was just reading way too much into verb tense. He wished he could be sure about Ike.

"What about those other problems you have?" Rhodes asked. "The hair, for example."

"What hair?"

Rhodes wasn't going to play that game anymore. "You know what hair, and here's what I know. I know you hadn't paid your bookstore bill and your tuition for the semester. I know you were about to have to drop your classes because of that. So what I think is that you stole the hair because you thought you could sell it somewhere and make some quick money. Why didn't you get it from your family or get a job?"

"You really think my father would let me work in town? Do you really think he has enough money to send me to college? Even if he would let me work here, do you think anybody would give me a job? Everybody knows whose son I am. They don't trust me because of that, any more than my father trusts them. Even if I get out of here on a personal bond, I still don't have a job. I still don't have any money, and I'm going to be in all kinds of trouble about what happened yesterday."

It was a bad situation, all right, but there had to be a way out of it. Rhodes couldn't think of what it might be, but he'd work on it if Ike would cooperate.

"Are you going to make that statement to the judge?" he asked.

"I guess I am. I don't want to stay in jail."

"Good. I want to talk to you again about all this. I'll be in touch."

Ike didn't appear to be thrilled at that idea. Rhodes left him there to mull it over.

Rhodes thought it would be a good idea to have an expert look at Wellington's cell phone, but since there were no experts at hand, he'd have to do it himself. He got the phone from the evidence room and checked it out.

All the voice mails, if there had been any, were deleted. So were all the recent calls. The contacts included only the college in Clearview and the main campus in another county. No help at all. Rhodes wrote down the number for the main campus and put the phone back in the evidence room.

Rhodes liked having a community college branch in Clearview. He liked it that the local students had a place to get an associate's degree without having to pay the high tuition and room and board costs at a university. So he didn't want the main campus to consider pulling out of town. He didn't think Wellington's death would give them any reason to do that, but it wouldn't hurt to have a talk with the college president and reassure him. That might even be a way to find out a little bit more about Wellington.

He made a call to the main campus number he'd gotten from Wellington's phone and got the switchboard operator, who put him through to the president's secretary. The secretary said that the president was in a meeting, but she was happy to give Rhodes an appointment to see him in an hour. That was fine with Rhodes. He could make the drive in a little more than half that time, so he could stop by the local branch first.

He told Hack where he'd be, and Hack made the usual protests.

"You oughtn't get too far out of pocket. You never know when we'll have an emergency around here."

"If we have any more wild hogs, call Alton Boyd," Rhodes said. "For talking water heaters, Buddy's the man."

Hack was going to protest further when Buddy came in.

"I'm here to pick up Ike," he said.

"What about that water heater?" Rhodes asked.

"Yeah," Hack said. "Did it cuss you?"

"Not much. You know how a water heater works?"

"I have a pretty good idea," Rhodes said, and Hack nodded.

Buddy filled them in, just in case. "When the water in it gets below a certain temperature, the heat comes on and the water starts to heat up. It makes a little bit of a noise when it does that. When the thing gets old, it might even make more of a noise. Anyway, Mr. Murphy had a pretty noisy one. He has a little bit of a hearing problem, and he's been watching too many old movies. Somebody gave him a big set of DVDs with a bunch of old movies from the fifties about space aliens and such. Must've given him ideas. Anyhow, I convinced him that his water heater wasn't talking to him. I think he believed me, but if he calls again I'll go back over and have another talk with him."

"Good idea," Rhodes said, thinking that if Benton had made the visit, he'd have made Mr. Murphy a tinfoil hat, which might have worked just as well, for all Rhodes knew. "You'd better get Ike now and get over to the courthouse. I'm going to be in Armistead County for a while this morning, and I'll want to know what happens with Ike."

"You goin' off again?" Hack said. "How come you can't stay here and do your job?"

"Because this part of the job means I have to go talk to some people in Armistead County, and I want to see them face-to-face. I'll take my cell phone."

"You better," Hack said. "You never know when we might have another wild hog emergency."

"Two words," Rhodes said. "Alton Boyd. He's the animal control officer, not me."

"That's more than two words."

"I'm leaving now," Rhodes said, and he did.

Rhodes decided that he didn't have time to stop by the local college, so he just drove past it on his way north. He also passed Max's Place and the little strip center where he'd shut down some eight-liners not so very long ago. A couple of other eight-liners had opened elsewhere, but so far no illegal gambling had been reported in either of them. Rhodes figured it was just a matter of time.

A little farther down the highway on the right was an old pond that Rhodes had fished in a couple of times when he was a boy. He wondered if anyone fished there anymore. He hadn't cast a bass lure in longer than he liked to think about. Maybe someday he'd have time to wet a hook again, but it wouldn't be today.

When Rhodes crossed the line from Blacklin County, the country looked no different at all. He'd have to drive all the way to Oklahoma to see much difference.

Off to his left, some distance from the highway, was the area known as Omega Ridge. A small community had been there once, but it was long gone now. Maybe a few tumbled-down houses were left, but Rhodes doubted that more than a trace of them was left. Around the turn of the last century the young men from

Omega Ridge had been known as the biggest hell-raisers within a hundred miles. They were well known in all the little towns in two counties. Like the houses, they were all gone now. Hardly even the memory of them remained.

Rhodes passed through the little town of Willene, which had even less of its downtown left than Clearview, mainly because there'd been a lot less of it to start with. It didn't take him long to pass through.

The next town was Swallow, which Rhodes assumed had been named for the bird rather than a physical action or a family. Barn swallows were thick in the air all over Texas most of the time, and Rhodes saw a couple of them swooping low over a field as he neared the town. Swallow was even smaller than Willene, and as soon as he was through it, Rhodes entered the interstate, driving across a long bridge over some often flooded bottom land. Not so often flooded these days, however, in the time of very little rain. Lots of cracked ground and dry grass filled the space where water stood less and less often.

After that it wasn't far to the town of Derrick City. The "city" part was a misnomer, since the population was only about double that of Clearview, and the derricks were missing, too. They'd been there once, however. Like Clearview, Derrick City had been an oil-boom town, and oil had been found there years before the Clearview boom, all the way back in the nineteenth century. The Omega Ridge boys had probably raised some of their hell in Derrick City, but now both Clearview and Derrick City were sleepy places where the boom days were long past and where even the derricks were gone, taken down because their metal was too valuable to be allowed to rust away in an old oil field.

The college buildings sat on top of a low hill and stood a little above the rest of the town. That made them easy to see from the highway.

Derrick City's growth, like Clearview's, was along the highway, and Rhodes turned off to drive through a cluster of convenience stores, fast-food outlets, and motels. He didn't have to go through the old downtown business district to get to the college, but he suspected it was about as deserted as the one in Clearview.

The college was prosperous, however. Its well-maintained main building had three stories, and the other buildings, if not as large, were equally well kept. Rhodes parked in a spot reserved for visitors and went into the main building. He looked at the directory on the wall and saw that the president's office was just down the hall.

Rhodes located it easily and went right in. He told the secretary, an attractive woman in her forties, who he was, and she told him to have a seat while she checked to see if President Arlan was ready to see him.

Rhodes sat in a well-padded chair with a seat and back covered with smooth brown leather. Two pictures hung on the paneled walls, both paintings of generals, one of Dwight D. Eisenhower and the other of Colin Powell. Rhodes had no idea what their significance was.

The secretary returned and asked Rhodes to follow her down a short hall to the inner office where President Arlan waited. She stood aside at the door, and Rhodes went inside, where the carpet wasn't quite deep enough to tickle his ankles, though it came close. Arlan stood behind a desk about the size of an aircraft carrier deck. Aside from a couple of pictures, a model spaceship, and an old-fashioned telephone set of the kind you saw only in offices these days, it was bare. Its top gleamed. If there was a speck of dust on it anywhere, it was the loneliest speck in town.

Arlan was an impressive man in an impressive navy blue suit, and Rhodes felt a bit underdressed. Maybe the badge in its holder on his belt would make up for his sport shirt and khaki slacks.

Arlan came around the desk and shook Rhodes's hand. He had a firm, dry grip, which was supposed to be a good sign, and, like the secretary, he asked Rhodes to have a seat. This time the leather chair covering was dark red.

When Rhodes was seated, Arlan sat behind his desk and said, "I've heard about Earl Wellington's death, Sheriff, but I don't know much about it. What can I do for you?"

Rhodes told him.

Arlan listened well. He didn't interrupt, and he maintained an interested look. When Rhodes had finished, he leaned forward with his arms on the desk and clasped his hands. "As you probably know, Sheriff, I can't comment on personnel matters. Those are confidential. At any rate, I don't think I know anything that would help you."

"You could tell me if Wellington had any problems here," Rhodes said. "He seems not to have been well liked by the faculty and students in Clearview."

"He was only part-time here, and I don't really keep up with the adjunct faculty. The department chair might know more, but I'm not sure she can tell you. Would you like to talk to her?"

"That would be fine," Rhodes said.

Arlan picked up the office phone and called his secretary. "Marian, please see if Dr. Sandstrom is in her office. If she is, tell her that I'm sending someone to talk to her about Earl Wellington."

He hung up and asked Rhodes what it was like to be a sheriff.

Luckily the phone rang almost immediately and Rhodes was saved from having to make up some kind of answer.

"Dr. Sandstrom is available," Arlan said, hanging up. "Marian will show you to her office."

He stood up, and so did Rhodes. Arlan didn't offer to shake hands again. He said, "I hope you can find whoever killed Wellington, Sheriff."

"I will," Rhodes said.

"You always get your man, is that it?"

"Pretty much," Rhodes said.

Chapter 14

▼

Dr. Sandstrom's office wasn't nearly as nice as Arlan's, but it wasn't bad. The carpet was a basic industrial weave, and the desk was standard size. The office reminded Rhodes in some ways of Seepy Benton's office, though the floor was clear of books and papers. Instead the books filled the bookshelves that lined the office walls. They appeared to be in no particular order, and they were more tumbled around than lined up. None of them looked like the kind of books that would interest Clyde Ballinger. Rhodes had seen some of the same or similar titles in Wellington's office, but he didn't see a copy of anything about Sage Barton.

There were books on Dr. Sandstrom's desk, too, held in place by bookends that were busts of Shakespeare. Rhodes remembered the face from a portrait he'd seen in a school textbook long ago.

Like Arlan, Sandstrom had a good handshake. She wasn't quite forty yet, Rhodes guessed, very thin, with only a touch of gray in her short brown hair. She wore rimless glasses and showed straight white teeth when she smiled. She asked Rhodes to call her Janet. The only chair in her office besides hers was beside the desk. The standard chair for student visitors. If a student brought reinforcements, they'd have to find their own chairs.

"Earl Wellington," she said when Rhodes sat down. "What can I tell you?"

"I'm starting to wonder if anybody will tell me anything," Rhodes said. "Seems like everything on a college campus is confidential."

"We worry about lawsuits," Janet said. "The administration does, at least. Not just here. Everywhere. Personnel matters are sensitive."

"Yet there's ProfessoRater," Rhodes said.

Janet grinned. "There's that, all right. Have you looked at it?"

"I have," Rhodes said. "Students don't mind saying what they think."

"They're not worried about lawsuits." She leaned forward. "Look, Earl was one of my adjuncts, and I want to help you if I can. Tell me what you're after, and maybe I can find a way to answer."

It was worth a try. "Did he have any enemies here? I'm talking the serious kind, the kind who'd follow him down to Clearview and get into an argument with him. A serious argument."

Janet thought it over. "I don't see why I can't answer that. It doesn't have anything to do with academics. You said you'd looked at ProfessoRater, so you probably know that Earl wasn't well liked by the students."

"That was true in Clearview, too," Rhodes said.

"He was a fussy man," Janet said. "You know the kind?"

"I think so. 'Picky' was the word they used in Clearview."

"As good a word as any. He was a stickler for the rules. His students couldn't be a minute late. They couldn't miss class. If they did, he called them at home. A couple of times he even went to a student's home to confront him. I had to call him in and speak to him about it. I told him never to do it again, but he couldn't seem to help himself. He was almost like a stalker. He wanted everybody to toe the line." She smiled. "That's a cliché, I know, but I was thinking about it today when I was grading papers. My students don't understand the meaning of the phrase, and they've started to spell *t-o-e* as *t-o-w*. It always makes me laugh to think of someone towing a line." She paused. "I'm getting off the subject. I try not to do that in class, but sometimes I do. I was telling you about Earl being fussy. Picky, you called it."

Rhodes hadn't called it that. Others had, but it didn't matter. He said, "Right. Did that cause trouble here?"

"Mostly with the students. He didn't seem to know how to talk to them. Some of them were insulted by him, but I don't think he meant any harm by what he said."

That squared with what Harris had told Rhodes.

"What about plagiarism?" Rhodes asked.

"Oh, my. He was death on plagiarism. It infuriated him, but then so many things did. He was one of the most prescriptive grammarians I ever met."

Rhodes didn't want to ask what that meant. It sounded bad.

"A run-on sentence was anathema to him," Janet continued, "and making the verb of a sentence agree with the object of a preposition drove him up the wall."

"With good reason," Rhodes said, thinking that he'd never heard anyone use the word "anathema" in a sentence before.

Janet gave Rhodes a look. "Are you making fun of me, Sheriff?"

"Not me," Rhodes said. "I never make fun of English professors."

"I'll just bet you don't. Let me tell you one more thing about Earl. He was so fussy, or picky, that he used to mark up the local paper with a red pen and send it to the editor. He even marked up a few of Dr. Arlan's memos and returned them."

"How to win friends and influence people."

"An appropriate allusion and use of sarcasm. Earl didn't have a lot of friends."

"Did he have any at all?"

"The only one I know was Francie Solomon."

"Who's Francie Solomon?"

"She's another adjunct. She teaches history. Would you like to talk to her?"

"Sounds like a good idea," Rhodes said.

The adjunct instructors had their own office. Just one office for all of them. It was sort of a bullpen, a big room with a few desks, some fabric-covered privacy panels whose haphazard placement didn't provide any privacy, and gray-painted steel lockers along one wall. Yet another step down from Arlan's office. Or several steps. Long ones.

Two people were sitting at old, scarred desks when Janet took Rhodes in. One of them was a tall man with long, lank hair who looked as if he hadn't had a good meal in far too long. The other was a woman in her middle thirties. She had short blond hair and blue eyes. She wore a Western-style shirt, boots, and jeans. Janet introduced her as Francie Solomon. She didn't introduce the man, who hadn't even looked up at them when they came in the room.

"Sheriff Rhodes is here about Earl," Janet said after the

introduction. "I have to go back to my office now, Sheriff, but would you please stop by before you leave?"

Rhodes said he would and asked Francie if there was somewhere they could talk.

"Right here's fine," she said with a wave at the panels. "We adjuncts don't get a lot of privacy. Pull up a chair."

It seemed as if everyone wanted Rhodes to be comfortable, or maybe they didn't want him looming. He located a metal chair by one of the other desks and pulled it over.

"You were a friend of Earl's," he said, sitting down. "How well did you know him?"

"Not very well," Francie said. "Nobody did. He was hard to know, and he didn't have a lot of friends. I kind of liked him, though." She shrugged. "Maybe I felt sorry for him. I was a little jealous when he got a full-time job, but now that he's dead, I really do feel sorry for him."

"What can you tell me about him that might help me?" Rhodes asked.

"Not a thing. Who'd want to kill Earl? Nobody that I know."

"It was more or less an accident, I think," Rhodes said. "An argument that got out of hand."

"Well, that I can believe. Earl liked to argue. One thing he didn't mind was confrontations. I think he even liked them, courted them. Some people do, you know. Not me, though. I try to avoid them. You being a sheriff, I guess you don't mind them."

"I take them as they come, but I don't go looking for them."

"Earl did. Go looking for them, I mean. Okay, he didn't do that exactly, but he gave his students such a tough time that he had plenty of them. He had them with the parents, too. And with Dr. Sandstrom."

Rhodes would have to ask her about that. She'd shuffled him off to Francie before he got a chance.

"You visited him in Clearview, didn't you," Rhodes said.

Francie looked surprised. "How did you know that?"

"I'm a trained lawman. You drive a black Silverado?"

"I do. You must be a really good sheriff to have found that out already."

If she wanted to think that, Rhodes would let her. No need to destroy her illusions.

"He was lonesome," Francie said. "I just went once. He gave me a call and invited me down for dinner. I went. I'd just broken up with my boyfriend and didn't have anything better to do. I'm back with my boyfriend now."

"That's good," Rhodes said.

"I guess. Sometimes I wonder. Anyway, Earl and I ate barbecue at Max's Place. You ever been there?"

"More than once," Rhodes said.

"Some guy was singing that night. Open mic night, maybe. He had some interesting songs. You ever hear him?"

"More than once," Rhodes said.

"Then you know what I mean. Anyway, in between songs Earl told me some of his troubles. He wasn't getting along with his chairman for some reason or other. He wasn't clear about it."

Rhodes thought he knew.

"Maybe it was the plagiarism problem," Francie continued. "Earl thought some kid had cheated on a paper. Earl couldn't stand that kind of thing."

"So I've heard."

"He said he was going to get the kid," Francie said. "He didn't say how, though. You think it was the kid who killed him?"

"I hope not," Rhodes said.

He talked to Francie for a while longer, but he didn't find out anything more. He thanked her and went back to talk to Janet Sandstrom. The man at the other desk still hadn't looked up.

Janet was in her office, but she told Rhodes that she had a class in fifteen minutes.

"I won't keep you long," he said. "I have to ask you about any clashes you might have had with Wellington."

"I hope you don't think I killed him."

"I don't. You probably had classes here yesterday, so you have the perfect alibi."

"How exciting." She didn't look excited. "I've never needed an alibi before."

"You don't really need one now," Rhodes said. "What about those conflicts?"

"Just the usual kind of thing. Students came in all the time about things he'd said in class, little sarcastic comments, things he thought were jokes but that came across as crude and insensitive." She paused. "Earl *was* a bit crude and insensitive, but I don't think he was aware of it. He lacked social skills. Maybe he had a mild case of Asperger's syndrome. Do you know what that is?"

"It means lacking in social skills," Rhodes said.

Janet laughed. "This time I know you're kidding me, Sheriff. I'm sorry if I sounded condescending."

"You didn't. It was a logical thing to ask."

"Maybe. Anyway, Earl had problems, but they weren't terrible ones. He could get by, and he was a conscientious teacher. He kept good records—excellent records, in fact. He never missed his classes, and he turned his grades in on time. You might be surprised to hear that not everybody we hire for adjunct work is like that. There's a good reason. We pay them very little, and we demand a lot. It's hard to blame them if they're a little lax, but Earl never was."

"So you didn't have any hesitation in recommending Wellington for a full-time job."

"That's right. He'd worked for several years here, and this was his chance to get paid an amount commensurate with his degree. He deserved it."

"You were getting rid of a problem, too."

Janet bristled. "That never entered into it."

Rhodes believed her, or he believed that she believed herself. He nodded and stood up.

"Have I been any help at all?" Janet asked.

"You have," Rhodes said, "and I appreciate your talking to me."

"Before you go," Janet said, "I have a favor to ask."

Rhodes couldn't imagine what sort of favor he could do for her, but he said, "I'll help if I can."

"I hoped you'd say that."

Janet opened the top drawer on the left side of her desk and took out a book. Rhodes's heart sank when he saw the title. *Piney Woods Terror Attack.*

"I know you didn't write it," Janet said, laying the book on her desk and opening it to the title page. "I hoped you wouldn't mind signing it, though. Everybody says you're the model for the main character."

"You must be disappointed that I left my pearl-handled .45s in the car," Rhodes said.

"Now you're making fun of me again."

"Not at all. I'll be glad to sign the book." That wasn't entirely true, but Rhodes didn't think he had any choice. "How do you want me to sign it?"

Janet handed him a pen. "Just your name and title would be great."

Rhodes wrote "Sheriff Dan Rhodes" in the book and returned the pen.

"These books are really well written," Janet said. She put *Piney Woods Terror Attack* back in the drawer. "Not that I plan to teach them in my classes, but I enjoy reading them. So do a lot of other people here."

"I'm not anything like Sage Barton," Rhodes said. "Just so you know."

Janet looked him over. "You're much too modest, Sheriff Rhodes. Much too modest."

"Now who's kidding whom?" Rhodes asked.

"Whom?"

"I'm not just some uneducated jerk," Rhodes said.

Janet smiled. "You really are a kidder, Sheriff."

"Not always," Rhodes said.

Chapter 15

▼

Driving back to Clearview, Rhodes wondered if his trip had been worthwhile. He decided that it had. While what he'd learned about Wellington hadn't been entirely new, it had helped him fill in his ideas about the man. It had already been clear that Wellington had problems with students and administrators, but added to that was that he seemed to enjoy the confrontations that resulted. Maybe he even encouraged them. He didn't have the social skills that would have helped him get along better with his colleagues and students, but he was a conscientious worker. He was more strict than most teachers and didn't mind speaking to his students when they did the least thing he considered wrong. He was exactly the kind of person who might get into an argument that turned violent.

Wellington had even mentioned Ike Terrell to Francie Solomon and had said he was going to "get" him. Rhodes didn't know what that meant, and Welllington was no longer around to tell him. Rhodes would have liked to ask him. It would have made things a lot easier.

Another thing that Rhodes had discovered was that Wellington's chairperson at the main campus had given him a good recommendation because she believed he deserved it. The question was, had she been telling the truth? Rhodes thought she had. She seemed like someone who could handle the kind of problems that Wellington caused without too much difficulty, so she might have expected someone else to have the same capability. Not everybody did, however. Harris seemed to have a little trouble handling things, or at least he was building up resentment because of the problems in his department.

That reminded Rhodes that Francie Solomon had mentioned something about Wellington having a problem with Harris in Clearview. There had been the plagiarism thing, but she appeared to have been talking about something else, even if she didn't know what it was. Wellington had trouble with everyone, though, so just one more might not make much difference.

It was a little before noon when Rhodes got back to Clearview, so he thought he'd stop by the college and see if he could talk to some people before they all left for the afternoon. He knew that lots of the instructors had evening classes, and those who did seldom spent much time on campus between lunch and the start of the later sessions. Also, there was no cafeteria in the building, so even the instructors who were there in the afternoon might leave the building to go home for lunch or to go to a restaurant.

Rhodes thought that Seepy Benton usually brought his own healthy lunch, whatever that might be. Green tea to drink, maybe, and vegetables to eat. Rhodes wasn't into healthy lunches himself.

He got to the building just as the eleven o'clock class was end-ing, and the hall was full of students, most of them already chat-ting or texting on their cell phones as soon as they cleared the classroom door. Rhodes wondered if they were telling someone what they'd learned that day or how awesome their instructor was. He didn't think it was likely, but anything was possible.

He went up to Seepy Benton's office. The door was shut, so he waited, hoping that Seepy would show up soon. He did, only sec-onds later. He was followed by a student who was asking some-thing about a chain rule and spatial variation and functions. Rhodes didn't understand a word of it.

Benton evidently did, however. He greeted Rhodes, opened his office door, and invited Rhodes and the student in. Before they could get through the door, Benton was at the dry-erase board, writing something that looked like fractions, except with letters. As far as Rhodes was concerned, he might as well have been writing in ancient Greek. As he wrote, he talked, and the student was jotting things down on a pad that he held.

When Benton was finished, he asked the student if he under-stood. Evidently he did, and he left with a smile.

Benton watched him go. "That's why I'm awesome," he said. "Well, that's *one* reason why I'm awesome. I can explain things so students understand them."

"Can't every teacher do that?" Rhodes asked.

"Could all of yours?"

"Maybe," Rhodes said. "It's been a long time. I can't remem-ber. That's not why I'm here, though."

"You're here on our case," Benton said. "I haven't done a lot of investigating, but—"

"Stop right there," Rhodes said. "You're not supposed to be

investigating. You're not a deputy. You're a college math teacher. You stick to that. It's better for everybody."

Benton looked pained. "But you need my help. You wouldn't be here if you didn't."

"You can help me by not getting in the way of the investigation."

"I wouldn't do that. Didn't you want to talk to some of the faculty members who were here when Wellington died?"

"Yes, but I didn't want you to talk to them first."

"I didn't plan to."

The words were hardly out of Benton's mouth when Mary Mason appeared at his office door.

"Am I interrupting anything?" she asked.

"We were just talking about you," Benton said.

"You were?" she asked.

"We were?" Rhodes asked.

"You wanted to talk to some of the people who hang out in the lounge in the mornings," Benton said. "Mary's one of them."

Mary wore a light blue blouse and navy slacks, with a blue turquoise pendant and earrings. She had blue eyes, too, not that Rhodes was really paying attention.

"Let's talk," Rhodes said.

Benton cleared books and papers off the two office chairs for Rhodes and Mary to sit in. Benton sat at his desk and tried to be unobtrusive, which didn't come easily for him.

Rhodes told Mary that he'd heard about Wellington being one of the early-morning visitors to the faculty lounge. She was one of those people who liked to talk, and that was enough to get her started.

"You should see it in the morning," she said. "People line up at the coffeemaker with their cups in their hands. Some of them are even shaking a little. They just can't wait for that first jolt of caffeine." She laughed. "I should talk. After all, I'm one of them. Usually the first one in the line."

"What about Earl Wellington?" Rhodes asked.

"He wasn't one of the bunch," Mary said. "Not really. He tried to be a couple of times, but it just never worked out. You know?"

Rhodes thought he knew, but he said, "I'd rather you told me."

"He was kind of standoffish, if that's the right word. He didn't have much to say, and when he did say anything, it was kind of . . . odd. Just . . . off. I can't really explain it, but when he tried to say something funny, it was never funny, and when he laughed at something someone else said, it was always too loud. Mostly, though, he didn't laugh because he didn't get the joke."

"No social skills," Rhodes said.

"That's the truth. I think he was never a part of the group because he didn't know how to be part of a group. He just couldn't fit in, and after a while he stopped coming by. There was more to it than that, though. Earl was a smoker, and there's no smoking in the building. He'd get coffee from a machine and drink it outside while he smoked."

"Everybody else got along just fine, though," Rhodes said.

"That's right. A very compatible bunch except for Earl."

"So nobody liked him."

"You could say that, but nobody *disliked* him, either. It was more like he was just a piece of the furniture. Mostly we ignored him." She paused. "That sounds awful, like we drove him away and made him go outside, but that's really not the way it was. I think that even if we'd all liked him, he'd have gone outside for that smoke. You know how people are about cigarettes if they're hooked."

"I've heard," Rhodes said.

Mary laughed. She had a nice laugh. "You don't look like a smoker. You're probably a teetotaler, too."

Rhodes thought about how much he'd like a cold Dr Pepper.

"Mostly," he said.

"You're not as much like Sage Barton as people say you are."

"I'm not like him at all," Rhodes said.

Mary gave him an appraising look. "I wouldn't say that."

Rhodes felt uncomfortable with the way the conversation was going, so he got it back on track.

"What about yesterday?" he asked. "Did Wellington come by the lounge?"

"No. He hadn't been by for at least two weeks. The usual bunch was there, but I'd left when I heard the news. I have to get the bookstore open about fifteen minutes before eight in case someone needs something for the first class."

Benton had told Rhodes that he was in his office when he'd heard the clamor in the hallway. The others had probably been gone from the lounge, too, when the body was discovered.

"Who was there that morning?" he asked.

"The usual bunch," Mary said. She turned to Benton. "You were there, Seepy."

Benton nodded. "I don't drink coffee, though. I don't do caffeine."

Rhodes wasn't surprised. "Who else was there?"

"I can't remember for sure. I know Charlotte Wilson was there. She's the volleyball coach. Beverly was there, too. Beverly Baron. She teaches accounting. I was talking to Tom Vance about mammoths, so he was there. He was telling me about one that was found around here a few years ago. You were mentioned, Sheriff."

Rhodes remembered the mammoth, not to mention the Bigfoot hunters and their convention that had been held around that same time.

"That must have been exciting," Mary said. "Not finding the mammoth bones, I don't mean that. I mean that fight to the death you had." She gave him an admiring look. "Just like Sage Barton."

"I wouldn't call it a fight to the death," Rhodes said. "I didn't kill anybody."

"It was thrilling just the same, the way Tom told it. The discovery of an old crime, the unexpected killer, just like a movie."

"It wasn't like a movie," Rhodes said. "Just another day."

"You Sage Barton types are so self-effacing," Mary said.

"Who else was in the lounge?" Rhodes asked.

Mary turned to Seepy again. "See what I mean? See how he changes the subject? Self-effacing."

"Like me," Seepy said, and Mary laughed.

So did Rhodes, but not for long. He asked again who was in the lounge. Maybe this time he'd get an answer.

"That's all I can remember." Mary said. "Wait. Will was there. Will Tracy. He teaches history."

"Anybody else?" Rhodes asked.

Mary shook her head. "That's really all I can think of."

"What about you, Seepy?" Rhodes asked.

"I think that might be all," Seepy said. "Those mornings all run together after a while."

Rhodes could see how that would happen. "None of those people could have had anything to do with Wellington's death, then. Nobody liked him, but nobody disliked him. The only people he clashed with were Dr. Harris and Dean King."

"Don't forget his students," Benton said.

"He had a lot of students. The only one who seems to have had it in for him was Ike Terrell, and I don't think he got into a fight with him. Wellington had plans for Ike, though. He told someone he was going to get him."

"Maybe he just meant he'd find a way to fail him," Benton said. "He could have worked something out, some kind of extra-hard test or a pop test on a day when Ike didn't show up for class."

"You have a devious mind, Seepy," Mary said. "I don't think a dedicated teacher would do that kind of thing."

"I wouldn't," Benton said, "but I'm not so sure about Wellington."

Neither was Rhodes, but he had something else on his mind.

"You two probably want to eat lunch," he said, "and I have some things to look into. Thanks for your help."

"I'm brown-bagging it," Seepy said. "Anyone care to join me in some sprouts and baked tofu? I just need to warm the baked tofu in the microwave in the lounge. It's great on sandwiches. There's plenty for everybody."

"No thanks," Rhodes and Mary said at the same time.

Chapter 16

▼

Mary Mason walked down the hall with Rhodes. She told him that she was going to eat at Max's Place.

"It has a great salad bar," she said, "and Seepy doesn't sing there at noon."

"That's something in its favor," Rhodes said, "but I have a few things to do. I'll eat later."

Mary smiled at him. "Some other time, then," she said and went on her way.

Rhodes didn't think there would be another time. Ivy wouldn't approve. He went looking for Harold Harris's office, and when he didn't see it, he went back to Benton's just in time to catch Seepy as he came out the door with a cardboard container in his hands.

"I'm looking for Dr. Harris," Rhodes said.

"I was hoping you'd had second thoughts about the baked tofu. You're sure you don't want some?"

Rhodes thought about the vegetarian meat loaf that Ivy made. "I'm sure. What about Dr. Harris?"

"His office is on the first floor. Number one-sixteen. He usually eats at home, though."

"I'll have a look," Rhodes said, and he left Benton to his baked tofu.

Harris's office was closed and locked. Rhodes went outside to his car and checked in with Hack.

"How long you been back in town?" Hack asked. "We might've needed you."

"I have the cell phone," Rhodes said. "I didn't get any calls while I was in Derrick City, and you didn't try the radio when I was driving back, so you must not have needed me."

"Might've thought it wouldn't do any good to call you."

"Never mind that. Is anything going on that I need to know about?"

"Just depends on what you need to know about."

"I'll leave it up to you," Rhodes said.

"Then you might wanta drop by the recycling place. Duke's there now, and you know how those people are."

"Tell him I'm on the way," Rhodes said.

The recycling center was only a couple of blocks in back of the Beauty Shack, but it looked as if it existed in a different world, a world like something in a postapocalyptic movie, with piles of scrap metal behind a rusting metal fence, and on the outside containers full of scrap and a number of huge empty metal tanks.

A new sign stood beside the opening into the center. It read, UNDER NEW MANAGEMENT. WE PAY CASH FOR YOUR SCRAP

METAL. That was interesting. Rhodes hadn't known that the previous owners were selling out. Duke might have known, however, and that would explain why he was visiting. The new owners might not be as worried about the sheriff's deparment as the previous ones had been after Rhodes had gotten finished with them.

Duke's car was parked outside the opening, and Rhodes parked beside it. He got out, and in the heat of the early afternoon he could almost smell the hot metal. He didn't see Duke, so he supposed the deputy must be in the office. Rhodes opened the door and went inside. He appreciated the cool of the air-conditioning.

Duke stood in front of a waist-high counter, talking to a big man with the name ERIC stitched over the pocket of his shirt. So the management might have changed, but the uniform hadn't.

"Hey, Sheriff," Duke said.

He was tall, and he looked even taller in his Western-style hat, which he hadn't removed. Rhodes never wore a hat, but now that his hair was thinning he might have to take up the habit. He'd already decided he wasn't going to wear a baseball cap.

"I've been having a talk with Eric here," Duke said. "I don't think he likes me. Isn't that right, Eric."

"Yeah," Eric said.

The uniform was the same, and so was the vocabulary. Or the lack of it.

"Eric's problem is that he feels put-upon because I'm here," Duke said. "He feels I'm accusing him of receiving stolen goods."

"Is that right, Eric?" Rhodes asked.

"Yeah," Eric said.

"Would those stolen goods he's thinking about be copper?" Rhodes asked. "The kind that comes from air conditioners?"

"They would," Duke said, "and the air conditioners would be

the ones at the Baptist church. They won't be conditioning any more air because somebody gutted them last night, and I thought Eric might know something about it. Not that I was accusing him of anything. Just having a little friendly talk."

"Yeah," Eric said.

He didn't sound sincere to Rhodes.

"What made you think Eric might know something?" he asked Duke.

"I'll tell you what," Eric said.

Rhodes turned to him, gratified to hear him speak a complete sentence.

"He thinks we're crooks, that's what," Eric continued. "Just because we buy scrap here. I told him he could look all around, anywhere he wanted to, across the street and everywhere."

The buildings across the street had once been cotton warehouses. Rhodes had searched them before. Besides a quantity of sizable rats, the buildings had at one time held stolen metal, but it had been removed before Rhodes got there.

"Is that right?" Rhodes asked. "You don't mind if he looks around?"

"Not a bit," Eric said. "He's welcome to go anywhere, just like I said, just so he has a search warrant."

"See how he is?" Duke asked. "A friend wouldn't be saying anything about search warrants. A friend would just invite me to look around and see what's what. Isn't that right, Eric."

"Yeah," Eric said, "but I'm not your friend. I'm an honest businessman who's trying to get along in a tough economy, and you're hassling me."

"Some other people out there are trying to get along in a tough economy by stealing copper out of church air conditioners," Duke said. "We can't have that, can we?"

"Doesn't have anything to do with me," Eric said. "I don't always know where something I buy comes from."

"Don't ask, don't tell," Rhodes said.

"Yeah."

Eric was within his rights. A few years earlier, the Texas legislature had made the theft of any amount of copper or aluminum a felony, but they hadn't imposed the same penalty on people who bought the metal. The law of unintended consequences had kicked in. Instead of decreasing, the number of thefts had soared.

Some large Texas cities, like Houston and Austin, had fought back by passing ordinances that required scrap metal buyers to report the receipt of materials they believed to be stolen. Clearview had no such ordinance, but as far as Rhodes knew, the ones in the cities hadn't done any good anyway. The penalties didn't have any teeth, and they were widely ignored.

"You're in the clear, Eric," Rhodes said, "no matter what. You haven't done anything that's against the law, so if you've bought any copper today, why not tell us who brought it in?"

"You gotta understand my position here," Eric said. "If I start calling the sheriff every time somebody brings in some scrap, people won't sell to me. I'll be out of business. You act like all of 'em are thieves, but they aren't. Maybe none of 'em are. They don't want me siccing the cops on them."

"Especially the thieves," Duke said.

"Yeah."

Rhodes could see they weren't going to get anything more out of Eric, and getting a search warrant wasn't worth the trouble. By the time they got back with it, the copper, if it had ever been there, would be long gone.

"Let's go, Duke," Rhodes said. "We'll leave Eric to tend to his business."

"You sure, Sheriff? I think he was about to come around. Isn't that right, Eric."

"Nope," Eric said.

Rhodes stopped outside the office and turned to Duke. "You have any evidence that the copper from the church wound up here?"

"Not a smidgen," Duke said. "It just seemed likely. More than likely, to tell the truth."

"You're probably right," Rhodes said. "It was worth a try. We'll have to keep an eye on the place. Right now I'm going to pay a visit to a college professor. You can follow me and be my backup."

"You need backup for a college teacher? Why?"

"I don't trust him."

"Why not?"

"He lied to me," Rhodes said.

Rhodes had noticed how nervous Harris was when they'd had their conversation about Wellington, and Rhodes remembered very well that Harris had told him he'd been in the faculty lounge the morning Wellington died. Benton had told Rhodes that Harris was part of the usual crowd, but neither Benton nor Mary Mason had remembered that Harris was there that morning. That didn't look good for Harris.

Rhodes called Hack and asked him to get Harris's address.

"What for?" Hack asked.

"I'm going to see him. Duke's my backup. What's the address?"

"Hang on."

The radio hummed and buzzed for a minute. Then Hack came back on and gave Rhodes the address.

"Why're you goin' to see him?" Hack asked.

"I need to talk to him," Rhodes said and signed off. He smiled, thinking that Hack's blood pressure was likely to be spiking.

The address Hack had given him was in one of the older parts of town, though there were still some people around who could remember when it had been one of the newer ones. When the houses were built, there had been no trees around them, but now tall pecan and elm trees shaded the no-longer-fashionable houses, most of which sat on large lots and had backyards with high board fences to shield them from the neighbors.

Rhodes parked at the curb in front of Harris's house. Harris wasn't one of those people who liked to work in the yard. The grass, where it wasn't shaded by the trees, was dead. The flower beds along the front of the house were filled with weeds, and there were no flowers in sight. Rhodes wasn't a yard person, either, so the sight didn't bother him in the least. He got out of his car and waited for Duke, who pulled up to the curb behind him.

"Ranch style," Duke said, joining Rhodes at his car. "From the fifties, right?"

"I think so. It's been kept up, though."

"Not the yard," Duke said.

"Not everybody likes yard work."

"I do. What're we after this college guy for besides that he lied to you?"

"I'm not sure," Rhodes said, "but something's going on with him. I thought it might be a good idea to have someone with me in case he assaulted me with a poetry book."

Duke hitched up his holster. "I'm your man."

"Let's go, then," Rhodes said.

They went up the cracked walk, and Rhodes knocked on the front door. No one responded, and Rhodes was about to knock again when he heard someone moving around inside. Harris's voice, muffled by the door, asked who was there.

"Sheriff Dan Rhodes."

The door opened, but only a little bit. Harris didn't take off the chain latch, and Rhodes could see only a bit of his face through the opening.

"I was about to go back to the campus, Sheriff," Harris said. "Can we talk there?"

"Better that we do it here and now," Rhodes said.

"Who's that with you?"

"Deputy Duke Pearson. He'll be sitting in on our discussion."

If Harris didn't want to let them in, there was nothing Rhodes could do, aside from kicking down the door, which might be fun but which wasn't strictly legal, no matter how many times it happened on TV shows.

Harris either didn't know that Rhodes didn't have a right to kick down his door or he didn't want to avoid Rhodes badly enough to take the chance. The door closed. Rhodes heard the chain slide out of the slot, and then the door opened.

Harris didn't look as dapper as he had on the previous morning. His eyes were red, as if he hadn't slept much, and he didn't have on a jacket and tie, just some khaki slacks, a white shirt, and a pair of scuffed loafers.

"I'm supposed to have office hours this afternoon," Harris said. "I really do need to get back to the campus."

"We won't keep you long," Rhodes said.

Harris gave in. "All right. Come on into the den."

Rhodes and Duke followed Harris into a paneled room with new carpet and bookshelves along two walls. The bookshelves were filled with neatly arranged volumes with colorful spines. If there was one thing Rhodes had learned so far in the investigation, it was that college English teachers owned a lot of books.

A big flat-screen TV set hung on a third wall of the den. The furniture looked as if it might have come with the house, but if it had, it had been well taken care of. Harris stood near the sofa. He didn't invite them to sit, so maybe he planned to do the looming this time if Rhodes gave him a chance.

Rhodes didn't. "We'll be here long enough for you to have a seat," he said.

Harris dropped down on the sofa. The inlaid mahogany coffee table in front of it held a couple of coasters and the TV remote.

Duke sat in an uncomfortable-looking chair, while Rhodes loomed.

"I have a couple of questions about yesterday morning," Rhodes said.

He waited a couple of seconds, but Harris didn't respond.

"You said you were in the faculty lounge when you heard about Wellington's death," Rhodes said.

Harris looked up at him. "I did? Then I must've been there."

"I don't think you were," Rhodes said. "I've talked to several people who were, and nobody remembers having seen you. You're usually on hand to get your early cup of coffee, so what happened to keep you away yesterday?"

"I'm pretty sure I was there," Harris said.

Harris had been nervous at the campus when Rhodes talked to him, but he was worse now. His voice was weak. He slumped, twisted his hands together, and didn't look up at Rhodes.

"Not according to the people I talked to."

Harris tried to buck up. He straightened his back and put his hands on his knees.

"They must be mistaken, then," he said.

"I don't think so," Rhodes said. "I think you're hiding something from me. Why don't you tell me now and save us both some time."

Harris was undergoing a transformation. He stood up and looked Rhodes squarely in the eyes.

"I don't know a thing, and it's time for me to get back to the college. Unless I'm under arrest. Am I under arrest?"

TV, Rhodes thought. Everybody watched too much TV.

"You're not under arrest," he said. "You can go whenever you want to."

"I thought so. You can go first. I'll see you to the door."

"No need of that," Rhodes said. "Come on, Deputy Pearson."

Duke hadn't said a word the whole time. He unfolded his lanky frame and got up out of the chair. It didn't look easy, but he managed it. Rhodes was halfway to the door when Duke caught up with him.

"He's guilty of something," Duke said. "I don't know what it is, but I know it's something."

"I'll find out."

"You think so?"

"I know so," Rhodes said.

Chapter 17

▼

Duke went back on patrol, and Rhodes went to the jail. He didn't have time for Hack and Lawton's banter, so to avoid it and to satisfy them, he told them pretty much what he'd been doing. They didn't have any good stories to entertain him with, so Rhodes worked for a few minutes on his reports. He had a feeling there was something he'd overlooked, maybe more than one thing. He figured it would come to him if he didn't worry about it, but there was a little itchy feeling at the back of his brain that wouldn't leave him alone. He'd almost figured it out when Buddy came in, and then Rhodes remembered what it was.

"How'd it go at the courthouse this morning?" Rhodes asked.

"The judge released the kid on a personal bond," Buddy said. "I hope that was the right thing."

"The boy needs him an education," Hack said. "Might as well let him get one. Without it he might end up like me, a broke-down old dispatcher for a sheriff who don't appreciate what-all he does."

"You know better than that," Rhodes said. "Everybody appreciates you."

"You think I'm broke down, though."

"I think you're healthy as a hog."

"Now you're callin' me a hog."

Rhodes looked at Buddy. "See what I have to put up with? It's all right, though. I'm used to it. Here's a question I've been meaning to ask you. Did you have to take Ike home?"

"Nope. Somebody picked him up."

"Who was it?"

"I don't know. I just know I offered him a ride, and he said he didn't need one. I never thought to look to see who it was that came for him."

"See if you can find out," Rhodes said. "Go back to the courthouse and ask around. Some of those guys who sit out under the pecan trees all day might be able to tell you."

Buddy left to do some asking. Rhodes checked his computer to see if Jennifer Loam had any breaking news to report. He immediately wished he hadn't checked because the top story, crowding Wellington's death down the page, was the epic tale of Sheriff Dan Rhodes versus the wild hog at Hannah Bigelow's house. There were even photos of the house, the pig, Hannah, and Mr. Wooton.

Rhodes looked over at Hack, who was sitting at his desk and trying to appear busy while affecting a look of childlike innocence at the same time. He wasn't pulling it off.

"Hack," Rhodes said.

Hack turned to face Rhodes. "You need somethin'?"

"I need to know if there are spies in this department."

"Spies? What kind of spies?"

"The kind of spies that're feeding information to Jennifer Loam for her Web site."

Hack's look of surprise was no more convincing than his look of childlike innocence.

"You thinkin' maybe Lawton'd do somethin' like that?" he asked.

"I'm thinking maybe *you'd* do something like that."

Hack looked hurt. Again, unconvincing. "Me?"

"You," Rhodes said. "This story quotes 'unnamed sources in the sheriff's department.'"

"That could be Lawton," Hack said. "Since it's unnamed and all."

Lawton was cleaning the cells and so not able to defend himself, but Rhodes didn't think Lawton was the guilty party.

"Besides," Hack said, "just because we work here don't mean we don't have freedom of speech. If somebody was to call here, and I'm not sayin' anybody did, and ask about what the sheriff was workin' on or if there was any big stories, well, a person would be obliged to tell 'em. We work for the public, and we gotta keep 'em informed about what-all is happenin' and how we're keepin' 'em safe from things like wild hogs and such as that."

"We don't have to tell them about hogs that aren't wild."

"Sure we do. That's the very kind of thing that folks care about. You think they care about people stealin' copper wire or car batteries? Well, maybe they do, a little bit, but what they *really* care about is a hog gettin' into Hannah Bigelow's house."

The sad thing about what Hack said was that Rhodes thought it was probably true.

"You ain't gonna start makin' us clear it with you when we talk to reporters, are you?" Hack asked. "That'd be like we were livin' in Soviet Russia in the days when there was such a thing. Censorship, that's what it'd be."

Rhodes didn't think it would be as bad as all that, but he couldn't really blame Hack for telling Jennifer the story. Hack might have made it sound more interesting than it had been, but Jennifer Loam was the one who'd gone out for the photos and the interviews, and Bigelow and Wooton exaggerated the whole thing because they enjoyed the attention. Unlike Rhodes, who could've done without it.

Rhodes couldn't even blame Jennifer, since she was trying to get more hits for her Web page. The more hits she had, the more advertising she'd get, and the more advertising she got, the more money she'd make.

Even though he understood how things worked, Rhodes didn't like it. He needed some help in finding out how Wellington had died and who was responsible, not publicity for getting a pig out of a house, especially when the hog wasn't even a real threat to anybody. Or even a hog.

"I'm not going to tell you not to talk to reporters," Rhodes told Hack. "I just wish the reporters wouldn't make such a big deal out of things."

"It's a big deal for around here," Hack said. "We don't have terr'ists blowing up stuff like Sage Barton does. We have to settle for hogs in an old lady's house."

"Another page from the story of my life," Rhodes said.

"Huh?"

"Never mind," Rhodes said, and he was saved from further conversation by the ringing of the phone.

Hack answered, talked awhile, then muted the receiver and turned to Rhodes. "Your pal Seepy Benton is on the line. He says he has some information for you, but he doesn't want to talk on the phone. Says he'd like for you to come to his office if you're not too busy savin' people from wild hogs."

"You're making that last part up," Rhodes said.

"Cross my heart," Hack said. "I guess he looks at the Internet like ever'body else."

"More than most, I expect. Tell him I'll be there in a few minutes."

Hack told him. Rhodes put things on his desk into a semblance of order and went to see what Seepy had to say.

"I heard some students talking," Seepy said.

Rhodes was in his office, and the same equation, or whatever it was, that Benton had written on the dry-erase board at noon was still there. It didn't make any more sense to Rhodes now than it had then.

"You're not investigating, are you?" Rhodes asked.

"No, nothing like that. You've stripped me of my badge. I just happened to overhear them. I was meditating in the restroom. They didn't even know I was there."

"There's not a faculty restroom?" Rhodes asked.

"This is a democratic community college," Benton said. "Nobody gets special treatment. Anyway, I was in the restroom—"

"I don't need too much personal information," Rhodes said. "Just tell me what you found out, if anything."

"I found out that Dr. Harris is an interesting guy."

Anything about Harris might prove to be of use to Rhodes, though the fact that he was interesting to students seemed like minor news. Seepy, however, like everyone else that Rhodes dealt with, never gave the important facts first.

"I assume you mean interesting in a way that might affect what I'm working on," Rhodes said. "So tell me."

"They don't like the way he teaches. They say he drones on and on about poetry. He tells them what to think about poems, and if they disagree with him, he gets upset."

That didn't sound interesting to Rhodes. "Kids always gripe about their teachers, don't they?"

"That's not the point," Seepy told him. "The point is that they looked him up on ProfessoRater before they signed up for his class. According to that source, he's almost as awesome as I am."

"And we all know that couldn't possibly be true."

Seepy didn't respond to Rhodes's crack. He turned to his computer and called up a Web page with a few strokes of his keyboard.

"Look at this," Seepy said. "They were expecting something a lot better than they got."

Rhodes moved over to the computer to see what Seepy had for him. It was Harris's page on ProfessoRater. According to the site, Harris was good. He was very good.

"You're right," Rhodes said. "He's as awesome as you are."

"Almost. I said he was *almost* as awesome, and that's what it says here, but the students didn't believe it. They said they'd both rated him low, and so had a lot of other students they knew. If that's true, it's not showing up here."

"Maybe there's a time lag."

"Not that much of one. The students who rated him had his class last year."

"So what does this mean?" Rhodes asked.

For once Seepy had to admit that he didn't have the answer. "I don't know. I can think of a couple of possibilities, but that's all."

"One possibility is that the students were just talking," Rhodes said, "and that they didn't really go to the trouble of doing the ratings."

"There's that," Benton said. "I don't think that's true, though."

"So what's another possibility?"

"That Harris has found a way to beat the system, that he hacked into it and changed his ratings."

Rhodes let that sink in.

"Suppose Earl Wellington found out about it," Seepy said.

"He was a stickler for the rules," Rhodes said. "He didn't like cheaters, and it wouldn't matter if they were students or faculty members."

"That's right," Benton said. "Am I a regular Sherlock Holmes, or what?"

Rhodes didn't bother to answer that. He was thinking of something Dean King had said: *It's always the English teachers.*

"Do I get my badge back?" Seepy asked.

"I'll put in a good word for you with Ruth," Rhodes said.

"She already knows I'm awesome. I'd rather have a badge."

"Not now," Rhodes said. "Right now I need to have a word with the dean."

As the campus's main administrator, Dean King was in her office all day, and sometimes even during part of the evening hours, so Rhodes had no trouble finding her. She didn't look at all busy, and he figured that the long days must sometimes be fairly empty. Even with committee meetings and student problems and her regular administrative duties, there couldn't be enough going on to occupy all her time. Nevertheless, she didn't appear happy to see him come in.

"Do you have good news for me?" Dean King asked when Rhodes was seated in her office.

Rhodes was impressed again by how imposing she was. Certainly she was large enough to have banged Wellington's head into the trash bin if they'd argued. He wondered if she got to the campus early each day. As the chief administrator, it was likely, and she'd been outside when Rhodes had arrived on the scene.

"No news at all yet," Rhodes told her. "Just some more questions."

Dean King hardly seemed to hear his answer. Rhodes thought she looked a bit distracted, and a few stray hairs had somehow escaped from their usual lacquered positions. He started off with an easy one.

"How's the replacement for Wellington working out?"

"He seems to be fine, though it's hard to say after such a short time. The students haven't complained, and they don't seem to miss Dr. Wellington at all."

"That must be good news."

"I suppose so," Dean King said, "but it doesn't put things to rest. I want to see this all come to an end, but I don't know what else I can do to help you."

"I'd like to ask about something you said, something about it always being the English teachers who caused trouble."

That question wasn't nearly as easy for the dean as the first one had been. She seemed baffled by it.

"I . . . don't remember saying that."

"Yesterday morning," Rhodes told her. "You said it had to do with academic problems."

"Assuming I did say it and that there were any problems, they'd be confidential," the dean said, putting a hand to her head to smooth down the rogue hairs. It helped for only a second, as they sprang out of place almost as soon as her hand moved away.

"I'm trying to find out about a Web site that you might be familiar with," Rhodes said. "ProfessoRater."

It could have been his imagination, but Rhodes thought the dean looked a bit apprehensive. She said, "I'm familiar with it. What does that have to do with anything?"

"I was wondering what might happen if someone, let's say an English teacher, just for the fun of it, managed to alter his ratings to make them better than they actually were."

"I don't think that could happen."

"Let's suppose that it could, and did. Then let's say another English teacher, one who liked for everything to go by the book, found out about it."

"That's a lot of supposing," Dean King said.

"I agree," Rhodes said, "but I'm just getting started. Let's suppose that this other teacher was already upset because of something, maybe a plagiarism case that he felt the dean and the teacher who'd altered the ratings hadn't handled right. Now this picky teacher would be even more upset. He might not be somebody with good social skills, so he wouldn't know that things had to be kept quiet, kept from the board of regents and the public. He might even threaten to expose everything. It would be a real scandal for the college if all that got out." Rhodes paused. "Assuming that it happened like that, I mean."

The dean just looked at him. Rhodes noticed that one of her hands was trembling a little.

"The guilty instructor might do just about anything to keep the news quiet," Rhodes said. "Don't you think so?"

"I'm sure I wouldn't know," the dean said.

"The administration would be very worried about something like that," Rhodes said. "An argument about it could get out of hand. Somebody might get hurt."

"I have no idea what you're getting at," the dean said, but Rhodes could tell that she knew, all right.

"I'm going to find out about all that," Rhodes said, "and then it won't be supposition. If you know anything at all, now's the time to tell me."

"If I knew anything that would help," Dean King said, "I'd tell you."

She didn't meet Rhodes's eyes, and he knew he was onto something. He didn't know exactly what it was, but he'd find out soon enough. The pressure was getting to both the dean and to Harris, and one or the other of them would crack. Judging from their behavior, Rhodes didn't think it would take too long.

Rhodes stood up. "I'll talk to you again about this. If you want to talk to me, you can call me at home or the jail. I'm easy to find."

"I'm sure you are," Dean King said. "I'll call if anything comes to me."

Rhodes didn't believe a word of it.

Chapter 18

▼

Rhodes went straight home from the college. He'd missed lunch so many times in his career that he hadn't even thought about it today, and he wanted a quick, nourishing snack before Ivy got home and presented him with something that was good for him.

It wasn't that he was trying to circumvent her good intentions or ruin his health. It was just that his food preferences didn't run to the healthy alternatives. So in order to be sure that he occasionally got what he needed, he'd bought a huge bag of M&M's, the kind with the peanuts inside. He kept them in the bottom drawer of an old desk, a drawer that Ivy never opened as far as he knew. He figured he had about fifteen minutes before she got home, plenty of time to get to the drawer and have a few pieces of the candy.

He parked in the driveway and was about to get out of the car when the radio came on. It was Hack with a message from Buddy, who had talked to some of the people who hung around the court-house.

"You know King Timmons?" Hack asked.

Timmons was in his eighties and loved courthouse intrigue. If there was any gossip to be had, Timmons would have it.

"I know him," Rhodes said.

"Buddy says he saw Ike Terrell get in the car with somebody."

"Did he know who the somebody was?"

"Nope, never saw her before."

"Was the car an old gray Pontiac?"

"King didn't know what kind of car it was, but it wasn't gray. He said it was maroon."

Rhodes hadn't seen a maroon car at the compound, which figured. Nobody left the compound, nobody except Ike, that is, so they wouldn't need any cars.

"Did he get a look at the driver?"

"You said you know King. Sure he got a look."

"Well?" Rhodes asked.

"It was a girl," Hack said. "Or a young woman. Real cute, King said. Said she had red hair and freckles. Whatever happened to freckles? You don't see a lot of freckles these days."

"A little speckled friend," Rhodes said.

"Huh?"

"Never mind," Rhodes said, and he racked the mic.

He was greeted by a dejected Yancey when he opened the front door of the house. The little Pom didn't even yip. He stood looking down at the floor.

"So you and Jerry aren't friends yet," Rhodes said. He bent down to give Yancey's head a gentle pat. "I'm sorry about that."

Yancey didn't respond, so Rhodes went into the unused bedroom where the desk was. He opened the bottom drawer and reached in for the bag of candy. It gave a satisfactory rattle. Rhodes opened it and stuck in his hand. Instead of encountering the smooth, round surface of the M&M's, he felt a piece of paper. He pulled the paper out of the bag and discovered that it was a note from Ivy.

"Caught you," it said.

Rhodes grinned. Ivy hadn't taken out any of the candy, so he popped a few pieces in his mouth and went out to feed Speedo. Yancey looked so pitiful that Rhodes picked him up. They went through the kitchen, where the cats lay near the refrigerator, both sleeping in approximately the same positions they'd been in when Rhodes had last seen them. Yancey, secure high above the floor in Rhodes's hand, squirmed and yipped.

"That's telling them," Rhodes said, though neither cat had so much as opened an eye.

In the backyard, Rhodes put Yancey down on the grass, and Yancey, forgetting about the cats, sped off after the chew toy. Speedo made a beeline for it as well, and Rhodes left them to it while he changed Speedo's water and put some food in his bowl. After that was done, Rhodes sat on the step and watched the dogs.

The day hadn't gotten any cooler, but the step was in the shade, so Rhodes was fairly comfortable. He thought about the girl with the freckles, and he thought it was time he found out her name. He knew someone who might know.

He took out his cell phone and looked at it. It wasn't one of the new smart phones. Rhodes didn't think he needed one of those, so what he had was an old flip phone, an anachronism in the age of phones that did everything but take your blood pressure. For all Rhodes knew there might even be one that would perform that little task.

As ancient as his phone was, however, it did have a place where contact numbers were stored. Seepy Benton's number was in there.

Seepy, of course, had the latest model of some smart phone or other. He'd once showed Rhodes how he could use it to read books, watch movies, make videos, search the Internet, and send e-mail. Maybe he'd showed Rhodes a blood-pressure app, too. Rhodes couldn't remember.

Rhodes was doing good just to be able to get to Benton's contact number. When he found it, he pushed the TALK button and heard the ringing begin.

Benton answered right away.

"You never mentioned that Ike had a girlfriend," Rhodes said.

"You never asked me," Benton said. "Anyway, I didn't know."

"A redhead," Rhodes said. "With lots of freckles. Probably not too many of those on campus."

"I can think of one. She's in the same class of mine that Ike is. Her name is Sandi Campbell."

"Thanks," Rhodes said.

"Do I get my badge back?"

"Not yet," Rhodes said. "Do you know who her parents are?"

"No. I have her phone number on my roster, though."

"That'll do," Rhodes said.

He got the number and used the phone to call Hack at the jail.

"I need a lookup on this number," he said and gave it to Hack.

It didn't take Hack long to get back to him with a name and address.

"Wade Campbell," Rhodes said. "Has the Dairy Queen franchise, right?"

"That's him," Hack said. "You gonna buy him out, spend your old age eatin' free Blizzards?"

"That's not a bad idea," Rhodes said.

"I want in on the deal," Hack said.

"You got it," Rhodes told him and hung up.

Rhodes gathered up Yancey and prised the chew toy from between his tightly clamped jaws. He pitched the toy on the grass, where Speedo grabbed it and ran to the back of the yard. He dropped it and looked up at Yancey, who yipped furiously. If Rhodes hadn't known better, he'd have thought Speedo was laughing.

Yancey continued to yip as Rhodes carried him through the kitchen. The cats weren't bothered, though Sam did open one yellow eye and look at them. Rhodes set Yancey down in the safety of the bedroom and went back outside.

Ivy was just driving up. She stopped beside the county car and rolled down her window.

"Leaving already?" she asked.

"I have to go interview somebody," Rhodes told her. "Want to come along?"

"Why not?" Ivy said. She pulled the car into the garage and joined Rhodes. "Who're we interviewing?"

"Sandi Campbell. I'm doing the interview. You can watch and learn. After I'm finished, we'll go out to dinner."

"Sometimes I wonder if you like my cooking."

"You know I do," Rhodes said. "It's just that we're going to be out anyway, and you won't have time to cook."

"Maybe you should do some of the cooking."

"You know my specialty," Rhodes said. "Nobody makes beanie-weenie better than I do."

"Spare me the beanie-weenie," Ivy said.

The address that Hack had given Rhodes was a county road leading off the highway that went to the small town of Obert. A small and exclusive housing addition had sprung up on the county road a few years ago, and the Campbell house was a two-story brick number with tall storm windows. It sported a neatly manicured lawn in front. Rhodes parked behind a maroon Toyota Camry in the driveway. He felt a certain amount of pride in the house, since his devotion to the Blizzard had helped to pay for it, after all.

Someone had told Rhodes some years ago that the cost of a Dairy Queen franchise in a town the size of Clearview would run as much as half a million dollars. By now that figure would've increased a good bit. Wade Campbell had taken over the Clearview franchise when it would have been somewhat less, and he'd obviously done very well for himself in the years since, if his house was any indication.

"This must be the place," Rhodes said.

"I'm impressed," Ivy said. "We should hire a torch to burn our house and then build one like this."

"Do we have enough insurance?" Rhodes asked.

Ivy worked at an insurance agency, and she kept up with that sort of thing. "I think so, but I'll check before we do anything. I know a guy whose uncle Charlie's done some torch jobs. There's only one problem."

"And the problem is?"

"Uncle Charlie's in prison in Oklahoma."

"Might have to find someone else," Rhodes said, getting out of the car.

Ivy got out on her side, and they went to the door. Rhodes punched the doorbell and heard chimes on the inside playing a familiar tune. He couldn't quite bring the name of it to mind, however.

"Aggie War Hymn," Ivy said.

"That explains the maroon car," Rhodes said.

The door opened, and a young red-haired woman stood there looking at them. She had an abundance of freckles. Rhodes thought that she was a bit too trusting to open the door to strangers, but maybe she'd seen the county car in the driveway.

"I'm Sheriff Dan Rhodes," Rhodes said. "Are you Sandi Campbell?"

"That's right."

"This is my wife, Ivy," Rhodes said, introducing her. "We noticed that your doorbell plays the Aggie War Hymn."

"I'm going to A&M getting my associate's degree."

"Great school," Rhodes said. "I'd like to talk to you for a few minutes if that's all right."

Sandi knew what he wanted to talk about without his asking. "About Ike?"

"That's right. It won't take long."

"I guess it's okay. Come on in."

She opened the door wider, and Rhodes and Ivy went inside. Rhodes asked if her parents were at home.

"Daddy's at the DQ, checking to make sure things are going all right. Mama's with him. They're going to eat burgers there. I don't much like burgers."

"The Blizzards are good," Rhodes said, and Ivy gave him a suspicious look. "So I've heard, anyway."

He and Ivy followed Sandi into the living area. It was immaculate. No books or bookshelves, no knickknacks. The rug didn't look as if anyone had ever walked on it, and the furniture was all like new, free of pet hair, scratch marks, and any impression that anyone had ever sat on it. Rhodes felt as if he were in some kind of well-cared-for public building.

Sandi asked them to have a seat. The couch didn't look comfortable, but it was. Rhodes started to brush off his pants before he sat, but he caught himself and didn't. He hoped he didn't leave any embarrassing Pomeranian hair on the cushions.

Sandi sat across from them in a big armchair. Rhodes got right to the point.

"I believe you had a little conflict with one of your English teachers," he said. "Earl Wellington."

"I thought this was about Ike," she said.

Something occurred to Rhodes as she spoke, something he should've thought of before. Why had Harris picked the incident with Sandi to tell him about? Of all the problems Wellington might have had, why did Harris bring up that one? Could it be that he knew Rhodes would find out who the student was and do exactly what he was doing now? Rhodes thought it was a good possibility. It was the kind of thing that could be used to cast more suspicion on Ike.

"I do want to talk about Ike," Rhodes told Sandi. "I'll get to that part. Am I right about the conflict?"

"Wellington was weird," Sandi said, avoiding a direct answer. Rhodes repressed a sigh. "I mean, I'm sorry he's dead and all, but it's the truth. He never looked at you when he talked to you, you know?" Rhodes nodded, and Sandi went on. "He was always saying things to some girl in the class, like what a nice outfit she was wearing or how good her hair looked."

"How was that weird?" Rhodes asked, who thought "inappropriate" might be a better word.

"It was the way he said it, I guess. It was like something he'd learned, you know?"

By this time Rhodes had figured out that Sandi wasn't really asking him if he knew, so he didn't bother to nod.

"Or like a robot," Sandi said. "You know?"

"His comment to you about being his little speckled friend was like that?"

"How do you know about that?"

"He's a trained officer of the law," Ivy said.

Rhodes resisted the impulse to tell her that she was supposed to be watching and learning. He said, "It came up in conversation with several people. How did Ike feel about it?"

"He thought it was insulting. It made him mad, you know?"

Rhodes knew, but he didn't get a chance to say so because Sandi realized what she'd just told him and tried to backtrack.

"I don't mean it made him *mad* mad. Just mad like a little upset, you know? It's not like he'd want to hurt anybody over something like that."

"I'm sure you're right," Rhodes said. "Did he tell you why he was in jail?"

"He did, and it really made me mad. Upset. Whatever. My daddy would have let him have the money to pay his bills, and if Ike didn't want to take it as a gift, he'd've loaned it to him. Ike doesn't want to take handouts, though. He wants to pay his own way."

"Burglary's not a good way to do that," Rhodes said.

"I know that. Ike does, too. He's really sorry about it. He made me take him by Mr. Wallace's shop this afternoon so he could apologize. He said he'd pay Mr. Wallace for the window and everything."

Rhodes was impressed. Not many people would've done that.

"Mr. Wallace was real nice about it," Sandi said. "He told Ike that he might not even press charges. He said he was going to talk to you about it. Has he called you yet?"

Lonnie hadn't called, but Rhodes wouldn't be surprised if he did. Lonnie was a softhearted sort.

"I'll check with the dispatcher later to see if he's called the jail," Rhodes said. "You mentioned that Dr. Wellingon was weird. Don't you think Ike is a little weird, living away from everybody down there in the compound?"

Sandi shook her head. "He won't be living there always. He's not like his daddy and those others. He wants to get out and do things. See things, too. He doesn't plan to stay there forever." She paused. "I shouldn't have said that. Don't tell anybody that, all right? His daddy doesn't know."

"I'm pretty good at keeping secrets," Rhodes said.

"Thanks. Ike's really sorry about stealing that hair, you know? It's partly my fault that he did it."

"How could it be your fault?"

Rhodes had plenty of experience with people trying to take the blame for the crimes committed by others. He hoped Sandi wouldn't do that.

"Mr. Wallace does my hair." She touched a strand of it. "I told Ike about how Mr. Wallace was getting some new things in and how he was trying to grow his business. I guess that's how Ike got the idea that he could steal the hair and sell it."

"He could've gotten the idea from TV," Rhodes said, glad to know that Sandi wasn't really shifting the blame to herself. "There are stories about people stealing hair extensions on the news all the time. It's an epidemic, like metal thefts."

"Well, he shouldn't've done it. He knows that now. I hope he won't have to go to jail."

"He probably won't," Rhodes said.

Ike didn't have a record, and the things he'd done had all been minor offenses. If Lonnie Wallace didn't want to press charges, Ike, being a first-time offender, would get off with probation at the worst. Probably he'd get off even if Lonnie did press charges.

"Good," Sandi said. "He didn't hurt Dr. Wellington, either. He told me he didn't."

"You believed him?"

"Ike doesn't lie to me. You need to look for whoever did it, because it wasn't Ike."

"You could be right," Rhodes said.

Ivy suggested that they have dinner at the Jolly Tamale, and Rhodes was happy to accommodate her. Mexican food wasn't quite as good as a Blizzard, but it was sure better than vegetarian meat loaf. Rhodes even indulged in a small bowl of chili con queso along with the chips and didn't feel at all guilty afterward.

In fact, he was feeling pretty good right up until his cell phone rang as he was about to pay the check. He took out the phone, noticing the youthful cashier's look of amazed contempt at see-ing such an antique piece of technology, and answered.

"Tracked you down," Hack said.

"I wasn't hiding."

"Couldn't get you on the radio. We got a situation."

Rhodes waited. If it was serious, Hack wouldn't indulge him-self in avoidance. It was serious.

"Got a call that somebody's stripping the wiring out of a house," Hack said.

Copper again. Air-conditioner innards and old wiring were favorite targets.

"Shelby answered the call," Hack said. "He's on the way, but he prob'ly needs some backup. You never know if those copper thieves are armed. The other deputy's down in the south end of the county and can't get there. It's the old Post place."

Rhodes knew where that was. He said he'd go and flipped the phone shut.

"I heard that," Ivy said as they left the restaurant. "Can I go, too?"

"You can go," Rhodes said. It was practical. The address Hack had given Rhodes was much closer to the restaurant than it was to Rhodes's house. "You'll have to stay in the car, though."

"Maybe we'll get into a high-speed chase. If we do, can I turn on the siren?"

"Why not?" Rhodes said.

Chapter 19

▼

Andy Shelby was the county's youngest deputy. He was a graduate of the same police academy that Ruth Grady had attended at
a community college near Houston, and he'd done well there. He
was new at the job, however, and sometimes apt to make a rash
decision. Rhodes hoped he hadn't made one at the old Post place.

As it turned out, he hadn't because he hadn't arrived. Rhodes
had been closer, and he pulled to the curb in front of the house as
Andy was rounding the corner at the end of the block.

It had gotten dark while Rhodes and Ivy were eating, but Andy
hadn't turned on his car's headlights. He pulled in behind Rhodes
and stopped.

Rhodes unlocked the shotgun from its stand.

"Do you think you'll need that?" Ivy asked.

"No, but it'll be a comfort to me."

"What about me?"

"You'll have to fend for yourself. Just be sure to keep the
doors locked."

Ivy grinned. "Leave me the keys. If anybody starts toward me, I'm turning on the siren and the light bar. I might even make a run for it."

Rhodes tossed her the keys, closed the door, and met Andy on the sidewalk, which was buckled and cracked. The Post house was in an old neighborhood, and it sat alone on a quarter of a block. There'd been a fire there some months before, and the place was festooned with NO TRESPASSING signs. The building sat on a high foundation, at least four feet above the ground. It was still intact, but all the window glass was gone, and the openings had been covered with plywood. Boards in the shape of an X had been nailed over the doorways. No one had lived there for at least fifteen years, maybe more like twenty, and Rhodes didn't recall who owned it now. Maybe some of the Posts' relatives who lived in some other town. Tall trees stood all around the yard, and bushes had grown up around the foundation.

The whole block was dark. There were a few other houses, but no lights showed in any of them.

"Spooky place," Andy said. He was a rangy youngster who could've used a few more pounds on his frame. "Wonder how anybody got inside."

"There's always a way," Rhodes said, thinking that the boards over the doorways would be all too easy to pull off. "Did Hack mention who called this in?"

"Nope. He did say it was somebody passing by who saw a light. I don't see one, though."

"Look down there," Rhodes said.

At the end of the right side of the house where the plywood wasn't well attached to one of the windows, a thin shaft of light glowed.

Andy pushed down on the hood that secured his Glock in its

holster and drew the sidearm. Rhodes carried a small-caliber pistol in an ankle holster, but he was more comfortable with the shotgun in this situation.

"Let's see if we can find out how they got in," Rhodes said. "Must have been the back door."

He started for the left side of the house. Andy was right behind him. The windows on that side were all dark. Rhodes smelled charred wood, and even in the darkness he could see black blotches on the white paint.

"Whoever's in there must have a car around here somewhere," Andy whispered. "Might be someone watching, too."

Rhodes had thought of both things, but he was glad that Andy had also. He stopped and pointed down toward the end of the block. Past the only other house and across an alley was a vacant lot, covered with bushes.

"Car's probably in those bushes," Rhodes said. "Too dark to tell. If there was a lookout, whoever's inside knows we're here. We'll have to be careful."

"My middle name," Andy said, even though Rhodes knew that wasn't the truth. They resumed walking.

Rhodes stopped at the end of the house and looked around the corner. He saw a barbecue pit and a small, high back porch with an iron railing. He also saw movement at the other end of the house, and before he could pull back, two things happened almost simultaneously. There was a gunshot, and a big chunk of wood flew off the corner of the house just above his head. Another shot followed, and the bullet splintered more wood.

"Damn!" Andy cried out.

Splinters in the face, Rhodes thought. "Stay back," he said, hoping that Andy was listening.

The shooter was too far away for Rhodes to do much damage

with the shotgun, but the noise the thing made was impressive and might put a scare in somebody. Rhodes turned the corner, dropping to his knees as he did so, and triggered off a blast. He shot high to miss the porch, and most of the shot went into the roof overhead. Rhodes, hoping the sound was enough to discourage the shooter, ducked back to safety.

He heard someone running down the back steps.

"Let's get him," Andy said. He was breathing fast, and Rhodes could almost feel the eagerness pulsing off him. Rhodes put up a hand to caution him not to take off in pursuit too quickly. The shooter might be waiting for that.

Footsteps pounded away from the house. Rhodes thought he could hear at least three people running. There shouldn't have been any more than that, two in the house and one outside.

"You okay?" he asked Andy.

"Just some scratches," Andy said.

"Let's go, then."

Rhodes and Andy went around the corner, and Rhodes saw two dark figures running across the yard and toward the back-yard of the only other house on this side of the block.

"Don't shoot," he told Andy.

Rhodes thought the house was occupied, and even if it wasn't, it was best not to risk a shot. He'd read too many stories about people who were asleep or sitting on a couch watching TV being killed or wounded by stray bullets. Anybody firing on the run was more likely to hit a house than he was to hit a person.

The figures disappeared into the brush in the vacant lot, and Rhodes heard a car start.

"The street," he said.

He turned and ran toward the side street just in time to see a car break out of the brush and turn down the street away from him. The car lights were off, and so was the streetlight at the end of the block. Rhodes wouldn't have been surprised if it had been shot out with a pellet rifle before the men started on the house. He couldn't tell a thing about the car except that it was gray or black. He and Andy stood in the middle of the road as it sped away.

"Want me to go after them?" Andy asked. He was still breathing hard.

"They have too much of a head start," Rhodes said, wondering how much adrenaline was still pumping through the young deputy's body. "You'd never catch them."

"We stopped them from stripping the house," Andy said, which was true enough, but Rhodes didn't see that they'd really accomplished anything by doing it. The house was never going to be used again, and Rhodes thought the city would soon force the owner to demolish it. On the other hand, if they'd caught the potential thieves, they might have stopped some future thefts.

"We did good," Rhodes said. He gave Andy a pat on the arm. "You did everything right."

Andy gave a weak laugh. "Well, I have to admit I got a little shook when they started shooting."

"So did I," Rhodes said, thinking about the first time he'd been under fire. He'd been weak in the knees for a couple of hours. "Who wouldn't get a little shook?"

"John Wayne," Andy said.

Rhodes was gratified that Andy knew the classics. He said, "Only in the movies. Give me your flashlight and let me take a look at your face."

Andy unclipped the light from his utility belt and handed it to Rhodes, who turned it on and shined it on the deputy's face. He saw a couple of bloody spots, but no splinters stuck out from the skin.

"After we finish here," Rhodes said, "you'd better stop by the hospital and get somebody to take a look at you, just to be on the safe side. Right now, we'd better check to see if anybody stayed behind."

Rhodes kept the flashlight and led the way up the back steps. When he reached the top, he saw that the boards that had been nailed across the doorway were lying on the floor of a small inside room atop broken glass from the windows. The odor of charred wood and smoke was strong even though the fire had been quite a while ago.

Holding the flashlight well away from his body, Rhodes directed the beam into the room beyond. It appeared to have been a kitchen, and Rhodes saw a burned table and some overturned chairs.

Rhodes listened for a minute or so. All he could hear was Andy breathing behind him and the usual noises of the night, a car passing on the street in front of the house and some insects buzzing.

Rhodes went inside, Andy still right at his back, and they went through the house a room at a time. Each room held burned furniture—a piano, a china cabinet, a desk, a bed—but there was no sign of anyone lurking in the darkness.

They did find where the Sheetrock had been torn away and some of the wiring stripped out, but that was all. When Rhodes was satisfied that there was nothing more to learn, he led the way back outside.

"You go on by the hospital now," he told Andy. "Have them patch up your face. When you get back on patrol, check by here fairly often. Those fellas might come back."

"I'll drop by every hour or so," Andy said.

Rhodes said every hour would be fine, and Andy went on his way. Rhodes went back to the car, and Ivy unlocked the door.

"I heard gunshots," Ivy said.

Rhodes locked the shotgun back in position and got in the car. "So did I."

Ivy gave him a stern look. "Don't you joke about this, Dan Rhodes."

Since she'd used his full name, Rhodes knew he was in trouble. "I didn't mean to. I was overcompensating."

"Don't give me any psychology, either."

Rhodes sat quietly, and after a while Ivy said, "I'm fine now. I don't like to think of you being shot at."

"I'm fine," Rhodes told her. "Nothing even came close to me. Somebody was just trying to warn us off."

He didn't believe that was true, but it seemed like the right thing to say.

"You don't have any prisoners," Ivy said, "so the warning must have worked."

"We'll get 'em next time," Rhodes said.

"I hope there's not a next time, not with guns."

"I could do without the guns myself," Rhodes said.

He got on the radio and called Hack to let him know what had happened. He also told him to have Ruth check the brushy lot for tire prints in the morning.

"Ain't rained in a month," Hack said. "Won't be any tire prints."

"Have her check anyway."

"If you say so."

"I do," Rhodes said.

．　　．　　．

Ivy didn't do any talking on the drive back home, and Rhodes tried to get his thoughts in some kind of order. He had a feeling that he had just about everything he needed to make a case against somebody, but the problem was that he didn't know which somebody to make the case against.

Harold Harris was clearly worried, probably about somehow being caught getting his score changed on ProfessoRater, and he'd lied about being at the faculty lounge the day Wellington died. That is, he'd lied unless both Mary Mason and Seepy Benton were wrong. Rhodes didn't think either of them was wrong. If Wellington had uncovered the problem with the scores, Harris could have argued with him and accidentally killed him. Harris might also have tried to shift suspicion to Ike. Rhodes still wasn't sure about that. Maybe it was just a coincidence that he'd mentioned Sandi Campbell.

Dean King was another possibility. She was intent on doing whatever was necessary to protect the college. She wouldn't want the word to get out about Harris's cheating, and she was easily strong enough to whack Wellington's head against the trash bin.

Ike Terrell was a puzzle. Rhodes was pretty sure he knew something, too, but he was caught between his father and his desire to get away from the compound. Rhodes didn't know how real that desire was. He had only Sandi Campbell's word for it, and a young man Ike's age was apt to say anything he thought a pretty girl wanted to hear.

There were a number of other things bumping around in Rhodes's head, too, and he figured that sooner or later they'd stop bumping into each other and line up in orderly fashion so he could look at them and sort through them.

"Why so quiet?" Ivy asked when they stopped in their own driveway.

"Thinking," Rhodes said.

One thing he was thinking was that she'd been the quiet one.

"Why don't we have some ice cream and talk about it," she said.

"We have ice cream?"

"I put some in the freezer the other day. I thought you'd have found it by now."

"I wasn't looking."

"You were going after those M&M's."

"I'd rather have ice cream."

Ivy got out of the car. "Then come along," she said.

Rhodes and Ivy sat at the kitchen table with bowls of vanilla ice cream in front of them. The cats were sitting up, grooming themselves without any interest in each other or anything else. Yancey sat in the doorway, looking into the kitchen with mournful eyes.

"Yancey will get over it," Rhodes said. "I give him one more day of trying to make us feel guilty, and then he'll be back to normal."

He took a bite of the ice cream. It wasn't a Blizzard, but it would do.

"Have you interviewed that Mary Mason yet?" Ivy asked. "I'll bet she has something to do with all of this."

"As a matter of fact, I did interview her, and she had some helpful information. She didn't have anything to do with Wellington's death, though."

Ivy looked disappointed. "Who did, then?"

"That's what I can't figure out."

Rhodes went through his various scenarios with her and asked her what she thought.

"I still think Mary Mason did it," she said.

Rhodes ate some more ice cream, slowly enough to avoid brain freeze. When he'd had a few bites, he said, "If only it were that easy."

"What about that Dr. Harris?" Ivy asked. "He's obviously hiding something. You should take him to the basement and give him the old third degree."

"There's a problem with that," Rhodes said. "Two problems, really."

"What?"

"First of all, we don't give our suspects the old third degree these days. I've heard they used to right here in Blacklin County, sixty or seventy years ago, but someone who's getting beaten up will confess to anything to stop the pain. When you get that kind of confession, you don't have much."

"I knew that," Ivy said. "What's the other thing?"

"The jail's like the Alamo," Rhodes said. "It doesn't have a basement."

"Darn," Ivy said. "That's inconvenient. I think Harris is the one, though. You just need to figure out how to get him to talk."

"I'll work on it," Rhodes said.

He finished off his ice cream and was considering getting another dip when the telephone rang.

"I'll get it," Ivy said.

"Never mind," Rhodes said, getting up. "It's bound to be for me."

It was Mayor Clement, and he wanted to know if Rhodes had anybody locked up for killing Wellington.

"Not yet," Rhodes said. "I have a lot of suspects, though. I'm

thinking about taking one of them down to the basement and giving him the old third degree."

Mayor Clement didn't think it was funny. "I don't care if you
waterboard the lot of them. I want a confession. I want this thing
wrapped up. You understand that, right?"

"I understand," Rhodes said.

"Good. Get it done."

"Shouldn't that be 'Git 'er done'?"

"What?"

"Never mind," Rhodes said. "I'm working on it."

"You'd better be," Clement said, and he hung up.

"It's always a pleasure to talk to our mayor," Rhodes said, sitting back down at the table.

"He does have a way of putting a smile on your face," Ivy said,
"but I could do a better job of that. Want to bet?"

Rhodes grinned. "You're on."

Chapter 20

▼

Rhodes's first stop the next day was the college. He got there early, before classes started, and went straight to Harold Harris's office, but the door was closed and locked. Rhodes knocked. No answer. Rhodes didn't think Harris was hiding in there, so he went to the faculty lounge. Seepy Benton was inside, chatting up Mary Mason and a man Rhodes didn't know. Among the others who were there, Rhodes recognized only Tom Vance. Everyone but Benton was drinking coffee. There was no sign of Harris, so Rhodes called Benton outside.

"Let's go to your office," Rhodes said. "I want to talk about Harris."

Benton didn't ask any questions. He just went to his office with Rhodes at his side. The formula Benton had written on the dry-erase board the previous day was still there, and Rhodes had to resist the urge to pick up the eraser and wipe it off.

"What about Harris?" Benton asked when they'd taken a seat.

"He's not here," Rhodes said.

"You think that's significant?"

"I do. I talked to him at his home yesterday. He's worried and maybe a little scared."

"You would be, too," Benton said, "if you'd been caught cheating on your ProfessoRater score."

"He hasn't been caught," Rhodes said. "We just think he might have done that. What I'm more interested in is why he told me he was in the faculty lounge on the morning Wellington died."

"You think he was outside with Wellington?"

"I don't know what to think. When I talked to him at his house yesterday, he wouldn't say anything helpful. I'm going back for another visit if he doesn't show up here soon."

"He's not in his office?"

"If he is, he wouldn't answer the door."

"You should check his schedule and see if he has an early class today," Benton said. "He'll have to show up there. I can just look the schedule up right here on my computer. Can I have my badge back?"

"Just check it for me, please," Rhodes said.

Benton turned to his computer and with a few mouse clicks had Harris's schedule displayed on the monitor.

"Here it is," Benton said. "He has an eight o'clock, all right. American Lit. In room two-sixteen. I can show you where that is."

"I can find it," Rhodes said. "You need to get ready for your own class."

Benton picked up a can of Pringles potato chips from beside his desk. Rhodes hadn't seen it there when they walked in.

"This is my lesson," Benton said, shaking the can.

"You're teaching a class in potato chips?"

"The potato chips are merely illustrative. What I'm teaching is hyperbolic parabaloids, of which a Pringles chip is a perfect example."

"Right," Rhodes said.

"It's an important part of multivariable calculus," Benton said.

"I should have remembered that."

"You certainly should. It's going to be on the final exam."

Rhodes was happy he wasn't going to have to take the final exam.

"You can use a graphing calculator on the final," Benton said. "If you need one, that is."

"That's good to know." The bell rang, for which Rhodes was grateful. Probably Benton's students were, too, now and then, though not as grateful for the bell to begin class as for the one to end it. "Time for class. Thanks for looking up the schedule."

"Anytime," Benton said.

Rhodes left the office and walked down the hallway to the room where Harris's class was to meet. Students went by, some of them texting on their phones, some of them talking on their phones, and one or two of them talking to each other. Rhodes wondered how much longer that would last. In a few years, maybe communication between two people sitting next to each other would be conducted by phone, too.

He noticed a student standing by the wall, holding up his phone and aiming it at Rhodes. Down at the end of the hall another student was doing the same thing. It took Rhodes a second or two to realize that they were either taking a picture of him or recording a video. He hoped the videos wouldn't appear on Jennifer Loam's Web site later that day with headlines like SHERIFF PROWLS THE GROVES OF ACADEME!

It wasn't impossible. Loam encouraged her readers to send in photos and video, and occasionally she got some interesting things. The sheriff appearing on campus wouldn't be among them, not as far as Rhodes was concerned, anyway.

Harris wasn't in the classroom, though there were students already seated. Rhodes stood outside the door and waited. He didn't have to wait long. Harris came hurrying down the hall with a thick textbook and a couple of manila folders.

"I don't have time to talk," he told Rhodes when he reached the door. "I have a class to teach."

"Your students won't mind waiting," Rhodes said. "They might even want to take video of us."

"You can't hold me out here against my will. I have an obligation."

"You're acting mighty funny for an innocent man," Rhodes said.

"Look, I want to talk to you, too," Harris said. "It will just have to wait until after this class. Come back in an hour, and I'll meet you in my office. Will that satisfy you?"

"I'll be there," Rhodes said.

Harris nodded and went past Rhodes and into the room, pushing the door shut behind him. Rhodes stood and looked at the door for a while before walking back down the hall, down the stairs, and out of the building.

Rhodes drove to the courthouse. It was where he always went when he needed a little time to think. Nobody ever bothered him there, except Jennifer Loam, and she didn't have any reason to track him down today, as far as he knew.

The hallways were mostly deserted since the courts weren't in session. He wished the barbershop chorus would come over and sing a couple of songs. The acoustics, with the granite floors and plaster walls and ceilings, would have made it a great place to practice. The people in the offices would appreciate the break, too.

Rhodes didn't bother to stop at the soft drink machine. He'd decided to continue his boycott of his favorite drink, and he still wasn't ready to change to something new. Maybe next week. Anyway, laying off the soft drinks had probably been good for him. He wasn't consuming as much sugar, and that was supposed to be a good thing, wasn't it?

He unlocked the office door and went inside. The room got a regular cleaning, but it always had an odd odor that Rhodes thought came from the fact that he hardly ever used the place. He considered opening a window to air it out, but it was cool in the office and hot outside. When it came right down to it, he preferred the cool stale air rather than the fresh outside air, a common failing among Texans in the summertime.

Sitting in his chair, Rhodes leaned back, ignoring the squeak, propped his feet on the desk, and thought things over. He'd seen a couple of examples in the last few days of people using their cell phones to take video. It was a common occurrence and had been for years, and Rhodes knew he'd overlooked something that should have been a standard part of his investigation. It wasn't too late to do something about it, and while it might turn out not to have any bearing on things at all, he'd have to give it a try. It was the kind of thing he should've thought of earlier, and he felt bad about it.

He still couldn't figure out Harold Harris, who didn't act exactly like a man who was guilty of killing someone, accidentally or not. He looked like a man who was guilty of something, though. Rhodes was sure of that, and Duke Pearson believed it, too, with the problem being that neither of them could figure out just what it was that Harris might have done. The ten o'clock meeting with Harris might provide an answer to that.

Rhodes thought about calling Hack to check on things around town, but Hack would have been in touch if there'd been a problem, and Rhodes didn't feel like dealing with him at the moment.

About ten minutes until nine, having reached hardly any conclusions, Rhodes got up and left. He didn't feel that his time had been wasted, even if it might seem as if it had to someone else. He never knew when his ruminations would bring something to the surface.

He was eager to hear what Harris had to say, so he went down to the car and got on his way.

Harold Harris's office was neat. No papers on the floor, no clutter on the desk, books neatly arranged on the shelves. The chair he had for students to use looked considerably more comfortable than those in Benton's office, and Rhodes chose to sit in it rather than to loom. Harris already looked nervous enough.

"I just got through talking to my students about Achilles," Harris said. Nervous or not, he was dressed again in what Rhodes thought was appropriate for a college instructor, with a blue blazer over his white shirt and patterned tie. "You know who Achilles is, of course."

The way he said it irritated Rhodes a little, but he didn't let it show. He said, "Sure. There was this thing about his heel. He was at Troy when the Greeks hid in the wooden horse. The thing about his heel isn't in that story, though."

Harris gave him an appraising look. "Indeed. Anyway, Achilles might have been an uncivilized ruffian by our standards, but he had something that a lot of us lack, a high sense of honor. He had that, and courage, too. He was a real hero, in a way a lot of our so-called heroes now aren't." Harris gave a weak grin. "Excepting Sage Barton, of course."

Rhodes repressed a sigh. Was there anybody who didn't read those books?

"As for me," Harris continued, "I've recently demonstrated that I'm just about the opposite of Achilles. And Sage Barton, for that matter. My students would think I'm a fraud, standing up there and reciting the virtues of a hero when I've been a coward so recently. You could see through me at once, I'm sure."

Rhodes decided that his best tactic would be to look inscrutable, which was easy enough for him to do, since he didn't have any idea where Harris was going with all the stuff about Achilles and heroism. While Harris might have been about to confess to killing Wellington, he could just as well be ready to admit that he'd somehow managed to alter his standing on ProfessoRater.

Harris waited for Rhodes to say something. When he didn't, Harris kept going. Rhodes felt clever for keeping his mouth shut.

"You knew I was lying about being in the lounge when Wellington was killed," Harris said, "and I wouldn't blame you if you thought I'd had something to do with it. That's not true, however. I'm completely innocent in that matter."

"If you're innocent," Rhodes said, "then what are we talking about here?"

Harris looked miserable, but he still didn't give the specific example Rhodes was looking for.

"I'm not proud of what I did," Harris said, without saying

what *it* was. "I know it was wrong, but I can't change that now. All I can do is admit it."

He looked at Rhodes as if asking for something. Rhodes didn't know what it was. Understanding or forgiveness maybe.

"I don't know anybody who's never done something he wished he could do over," Rhodes said. "We don't get do-overs, though, so we just have to muddle through. I've heard plenty of stories people didn't want to tell me, but they eventually realized they had to. You might as well tell me yours."

"I'm embarrassed about it," Harris said, "and I'm ashamed of myself."

"If it's about ProfessoRater, you don't have anything to worry about. Not from me, anyway. That's college business, not mine. I don't care about it at all, not unless it caused you and Wellington to get into an argument that left him lying out by the trash bin."

Harris sat up a little straighter. "How did you know about the ProfessoRater?"

"Just doing my job," Rhodes said. "I try to find out all I can about the people involved in a case I'm working on."

Harris squirmed a little in his chair. "I . . . don't want to talk about that. That's between me and the dean. It's over and done with. Everything's settled, and it has absolutely nothing to do with you or with Wellington."

"He knew about it," Rhodes said.

"Knew what? I said I'm not going to talk about that. The dean and I have reached an agreement. It's a dead issue."

Rhodes was frustrated, and it showed. "If that's not what we're here for, you'd better get to the point."

"All right. I'm sorry for going all the way around Robin Hood's barn to get to the point. This isn't easy for me." Harris paused and took a deep breath. "I was a little late day before yesterday, and I was hurrying across the parking lot to get to the lounge and have some coffee before class. I happened to glance over at the Dumpster, and I saw Wellington lying there. I went over to see if I could help, thinking maybe that he'd fainted or something like that, but when I got to him, it was obvious he was dead. I saw the blood and I panicked." Harris paused and rubbed a hand across his forehead. "I ran back to my car and sat behind the wheel. I was hyperventilating. After I got myself under control, I went home." Another weak grin. "Not like Sage Barton would have done. I didn't get back in time for my class, not that anybody noticed. I'd hardly gotten back on campus before Dean King called me to see you. I'm sure you could tell how nervous I was. Hardly the kind of behavior that Sage Barton would approve of."

"Let's forget Sage Barton," Rhodes said. "He has less to do with this than your ranking on ProfessoRater. Why didn't you tell me all this to start with?"

"I know I should have," Harris said. "It's just led to even more trouble for me."

"More trouble? How?"

"Someone thinks I saw more than I did, someone menacing. I got a call here in the office that afternoon. It was frightening, and it had an effect on me. I was scared. I admit it. I should've told you about it when you came by my house, but I didn't."

"Who called?" Rhodes asked.

Harris looked surprised that Rhodes would ask. "He didn't give a name."

"What did he say?"

"He said I'd better keep quiet. If I didn't, I'd get the same thing that Wellington did."

"Keep quiet about what?"

"That's what I don't know. I didn't see anything or anybody. Well, that's not entirely true. I saw a car leaving the parking lot as I came in, but I hardly glanced at it. I certainly don't know who was driving or even what kind of car it was."

Someone was giving Harris's powers of observation far too much credit. Rhodes had dealt with countless people over the years, and their lack of attention to what went on around them no longer surprised him. He'd heard three or four people who witnessed the same event describe what had happened, and most of the time they might as well have been in different towns for all that their accounts agreed. It was no wonder that lawyers dreaded eyewitness testimony. It was the most unreliable evidence in the world.

"There's some good news, however," Harris said.

Rhodes didn't see what that could be, but he said, "Tell me."

"I preserved part of the conversation," Harris said. "When I finally realized what the man was saying, I recorded the rest on the answering machine."

Rhodes was amazed. He wouldn't have thought that Harris would've had the presence of mind to do it. It might not help, but at least it was something.

"It's not all good news," Harris said. "The man was obviously disguising his voice."

Rhodes was disappointed, but maybe he could get some kind of clue from the man's phrasing.

"Let's hear it," he said.

"Let me see if I can find it," Harris said.

He punched a couple of buttons on the phone, and Rhodes heard a man's voice. It sounded as if the man had something stuffed in his mouth, so the voice was effectively disguised, all right.

There was just one problem. Not for Rhodes, but for the caller. Duffy could disguise his voice, but he couldn't disguise his sniffles.

Duffy had been right about one thing. You never knew who might be recording your calls.

Chapter 21

▼

Rhodes left the campus and went to the jail. He had things to do. While it was nice to have Duffy's voice on Harris's phone message, it didn't prove anything. Rhodes wasn't sure they could prove it was Duffy's voice, even with the sniffles, and since no amount of prodding had gotten anything further out of Harris, Rhodes was stuck again. If all else failed, he could confront Duffy and Terrell with the phone message, but they'd just laugh.

Rhodes wasn't sure about Terrell's involvement. He remembered now that Duffy had told him, several times, that Terrell never left the compound, never even went outside the fence. Duffy, however, had never said that *he* didn't leave the compound. Rhodes had gotten that impression, as Duffy had no doubt intended, but in thinking back over everything that had been said that day, Rhodes was sure Duffy hadn't actually said it. Some people had a way of shading a thing like that to avoid being caught in a lie later on.

There was something Rhodes needed to do, something that might give him a clue as to why Duffy had fought with Wellington, if indeed he had. Duffy had been pretty worked up about the plagiarism problem, but Rhodes didn't think that could have been what set him off. He'd helped Ike with his math, not his papers. It didn't seem likely that he'd have been so involved in the matter that he'd have wanted to hurt Wellington because of it.

At any rate, Rhodes had plans for what to do with the rest of the morning. Hack and Lawton, however, weren't going to let him carry them out immediately. They had other things in mind.

"Big emergency at the Pizza Hut," Hack said as Rhodes came through the door. "Some fella out there just called it in. Ruth's on the way, but you might wanna run out there and help her out."

"Get Buddy or Duke to go," Rhodes said. "I have work to do here."

He used his no-nonsense tone, but Hack ignored it, as he often did. "I called Buddy. He's on the way, but he's out close to Milsby. It'll take him ten minutes or so to get there. You could do it in less."

"Not much less," Rhodes said, "and I'm busy."

Hack turned to Lawton. "The sheriff's always busy. Too busy for little things like a riot at the Pizza Hut."

"Riot?" Rhodes said.

The Pizza Hut wasn't far from the college, and Rhodes hadn't noticed anything happening there when he'd left the campus. It was a little early for a riot, anyway. The place couldn't have been open more than ten or fifteen minutes.

"Sort of a riot," Lawton said. "Lots of screamin', anyway. I could hear it comin' over the phone when Hack took the call."

"That doesn't make a riot," Rhodes said.

"Fightin', too," Hack said. "Hair pullin'. Bitin'. I'm not a hundred percent sure Ruth can handle it."

Rhodes was curious in spite of himself. "How many people are involved?"

"Not many," Lawton said.

"That's not very exact. Give me a number."

Lawton looked at Hack. Hack said, "Two."

"Two," Rhodes said. "That's not a riot. That's an argument. Ruth can handle it."

"Might get bigger. It's inside. Innocent bystanders might get hurt."

"Look," Rhodes said, "I have a lot on my mind today, and I'm not going to the Pizza Hut. Just tell me what's going on."

"Couple of women," Lawton said.

"One of 'em got the other one's to-go order," Hack said, "or that's what it sounded like. The kid who called it in wasn't too clear on that. Anyway, the one who got the order must've decided she liked it better'n what she'd ordered for herself. She ran for the door, and the other woman tripped her."

"Pizza on the floor," Lawton said. "Messy."

"That's when the fight started," Lawton said. "It got messier. The kid said they were rollin' on the pizza."

"That sauce makes a bad stain," Hack said. "Hard as the dickens to get out."

"Yeah," Lawton said. "One time—"

"Never mind," Rhodes said. "Ruth can handle two women fighting over a pizza. She doesn't need me to help her. By now it's all over and they're more worried about getting pizza stains out of their clothes than what they were fighting about. If they aren't, Ruth will settle them down, and when Buddy gets there, he can give them cleaning advice. I can't be running off every time there's some little something to handle."

"Gettin' touchy again," Hack said. "I heard that happens when people get older."

"Yeah," Lawton said. "Never happened to me and you, though. Wonder why that is?"

"We're just on an even keel all the time," Hack said. "Some people are like that. There's a word for it. Big word. I can't always remember it. Pragmatic or somehin' or other like that."

"Phlegmatic," Lawton said. "I can even spell it. Don't remember where I heard about it. Back when I was in school as a kid, maybe. We learned a lot more back then than the kids do now. You ask one of them what phlegmatic means, why, they wouldn't have any idea that it was even a word, much less that it meant people like you and me. Cool as cucumbers, that's us."

Hack nodded. "Phlegmatic. Ain't you glad we're like that, Sheriff? Be nice if you were more phlegmatic yourself."

Rhodes had tuned them out by that time. He was on his way to the evidence room to get Wellington's cell phone and make another check on it. He should've let Seepy Benton do it to begin with. Seepy would never have overlooked something so obvious.

He signed out the phone and brought it back to his desk. Hack and Lawton had lost interest in tormenting him, so he sat down and looked it over without interference. While he didn't have a smart phone himself, he knew how they worked.

First he had to turn it on, and when he did that, he saw that the battery level was very low. He didn't have a charger for it, so he'd have to be sure he got things done before he ran out of power.

He looked for the PHOTOS icon and found it easily, but the photos themselves were disappointing. Rhodes had hoped there was some kind of overlooked evidence, but all he found was pictures of the black and white cat that was now named Jerry and happily residing in Rhodes's kitchen.

Rhodes had thought that possibly Wellington's obsession with Ike and his comment to Francie Solomon that he was going to get him might have meant that Wellington had taken some kind of action. Janet Sandstrom had said he was the sort of person who'd harass students who missed class by calling them and even showing up at their homes. He couldn't have shown up at Ike's home, but he could have staked it out.

Rhodes had been looking for photos of Ike breaking into the Beauty Shack. Wellington could have taken them and gotten back to the college before Ike arrived. He could have been smoking his morning cigarette by the trash bin when Ike got there, accosted Ike, and gotten his head smacked against the sharp end of the Dumpster for his trouble. There was nothing like that, and photos of a cat weren't going to give Ike much of a motive.

Rhodes put the phone down and thought about it. Hack took advantage of the opportunity to ask Rhodes what he was doing.

"Looking for pictures on this phone," Rhodes said. "I didn't find any worth talking about."

"Why'd you care about the pictures?" Hack asked.

"Evidence."

"Did you check the videos?"

"I was planning to do that next," Rhodes said, which was true. He should have done it two days ago.

"Always check the videos," Hack said. "Ever'body in town's got a video on that Jennifer Loam's Web site. There was one today of those kid goats of Vernell Lindsey's. You know about 'em?"

Rhodes knew about the kid goats, all right. Vernell had three goats, Shirley, Goodness, and Mercy. All three had a penchant for escaping their enclosure, and Shirley had strayed far enough to get herself in trouble. Now she was a mother.

"Those kids are pretty cute," Hack said. "Cut all kinda capers."

"I'm sure," Rhodes said.

"Vernell did the video herself," Hack said. "With her phone. It's amazin' what a phone can do these days. You say you're gonna check Wellington's phone for videos?"

"As soon as people will leave me alone long enough to let me."

"Touchy," Hack said, turning away. "Just plain touchy."

Rhodes hoped the battery hadn't run down while Hack was talking, but the phone had turned itself off to preserve power, so things were okay. Rhodes turned it back on, located the video icon, and discovered that there were four videos on the phone.

The first one was of nothing at all. Not really nothing, exactly, but it looked as if Wellington had been trying to figure out how to use the video function and hadn't quite gotten the hang of it. There were a few seconds of a rug, and then the camera swung up to get a ceiling. It steadied a bit, and Rhodes glimpsed chairs and bookshelves. He was looking at the inside of Wellington's apartment, but by the time he realized it, the video had ended.

The second video was of Jerry, and Wellington seemed to have figured things out. It was far from professional quality, but at least the camera wasn't jumping all over the place. Jerry wasn't doing much of anything other than sitting in the room and looking at the camera. A small rubber ball rolled into the frame, and a voice that Rhodes assumed was Wellington's said, "Chase the ball, Ginsberg. Chase the ball." That was all.

Two things struck Rhodes. One was that this was the first time he'd heard Wellington's voice. Nobody would ever hear it again unless they watched this video.

The second was that Ginsberg was a pretty good name for a cat. He'd have to mention it to Ivy.

Rhodes looked at the third video. He'd been right about Wellington stalking Ike. The video was taken after dark, so it was hard to see anything clearly, but Rhodes knew it could be enhanced at the state lab if necessary. For the moment he could see enough to tell that the video was of a car coming onto the highway from the road leading to the Terrell compound. It was the old Pontiac that Rhodes had seen on his visit.

That was all there was, however. Just a car leaving the compound. Not exactly the kind of evidence that was going to get anyone convicted of anything.

Rhodes had been thinking for a while about how the compound kept going. No matter how self-sufficient Able Terrell wanted to be, and no matter how much he tried to cut himself off from civilization, there had to be money from somewhere. The satellite bill and the electric bill had to be paid.

Rhodes punched the last video. Jackpot. It had been the Pontiac in the other video, all right, and it had apparently carried Duffy to town and to the church where the air conditioners had been stripped. Wellington had managed to follow him and get video. Duffy had used a light, so he showed up clearly enough for identification. There was another man with him, but it wasn't Ike, and it wasn't Able. Now Rhodes knew how the compound dwellers got their income, and he also knew that Duffy had a motive for fighting with Wellington.

The video ended abruptly. Rhodes wondered if Wellington had been spotted. It could have been like that, and he could have done something really stupid, like letting Duffy or the other man follow him home. If so, they'd done nothing that night, or any night for a while. The church air conditioner in the video was at the Nazarene church, and that one had been stripped several days ago. Somehow Duffy had discovered that Wellington had the video, and he'd done something about it.

Ike hadn't been one of the men with Duffy, Rhodes thought, at least not that night. If he had, Wellington would have turned him in. Or maybe Wellington just hadn't seen him. Wellington might never have done anything with the video at all, but Duffy couldn't be sure of that, so he confronted him. Maybe.

It could have happened like that. All Rhodes had to do was prove that it had. That was going to be the hard part.

Rhodes was almost certain now that Duffy had been in the Post house the previous evening to strip the wire and that the gray car leaving the brush down the block had been the Pontiac.

"Did you have Ruth look for those tire prints?" he asked Hack.

"You told me to, didn't you?"

"Right."

"So I told her. I always do what I'm told, even if I don't get any credit for it around here."

Rhodes ignored the whining. Hack didn't mean it, anyway. He just liked to whine.

"What did she find?"

"Found just what I said she'd find, which was nothing. Ground's too hard to take any prints. Some of the bushes was broken, but that's no help to you."

Rhodes got the feeling that Hack was holding something back. That was his usual method of operation.

"There's more," Rhodes said. "Tell me."

"Well, she did say that there was a little bit of something stuck on one of the bushes, maybe a piece of cloth from somebody's shirt. Anybody could've been in that vacant lot, though, so it won't do you much good as evidence."

"It might," Rhodes said. "She saved it, of course."

"Sure she did. You think she's not good at her job? Got it all locked up in the trunk of the car. She'll bring it in at the end of her shift."

"Good. I'm going back to the college. I need to talk to Ike Terrell."

"He don't strike me as the talkative type," Hack said.

"He'll talk to me this time."

"You really think so?"

"I know so," Rhodes said.

Rhodes got to the campus just as the eleven o'clock class was ending. It would be the last class of the day for many of the students and for a lot of the faculty members. Rhodes went to Seepy Benton's office. He didn't want the students to see him accosting Ike in the hallway, so he sent Seepy Benton to fetch him.

"Do I get a badge?" Seepy asked.

"No, you don't get a badge. Just do it as a favor to me."

"If that's the way you want it."

Seepy left and returned shortly with Ike Terrell. Tagging along was Sandi Campbell.

"She insisted," Seepy said when he saw the look on Rhodes's face.

"You two go have a talk about the quadratic equation somewhere," Rhodes said. "I need to talk to Ike privately."

"I'm not so sure that's a good idea," Sandi said. "He might need somebody with him. Maybe a lawyer."

"This isn't about anything he's done," Rhodes said. "Just a friendly little talk."

"You say that a lot," Ike said.

"It's always true, too," Rhodes said. "I think you'll want to hear what I have to say."

Ike looked at Sandi and nodded. "All right," she said, "but I'm not going to talk about the quadratic equation. Whatever that is."

"How about Pringles potato chips?" Benton said, picking up the can that sat on his desk and giving it a little shake. "I know some fascinating stuff about potato chips."

"Really?" Sandi said.

"Really," Benton said. "Come on with me. We'll go down to the student lounge and I'll tell you all about it."

Ike nodded again, and Sandi followed Benton out of the office. When they were gone, Rhodes shut the door and said, "She's in for a big surprise."

"What?" Ike asked. "You mean he doesn't know anything about potato chips?"

"I mean he *does* know a lot about potato chips. Just not the kind of things Sandi might be expecting."

"What about you?" Ike asked. "What are you expecting from me?"

"Let's sit down and find out," Rhodes said.

Chapter 22

▼

Rhodes got right to the point by telling Ike that he knew all about Duffy's nighttime excursions into town to steal metal.

"I wouldn't be surprised if he's been stealing it all over the county," Rhodes said. "He's pretty good at it. I don't know who's with him, though. Last night there were two others. They were at a vacant house, the old Post house." He paused to let that sink in. "Was one of the others you?"

Ike looked at the floor. "You said this was a friendly talk."

"I'm not accusing you of stealing metal," Rhodes told him. "I'm just curious. I know it was you at the Beauty Shack stealing hair, so I wondered. Was Duffy with you then?"

Ike raised his head. "No. I did that on my own. Duffy didn't know about it. Nobody knew about it. It was stupid, but . . . but I did it. That's all, though. I never stole anything else. Never."

"You ran when I got to the college a couple of days ago. It wasn't just because of the hair in your trunk. I wouldn't have had any reason to search the car, and you knew that. So why did you run?"

Ike's gaze went back to the floor. "I was scared."

"I'll bet you were, but I don't think you were scared of me. I think you were scared of Duffy. He knows that Dr. Harris saw him on the campus. He's threatened Harris by phone. I don't think he'd like it if he knew you'd seen him, too. You did see him, didn't you?"

"You don't understand what it's like," Ike said. He looked off at Benton's messy bookshelves, but Rhodes didn't think he was seeing anything.

"You might try telling me," Rhodes said. "Maybe I can help."

Ike sat there for a minute, staring at the bookshelves. Then he said, "All my life I've been at the compound. It wasn't so bad when I was a kid. We had some space there to roam around in. We had woods and trees, and I got to shoot pistols and rifles and cross-bows. We had TV." He paused. "The TV was probably a mistake."

"Lots of people think TV is a mistake," Rhodes said.

"Not for the reasons it was a mistake for me to see some of the programs. I found out about what life was like outside, and I wanted to try it. I wanted to see things for real instead of being inside a fence. My father wouldn't let me, not for a long time. Finally I started getting away now and then. He didn't like it, but he knew if he didn't let me out occasionally, I'd run away forever."

"Might not have been a bad idea," Rhodes said.

"Don't take what I said the wrong way," Ike said. "I liked it at the compound a lot of the time when I was growing up. There were some other kids, and going to school at home was okay. Sure, Duffy was a terrible math teacher, nowhere near as good as Dr. Benton, but my mother was pretty good with English, and I could learn a lot of stuff from the Internet. It wasn't enough, though. You know what I mean."

"You wanted some help with your math, for one thing."

"Yeah, school was part of it. Not all."

"Hormones?"

Ike looked at Rhodes and grinned. "That was part of it, for sure. My father knew he couldn't keep me there away from girls all my life, but it's hard to meet anybody when you're cooped up most of the time. He finally gave in and let me come to the college, and I met Sandi. I like her a lot."

"She's not thrilled about what you did at the Beauty Shack."

"I know that, and I don't blame her. I meant it when I said it was stupid. I can't take it back, though. She knows that, and I'll take what's coming to me. I hope I can finish the semester, but if I can't, that's just too bad."

Rhodes didn't think this was the time to mention the possibility of probation. He needed to get the subject back to what really mattered.

"It must've been hard to keep secrets in the compound. Everybody in this town knows everybody else's business. In the compound it had to be a hundred times worse."

"You know it. Sometimes I felt like I couldn't even breathe. Just one more reason I needed to get out. My father thinks the world has gone crazy. He thinks the government's going to collapse, and he's ready to defend his little compound when that happens. I don't believe he's right. He's been thinking it for twenty years, and the world's still going on. He's the one who needs to get outside and see what's what."

Rhodes wanted to talk about secrets, not about Able Terrell's views, as interesting as they might be.

"Duffy gets outside," Rhodes said. "He strips air conditioners and houses. He probably steals a few pickup tailgates, too. Lot of those going missing around town lately. Able had to know about it. You did, too."

"I don't know what my father knew." Ike looked at the dry-erase board, but Rhodes didn't think he was interested in the equation. "He never talked about Duffy."

"What about you? Did you know?"

Ike still wouldn't look at Rhodes. "I kind of got the impression that Duffy was doing something wrong. I found out what it was one day when I overheard him talking to Alf Dewberry."

"Who's Alf?"

"Another guy who lives in the compound. He goes outside with Duffy now and then."

"If you knew all this, your father must have known it, too."

Ike shrugged. "Maybe. If he did, he never told me. It wasn't exactly the kind of thing we talked about."

Rhodes didn't think it was possible for Able not to have known, but it didn't matter when it came to Wellington's death.

"You saw Duffy leave the campus the morning Wellington was killed," Rhodes said. "Isn't that right?"

"I didn't see him leave the college." Ike was emphatic. "That's not true."

"You saw something, though."

Ike thought it over for a while. Finally he said, "Yeah. You could say that."

Rhodes felt as if he were finally getting somewhere. "So tell me what it was."

"I saw Duffy on the road from the college. He was coming up the overpass as I was going down. He didn't notice me. When I got to school, I knew something was wrong, and I didn't want to get involved in it." He shook his head. "I should've just parked and stayed in the car. I wouldn't be in this mess now if I'd done that."

"You might be in a bigger one," Rhodes said. "You can't ever tell. Where were you going to sell the hair?"

"I hadn't thought it through. I knew it was easy to sell, though. I heard about it on TV."

Suspicions confirmed. "You'd have to leave the county to get rid of it."

"Yeah, I thought of that. I could do it easy. I'll bet there were places in Derrick City I could've sold it, but I didn't get a chance. You stopped me, and I appreciate it."

Ike sounded sincere, but sound and meaning weren't always the same, as Rhodes well knew.

"How about Duffy? Where does he sell the metal?"

"I don't know," Ike said. "I guess he has a way to get rid of it if he's stealing it, but I don't know what it is."

Rhodes figured that Duffy probably had someone meet him at the recycling center at night, or maybe he just turned it over to someone at an arranged meeting spot and let a third party sell it for him. He might even be selling it in Derrick City instead of at the recycling center. It didn't matter. Duffy was going to be shut down soon enough.

"What're you going to do?" Ike asked. "About Duffy?"

"I'm going to arrest him," Rhodes said.

Ike didn't look happy about that. "I don't see how you can. You can't get into the compound. Nobody can get in there if my father doesn't want them to."

"We'll see," Rhodes said. "How many people are usually inside?"

"There's Duffy and Alf and Cleon, plus Alf and Cleon's wives. There's AJ. He's not married. Alf has two kids, a boy and a girl, about ten and twelve. Cleon has a son. He's twelve, too. There's my father and mother."

"How much resistance will they put up?"

"I can't say. Duffy's not going to volunteer to come with you, though, and my father's not fond of the law. Neither is anybody else in there. They won't send Duffy out, and you can't get in. You'd better just leave well enough alone."

Rhodes didn't want to get into some kind of prolonged stand-off, and he didn't want to create a situation where anybody was going to get hurt, much less killed. He'd just have to hope that Able would decide to cooperate. That would be the easiest thing for everybody.

Or he could leave well enough alone. If Duffy never came back out of the compound, wouldn't that be just the same as being in prison? Able didn't think so, but Ike would agree that it was.

Nevertheless, Rhodes was going to arrest Duffy. Or try. That was his job, and he didn't believe in not doing his job.

"I'll go down there and talk to him and see what happens," he told Ike. "You can stay out of it."

"Don't worry," Ike said. "I'm a law-abiding citizen. I want to do what's right."

It sounded good to Rhodes, and he wanted to believe it.

Rhodes left Ike at the college and went back to the jail. He told Hack to call the deputies on duty and tell them to meet him at the courthouse.

"What for?" Hack asked. "Why the courthouse? What's goin' on?"

Rhodes knew that if he didn't tell Hack, the dispatcher would pester him endlessly and would never forgive him.

"We're going to the compound to arrest Duffy."

"Can I go?" Jennifer Loam asked.

Rhodes hadn't heard her come into the jail. He'd been too wrapped up in his thoughts about Duffy and the compound. He turned to Jennifer and said, "No. You can't go."

"I'll stay out of your way."

"I'm sure you would, but you don't need to be there."

"Freedom of the press. First Amendment. Who's Duffy, by the way?"

"That's what I want to know," Hack said. "I talked to him on the phone, but I don't know who he is."

"He's a suspect in the death of Earl Wellington," Rhodes said, "and a suspect in a lot of thefts that have been going on in the county." He looked at Jennifer. "That should be enough for your Web site. I'll give you everything else later." He turned to Hack. "Get the deputies now. I'll be at the courthouse."

"Might's well meet 'em here," Hack said. "Now that ever'body knows what's goin' on."

He had a point. "All right. Call them in."

"Can I stay?" Jennifer asked. "I'll be quiet. Promise. I won't say a word."

"No video," Rhodes said. "No photos. No note taking."

"You're a hard man, Sheriff."

"Tell me about it," Hack said. "He's touchy, too. You're lucky he ain't started snappin' at you by now."

"Call the deputies, Hack," Rhodes said.

"See how he is?" Hack said, but before Rhodes could say any more, he turned to the radio and started making the calls.

Jennifer Loam did as she promised. She sat on the opposite side of the big room and didn't say a thing while Rhodes went over the situation with Buddy, Duke, and Ruth.

"I've been telling you that this county needs a SWAT team," Buddy said. "Mikey Burns agrees with me, too."

Commissioner Burns had once told Rhodes that what the county really needed was at least one M-16 rifle. For firepower. Rhodes had thought at the time that it was a goofy idea. Maybe he'd been wrong.

"You and Burns can discuss that some other time," Rhodes said. "Since we don't have a SWAT team, we'll just have to go with what we've got, and that's us."

"What's the plan?" Ruth asked.

Rhodes explained what the compound looked like and what the layout was on the inside. "There are five men, three women, and three children in the compound. I don't know what will happen when we get there. Able might decide to turn Duffy over, but I doubt it. I'm sure that the other men are involved in the metal thefts with Duffy. Maybe Able is, too. That makes it tricky."

"What about the walls?" Duke asked. "How solid are they?"

"Solid and braced. We might be able to pull them over, but that would mean an all-out fight. I hope we can avoid that."

"If we can't avoid it, then we can't," Buddy said, sounding a little too eager. Rhodes wanted to be sure he never sent Buddy and Shelby out together.

"I don't want anybody to be hurt," Rhodes said. "Not them, not us."

"Especially not us," Ruth said.

"That's right," Rhodes said, "so let's not get excited. No shooting unless I tell you. We're just there to make a peaceful arrest."

"If they'll let us," Buddy said. "What if they won't?"

"We'll see," Rhodes said.

Hack, who hadn't made any promises to be quiet, said, "Seems to me you need yourselves a plan B."

"I'll come up with one," Rhodes said.

"You gonna tell us what it is?"

"I don't remember you being a part of this discussion."

"Just tryin' to help," Hack said. "No need to get touchy about it. You're always gettin' touchy."

"I'm touchy because I don't have a plan B," Rhodes said.

Rhodes led the caravan to the compound. The county cars were almost bumper to bumper as they left the highway and navigated the dirt road through the trees. When they came to the clearing, Rhodes drove off the road and stopped well away from the compound fence. He got out of the car as the deputies stopped nearby. They joined him, and Buddy said, "Now what?"

"Now I make a phone call," Rhodes said.

He took out his flip phone and punched in the number that Duffy had used to call the jail. He'd gotten the number from Hack before they left, and he hoped it would work.

It did. Duffy answered.

"That you, Sheriff?"

"It's me," Rhodes said. "How'd you know?"

"We're real up-to-date here. Got caller ID and everything. Plus you made quite an entrance."

"I thought you might notice."

"I bet you did. What can we do for you?"

"I want you to come on out, Duffy."

"Why would I do that?"

"One reason would be that you're under arrest."

Duffy laughed. "Nope. You got that all wrong, Sheriff. I'm in here, you're out there, and I'm a free man. Not coming out. You might've brought some friends along to help you, but it won't do you any good. You can't arrest me if you can't get to me. Besides, I didn't do anything."

"You stole metal from air conditioners. I've seen Wellington's video."

"Don't know what you're talking about. Never heard of Wellington. Must be a case of mistaken identity. I'll be hanging up now."

"Put Able on. I'd rather talk to him anyway."

"He doesn't want to talk to you, though."

Duffy broke the connection.

"That didn't go too well, did it," Ruth said.

"Not well at all," Rhodes said.

Rhodes was afraid that it had gone even less well than it appeared. Something in Duffy's tone was a little off, and Rhodes wondered what was going on in the compound. It sounded almost as if Duffy might be in charge. Maybe he'd staged a coup. If that had happened, it would change things considerably. Rhodes needed not only a plan B but a plan C as well. A plan D would also come in handy.

"You remember what happened at Waco?" Buddy asked.

Rhodes remembered. It had been a long time, but Rhodes didn't think anybody had forgotten the siege at the Branch Davidian compound. It had ended very badly indeed for all concerned.

"This isn't the same thing," Rhodes said. "Much smaller scale, and we're not going to stay here for fifty days. Or call in the Feds, for that matter. We can handle it."

"Good," Duke said. "How?"

"I was thinking you and I could throw Buddy over the fence. Then he could open the gate for us."

"Ha ha," Buddy said.

"I had a feeling you wouldn't go for it," Rhodes said, "but that's all right. I have a better idea."

"What's that?" Ruth asked.

"*I'm* going over the fence," Rhodes said.

Chapter 23

▼

Never having besieged a compound before, Rhodes didn't know what the inhabitants expected him to do. He did, however, have a pretty good idea of what they didn't expect.

They didn't expect he'd go back to town, at least not right away.

They didn't expect he'd start shooting, because they remembered Waco for sure. Able probably showed videos now and then just to remind them.

They certainly didn't expect a fat old man like him to come over the fence.

Not that Rhodes thought of himself as being either fat or old, but he suspected the men behind the fence did. They wouldn't have a lot of respect for any kind of lawman, and even less for the local sheriff. They wouldn't think he could scale a ten-foot fence.

Neither did the deputies, for that matter.

"You're kidding us," Buddy said.

Ruth and Duke didn't say anything, but Rhodes could tell

from the looks on their faces that they didn't believe for a second that he could do it. Maybe he couldn't, but he thought it was worth a try.

"We could bring in ladders," he said, "but they'd have too much time to prepare if we tried something like that. They'll be so surprised at one person coming over the wall that I'll have time to do plenty before they know what's happening. They might not even see me."

"For them not to see you," Buddy said, "you have to get over the fence."

"I get the impression you don't have a lot of confidence in my abilities," Rhodes said.

Buddy backtracked a little. "It's not that. It's just that the fence is really high. It won't be easy."

"Ten feet," Rhodes said. "That's no hill for a climber."

Buddy looked at the fence. He looked back at Rhodes. "It's a fence, not a hill, and you can't climb it. You'd have to jump it."

"That's the plan," Rhodes said.

"Plan B," Duke said.

"Right."

"Go for it," Ruth said. "If you break a leg, we'll get you to the ER in five minutes."

"Thanks for the encouragement."

"Just kidding," Ruth said, but Rhodes wasn't sure that was true.

"They're bound to be watching us," Duke said. "They'll see you."

Rhodes had thought of that. "No they won't. You're going to distract them."

"How will we do that?" Buddy asked, so Rhodes told him.

*   *   *

Rhodes slipped through the trees as quietly as he could, circling around to the back of the compound. What he hoped to do was simple enough. He'd sprint across the open space between the trees and the fence, go over the fence, and drop down inside the compound.

The only problems as he saw them were sprinting, going over the fence, and dropping down inside the compound. Aside from those things, it would be a cinch.

Rhodes knew how to sprint. In high school they'd called him the Will o' the Wisp because of his speed and elusiveness. That was before he'd injured his knee, of course, and he hadn't sprinted in a while. Since high school, maybe. Running, sure, he'd done some of that. Sprinting, not so much.

He knew the theory of going over the fence well enough. The problem was doing it.

Dropping down inside should be easy. Gravity would take care of that if Rhodes could pull himself over the top of the fence, but landing might be a little dicier. Rhodes wasn't as elastic as he'd once been.

What it came down to was that they had to get the gate open, and to do that someone had to get inside. Rhodes was the sheriff, so it was his job. He could have delegated it, but Buddy and Ruth were too short, and Duke was too heavy. Besides, he looked even less like a sprinter than Rhodes did. So Rhodes was elected.

He'd brought some gloves with him, and he slipped them on. They'd help him grip the top of the fence if he managed to reach it. He'd also brought a .38 revolver that he wore in a holster at the small of his back. His little ankle pistol wasn't going to be enough if he needed a gun inside the compound. For that matter, even the .38 might not be enough. He was counting on surprise and confusion to help him out before Duffy gunned him down with an AR-15.

Rhodes got to the rear of the compound a little quicker than he'd thought, so he stopped at the edge of the trees and waited for the distraction. The sky had clouded over, and it was dark back toward the west. A little wind had kicked up, and Rhodes smelled rain on the air. It hadn't rained for a long time, and Rhodes hoped they'd get a drenching, but not until after he'd done what he came to do.

The distraction came a minute or so later. Rhodes had asked the deputies to turn on their sirens and lightbars at the same time. The noise and the flashing lights would be enough to draw the attention of everyone in the compound to the front. Rhodes didn't know how long their attention would be diverted, so he'd just have to hope it was long enough for him to get inside. Assuming he could get inside.

As soon as the noise began, Rhodes took off. He knew that he had to hit the wall with his left foot about waist high. If he didn't, his shoe wouldn't grip. It would just slide down, and he'd bounce away from the wall. When his foot hit he had to use all the power of his leg to propel himself upward, keeping his hands and his chest away from the wall. When his leg straightened, he'd grab the top of the wall, get his chest above it, swing himself over, and drop down.

Rhodes tried not to think about any of that. If he thought about it, he wouldn't be able to do it. Clear the mind. Let the body take over.

His foot touched the wall. He stepped as powerfully as he could. His arms shot up. He was over six feet tall and had a good reach. He could do it.

His fingers cleared the top of the fence, and he gripped it hard, pushing down with his arms and using his momentum to shove his chest above the top of the fence. He swung his right leg up, rested it for a fraction of a second on top, and pushed himself over. He caught the top of the fence as he swung around and hung on. He let himself dangle for a beat, then dropped to the ground.

Sage Barton couldn't have done it better. Nothing to it.

Nothing except that if anybody came at Rhodes at that moment, he was doomed, because unlike Sage Barton he had to stand there for a while to catch his breath, let his heartbeat slow down, and calm the quivering in his arms.

The sound of the sirens crashed in on him, and Rhodes realized he hadn't heard them since he'd sprinted for the fence. It wasn't that they'd stopped. He'd blocked them out somehow.

As his breathing returned to normal, Rhodes looked around the compound. He didn't see anyone. He picked out Able's house, went to the back door, and turned the knob. The door wasn't locked, but why should it be? Who would Able be locking out? The few people in the compound would all trust each other. It wasn't as if they were living in the wicked outside world.

Rhodes opened the door and went inside. He found himself in the kitchen. It still smelled a little like beans. They must eat a lot of beans in the compound. Cheap, and if they were dried they'd keep forever. The door to the right was closed, but the doorway in front of Rhodes led to the room where he'd met with Duffy and Able.

Rhodes had started across the kitchen when he heard something thump against the door to his right. The noise of the sirens was loud even in the house, and he wasn't sure. He stopped and went to the door. Something thumped against it again. Rhodes drew the .38 from the small of his back and tried the knob. It turned, and he opened the door to discover Able Terrell trussed up in a storage closet with silver duct tape over his mouth.

"Hey, Able," Rhodes said, not really expecting Terrell to hear him.

Terrell looked at him and mumbled something. Rhodes knew because he could see his mouth working behind the tape. Rhodes couldn't decide whether to risk removing the tape or not.

"Should I let you talk?" Rhodes asked. He holstered the pistol. "I guess so. You seem to be on the outs with the folks here."

Rhodes reached out and got a grip on the left edge of the tape. "Ready?"

Even if Able couldn't hear, he understood what Rhodes meant. He nodded, and Rhodes ripped the tape off his face.

"You and Duffy having some differences?" Rhodes said, loudly enough for Able to hear.

Able took a couple of deep breaths. "That son of a bitch. Untie me."

Rhodes couldn't think of any reason why not. He went into the kitchen, found a butcher knife in a wooden knife block, and cut the ropes that held Able.

Able stood up, bracing himself on the door frame with one hand. "Duffy came in and held a gun on me while Alf tied me up. What the hell's going on here?"

"You tell me," Rhodes said. "Better yet, we can talk about it later. Where are your guns? We might need them."

Able took Rhodes into another room, where a gun cabinet occupied about half of one wall. It wasn't the collection that Rhodes had heard rumored, but it was impressive nevertheless: a couple of semiautomatic shotguns, both 12-gauge; a Winchester .30-30;

a Winchester .44 Magnum; two AR-15s; and three AK-47s. No rocket launchers, however.

Able took one of the AK-47s. Rhodes grabbed a shotgun. It was loaded. Rhodes looked at Able.

"What's the use of having an unloaded gun?" Able asked.

Rhodes didn't have time for a discussion. "We'd better get outside before Duffy and his friends figure out what's going on. Where are the women and children?"

"I don't know. Duffy probably stuck them in one of the other houses. He wouldn't let anything happen to them."

Rhodes wasn't so sure about that, but he led the way to the front room and took a look out the window. Duffy and two other men, Alf and Cleon, Rhodes assumed, stood about ten yards away, looking toward the gate. All three were armed. Duffy had an AR-15, and the others had conventional rifles. They were talking, maybe about the noise and flashing lights, but they'd get tired of that soon enough.

Rhodes stood next to Able so he could speak into his ear. "I'm going out. I'm going to arrest Duffy."

"What for?" Able asked.

"Theft. You must know what he's been doing to bring in money."

Able looked puzzled. "He told me he had an inheritance."

Rhodes would have loved to hear more, but the men outside were getting bored with the sirens. "We'll talk about it later. You can back me up on this. Go open the gate when I get things settled down."

Rhodes went to the door and opened it. He stood in the doorway with the shotgun pointed at the three men. Duffy turned and saw him first. Without hesitation he brought up the AR-15, firing as he did so. He'd altered the rifle to fire on full auto, and the bullets stitched a line through the dirt and up the wall of the house. Duffy's trigger finger was broken, so that explained why his shooting was a little off, Rhodes thought as he ducked back inside and hit the floor.

Alf and Cleon started shooting, too. The hammering of the gunfire was easy to hear even over the howling sirens. Window glass blew inside the room.

Rhodes looked around for Able and saw him lying behind the couch with his eyes closed. No matter how much training you had or thought you had, the real test was whether you could act when you were under fire. Able apparently wasn't able. Rhodes grinned at his own sad attempt at humor. Even if nobody else liked his jokes, he had an appreciative audience of one.

Meanwhile, Duffy and his pals were plenty able. They'd switched out magazines and were firing again. Bullets buzzed above Rhodes's head and smacked into the wall.

Rhodes slithered to the window, took a quick look outside, and cut loose with the shotgun, spraying number 12 buckshot all around the yard. He heard a couple of yells and took another look. One man was down. It wasn't Duffy. He and the other man were running for cover.

Rhodes got up and went into the compound. He heard barking. The hounds had been released.

Rhodes didn't like the idea of killing dogs. He'd never had to do that in the course of his job before, not even a rabid one, and he didn't want to start now. The dogs, all four of them, came around the corner of the house, nearly tumbling over each other in their eagerness to get at Rhodes. They barked and snarled and showed their teeth. There was no doubt that they intended to rip Rhodes into bite-sized chunks and dine on sheriff until they were full. They weren't giving Rhodes much choice. He raised the shotgun.

"Stop!" Able called out. He'd come out of the house and stood behind Rhodes. "John! Paul! George! Ringo! Stop! Sit! Stay!"

The dogs were well trained. They stopped and sat and stayed. That is, they stayed until the jeep came roaring in their direction. Then they scattered like frightened chickens.

The jeep was headed straight for Rhodes. He fired the shotgun at the radiator and dived to the side. The jeep swerved away from him, and Rhodes caught a glimpse of the man fighting the wheel. It wasn't Duffy.

The jeep came to a dead stop. Rhodes hopped to his feet and yelled at Able to open the gate. He didn't wait to see whether Able responded. He ran toward the back of the house to find Duffy, but he didn't see him anywhere.

Rhodes didn't think Duffy had gone over the fence. He must still be somewhere inside the compound, so Rhodes looked around for any signs of where Duffy might be hiding. Not many places presented themselves, other than the hay bales and the Pontiac.

The sirens stopped. Rhodes heard thunder in the west, and it was followed by the crack and flash of lightning. The wind picked up dust from the ground and stirred it around.

Rhodes looked at the house. Concrete blocks held it about a foot off the ground. Duffy might have squeezed under it. Rhodes went to see if he could spot any marks in the dirt. As he bent down near the back steps, he heard something behind him. He turned to see Duffy rising above the hay bales.

Rhodes got the shotgun to his shoulder in time to trigger off a couple of rounds into the hay. Hay flew everywhere, the wind carrying it up and around, and Duffy dropped out of sight behind what remained of the bales. Rhodes went after him.

Duffy still had his AR-15, but he didn't see Rhodes because he was pawing straw and dust out of his eyes with his left hand.

"Put down the rifle, Duffy," Rhodes said. "I'd hate to shoot you with this shotgun. It would be too messy. For both of us."

Duffy didn't argue. He dropped the rifle and continued to paw at his eyes.

"I'll cuff him for you," Buddy said, walking up to Rhodes.

"Be my guest," Rhodes said.

"I knew all along you could get over that fence," Buddy said.

"Sure you did," Rhodes said.

"I did, too," Jennifer Loam said.

Good grief. Rhodes turned around. Jennifer stood there wearing a Kevlar helmet and vest. On the vest bright yellow letters spelled out INNOCENT JOURNALIST. Jennifer had a small video camera in one hand.

"Nice outfit," Rhodes said. "Where did you come from?"

"Thanks. I followed you out here, but I stayed back out of the way until I saw you sneak off through the trees. When the sirens went off, I decided I could show myself. I asked where you were, and Ruth told me about the fence." She held up the camera. "I was hoping you'd re-create getting inside so I could shoot it. It would really look good on my Web site."

Rhodes looked at her and shook his head.

"No way," he said.

Chapter 24

▼

When things were sorted out, the deputies hauled Duffy, Cleon, and Alf to the hospital and the jail. Alf had a good bit of buckshot in his leg, but he'd be all right. Cleon had banged his head against the steering wheel of the jeep when it made its sudden stop, but he wasn't hurt enough to matter.

Jennifer Loam went back to town to write the story for her Web site. Rhodes dreaded what it might say, but he knew he'd find out sooner or later.

Able located the women and children, got them settled down, and then talked to Rhodes, who sat in the same chair he'd sat in when they'd had their first talk. This time Able sat down, too. The room was a mess, but Able said he'd worry about that later, which was fine with Rhodes. Outside a gentle rain was falling, and Rhodes heard it running off the roof. Some of it had blown in through the broken window and wet the floor, but the wind had died down now. It was much cooler than it had been earlier.

"One thing before we get started," Rhodes said. "John, Paul, George, and Ringo? Really?"

"My parents were fans," Able said. "I grew up with the music." He shrugged. "Seemed like a good idea at the time."

"Lots of things do," Rhodes said, having had some experience along those lines. "Tell me about Duffy. What happened here?"

"I'm not sure," Able said. "I guess it's your fault. He came in here this afternoon, nice as pie, and asked me if I'd do him a favor. I said, sure, what was the favor? He said something like 'Look over there,' and I looked. He hit me in the back of my head and tied me up. That's all I know about it."

Rhodes thought about that for a minute or so. "Let's get back to Duffy's money. Tell me about it."

"I told you already. He supposedly had an inheritance. That's what he said. His uncle or somebody had died and set up a little trust fund. Now and then he'd go to the post office and pick up a check."

"So he wasn't like you. He left the compound now and then."

"People aren't prisoners here. I never leave. This is my little patch of ground, and I'm sticking to it. Anyone else can leave as he pleases. Ike does. You know that."

"I got the impression that he didn't leave for a lot of years."

"That's because he didn't have any transportation. When he could drive without getting arrested, he could leave, and he did. Not often, until lately, but he left."

"Didn't it strike you as funny that Duffy went out at night so much?"

Able shook his head. "He didn't go out that much. Once or twice a week. Alf would go with him some. They said they felt cramped in here."

Rhodes would have felt cramped, too. "Didn't they share your ideas?"

"They don't like the government any more than I do, if that's what you mean. They liked having a safe place to live when the time comes and things fall apart."

Rhodes didn't want to get into that discussion. He said, "Duffy didn't have any trust fund. He was stealing copper from air conditioners and abandoned houses. Probably stealing tailgates, too, and selling them. That's where he got his income. You'll need to find another source of money."

"The Lord will provide," Able said, but he didn't sound convincing. "I want to thank you, by the way, for what you did for Ike. He was really happy you got him out on that personal bond. It was the right thing to do."

Rhodes didn't want to talk about that. "It seemed like a good idea at the time."

"It's just as well he wasn't in on this," Able said.

"For sure," Rhodes said.

He was convinced that Able didn't know about Duffy's illegal activities or what had happened to Wellington. Duffy might have a different story to tell, but Rhodes would deal with that when the time came. For now it was enough that Duffy was in jail.

"I don't know what came over Duffy," Able said. He ran his hand over the gray streak in his hair. "He could've asked me to help him instead of tying me up and dumping me in a closet."

"If he'd asked for help, what would you have done?"

Able looked at the floor. "I'm not sure."

"I hope you'd have given me a call. Duffy must have thought you would."

"Maybe I would have. I don't know. It's still hard to believe this has happened. I thought we were safe here."

"You can't fence out the world," Rhodes said.

"I have for a long time."

"Yeah," Rhodes said. "I guess you have."

Rhodes had one more thing to do before he went to the jail to check on the prisoners. He drove out to Wade Campbell's house. The county road was still damp from the rain, but it would be entirely dry before long. Rhodes thought it hadn't rained enough to do much more than green up the grass for a few days, but that was better than no rain at all. Not much better, but at least it was something.

He parked in the driveway behind the same maroon Camry he'd parked behind the first time. He went to the door, rang the bell, and heard the Aggie War Hymn. Sandi Campbell came to the door. Ike was with her. Rhodes had thought he'd be there.

"Come in, Sheriff," Sandi said. "We've been wondering how things went."

"Ike told you about that?" Rhodes asked.

Sandi nodded. "He said you were going to arrest somebody at the compound. He said it wouldn't be easy."

"He was right about it," Rhodes said.

Sandi stepped aside from the doorway. "Come on in. We can sit down while you tell us."

They went into the spick-and-span den. Rhodes let Sandi and Ike sit down. Rhodes loomed.

"Is my father okay?" Ike asked.

"He's fine," Rhodes said. "Duffy and the other two men are in jail."

"I'm kind of surprised you got them. I didn't think you could get inside the compound."

"I know," Rhodes said. "Especially if somebody warned them that I was coming and told them why."

"What do you mean?" Sandi asked.

"Exactly what I said. Somebody called Duffy and told him what was up." Rhodes turned to Ike. "Why'd you do it?"

"I didn't," Ike said. "Not me."

"All we have to do is check your cell phone records," Rhodes said. "It's easy. Duffy knew we were coming. He was all set for us. Only one person could've told him, and that was you."

Sandi looked at Ike. Ike avoided her eyes and didn't say anything.

"I made a mistake about you," Rhodes told Ike. "I believed you, and I was wrong. Here's what I think happened. I think you and Duffy went to the college to confront Wellington about your paper. I don't know if you plagiarized it or not, but it doesn't matter. You were still angry about it, and Duffy didn't mind doing a little strong-arming for you. What happened to Wellington was probably an accident. A little intimidation and then a scuffle that got out of hand. If Wellington had hit his head anywhere else on the trash bin, he might not have died, but that corner was sharp and punched in his skull a little too far. Bad luck for him. Bad luck for everybody."

Sandi looked horrified at what Rhodes had said. Ike still wasn't talking.

"Or maybe you did it yourself," Rhodes said. "I think you were on some of those copper-stealing trips with Duffy, too. If you were, he'll tell me. He'll tell me if he was with you that morning at the Beauty Shack. You can be double sure he'll tell us if he didn't scuffle with Wellington."

Rhodes stopped talking and waited. After a few uncomfortable seconds, Ike looked up at him.

"It was Duffy," Ike said. "I was afraid to tell you. I didn't mean for it to happen, not any of it."

"So you warned him we were coming because you were afraid he'd tell us your part in everything."

"Yeah. I didn't think you could get to him in the compound, not if he was ready for you. I thought everything would be all right. I thought the compound was built to keep out an army."

"You were wrong," Rhodes said.

After Rhodes booked Ike on the new charges and Lawton got him in a cell he questioned Duffy. When he returned, Hack asked if he'd seen Jennifer Loam's web site that evening.

"No," Rhodes said. "I'm not sure I want to."

"She just got it updated," Hack said. "Me and Lawton took a look." He tapped his computer. "You wanna see?"

Rhodes was feeling a little low. He'd misjudged Ike Terrell and believed him about too many things. At least Duffy had admitted that he'd killed Wellington when Rhodes questioned him. So Ike was off the hook for the murder. It didn't matter a bit to Wellington, however.

"I have to call Able Terrell," Rhodes said, "and give him the bad news."

"You oughta look at this story first," Lawton said. "It's real good."

Rhodes knew that the quickest way to quiet Hack and Lawton down was to humor them, so he stepped over to Hack's desk to see what Jennifer Loam had to say about the day's events.

"Look at that," Hack said. " 'One-man army storms compound.' "

"Yeah," Lawton said. " 'Heroic local sheriff puts Sage Barton to shame.' "

Hack tapped the screen. "It's got a video of the heroic local sher-iff 'bout to blow some guy away with a shotgun. Wanna watch?"

Rhodes had seen enough. "I have to make that call now."

"Able's gonna be mighty disappointed about that boy," Hack said.

"So am I," Rhodes said.

It wasn't until he got home that evening that Rhodes thought about having missed lunch again. He mentioned it to Ivy as she was getting ready to make dinner.

"I'll fix you an extra burger," Ivy said.

"Burger? A real one? With meat?"

They were in the kitchen. The two cats were asleep, and Yancey was looking in from the doorway. He looked a little more cheerful than he had that morning, Rhodes thought. Rhodes wasn't too cheerful himself, not with all that had happened that day, but the idea of a real hamburger made him feel a little better.

"I thought a hamburger might be all right just this once," Ivy said. "I got some fresh ground sirloin on the way home."

"Did you get any cheese?" Rhodes asked.

"As a matter of fact, I got some sliced cheddar. Will that be all right?"

"More than all right," Rhodes said. Thinking about it made his mouth water.

The phone rang, and Rhodes got up to answer it. It was Clif-ford Clement, who started off with a simple question, "Well?"

"That's a deep subject," Rhodes said.

"Don't get flip with me, Sheriff. You know what I'm asking about."

"We have someone in custody for Wellington's death," Rhodes said. "We've even solved the copper thefts, or some of them. Now, if you don't mind, I'm about to have dinner. You can take a look at Jennifer Loam's Web site. She has the whole story."

"I'll do that," Clement said, and he hung up.

Thinking about Clement reading what Jennifer had written made Rhodes smile, mainly because it wouldn't make Clement smile. Rhodes might be able to develop an appreciation for the Web site after all.

"You're smiling," Ivy said. She was kneading the ground meat into patties. "Are you thinking about that extra burger?"

"That's part of it," Rhodes said.

"I just want you to know that I'm proud to be married to the heroic local sheriff," Ivy said.

"You heard about that?"

"I know how to use a computer," Ivy said, "but I knew all along you were heroic. That's the real reason you're getting the extra burger."

Yancey came into the room and yipped. Hearing him lightened Rhodes's mood even further. Yancey walked over to the cats and growled. The cats ignored him, and Yancey pranced away. He sat down by Rhodes's chair.

"I'm glad to see he's recovered," Rhodes said.

"I read him that article on Jennifer's Web site. I think that helped. He was inspired."

Rhodes gave Yancey's head a light rub. Yancey lay down and rolled over to let Rhodes rub his tummy, too.

"I might be a heroic local sheriff today," Rhodes said, "but tomorrow I'll be chasing wild hogs out of somebody's house again."

Ivy dropped the ground sirloin into the hot pan. The meat hissed and popped. Yancey jumped up and ran out of the room.

"Still a little skittish," Rhodes said.

"Unlike you," Ivy said. "Always ready for anything."

Rhodes thought that over. He smiled. "It's not a bad job. There's always something going on. I think I'll keep going to work for a while."

"Good," Ivy said. "Now get out the hamburger buns."

"Yes, ma'am," Rhodes said, and he did.

9-13